FIELD AGENT

ERIC SWAN THRILLER #4

DOM TESTA

PROFOUND IMPACT GROUP, LLC

Field Agent: Eric Swan thriller #4

By Dom Testa

Published by Profound Impact Group, LLC

PO Box 506

Alpharetta, GA 30009

Reach us at EricSwan.com

ISBN: 978-1-942151-15-9

Cover art by Damonza

JOIN THE SWANIVERSE - GET FREE STUFF

Eric Swan is
The Spy Who Can Never Die

With each new tale you'll learn a little more about Q2's super spy, Eric Swan.

If you'd like to be among the first to learn of each new adventure *before* they're published, just let me know where to find you.

As a thank you for joining the Swaniverse, you'll be treated to a **free** Eric Swan short story, along with other bonus treats.

It's simple: Just go to EricSwan.com.

Thanks, and happy reading.
Dom Testa

MORE ERIC SWAN BOOKS FROM DOM TESTA

Power Trip: Eric Swan Thriller #1

Swan takes on diabolical twins determined to bring down the power grid. If he fails, the country will slip into a dark age of chaos and anarchy.

Poison Control: Eric Swan Thriller #2

A treacherous madman is intent on poisoning the water supply. Swan must outsmart this rogue scholar before he can release his apocalyptic toxin.

God Maker: Eric Swan Thriller #3

Agent One has resurfaced, and he's kidnapped the mother of Q2's investment technology. Swan must not only battle this psychotic killer, but come to grips with his own fears.

CONTENTS

The intoxicating scents reached all the way to the parking lot. With a window down they began the assault before we'd even finished parking the car, which seemed unfair. It was a psychological ploy, predicated on natural human weaknesses, no different than movie theaters walloping you with the overpowering aroma of buttered popcorn the second you walked in the door.

In this case it wasn't a theater, but a farmers market on a sunny Saturday morning. I used to be fooled by the name, conjuring up notions of wall-to-wall healthy food choices, straight from the soil to my pantry. If that had been the original intent, then evil forces had somehow snaked their way in, until now every third booth promised sugary or chocolatey delights.

And I loved every one of them. After six weeks of convalescence, they provided a strong enticement to leave the house and join my wife as she did a bit of shopping.

Christina hadn't come right out and said it, but she was ready to get rid of me. Not permanently; just back to work. I, on the other hand, not only hadn't decided if I was ready yet, but couldn't say for sure I even wanted to keep my old job.

For a spy and assassin, down time can have one particularly strong drawback. Hours spent off the clock run the risk of becoming hours spent analyzing the past. In this case, my mind had hovered over the image of the last man I'd killed. Edwin Bolt, a large, brutish man, had been merely a pawn in another criminal's game. Now, weeks later, I reflected on the possibility of the late Mr. Bolt being the last kill of my career.

How many had I racked up over the years? On one hand I was ashamed to say I didn't know, because a cavalier attitude over the taking of human life would normally be associated with sociopathic behavior. On the other hand, I'd dispatched every one of them—including burying a butcher knife into the eye of Edwin Bolt—because my government paid me to do so. Besides, they all had it coming.

I don't enjoy ruminating over dead criminals left in my wake, especially on such a pleasant day. But because my status as a field agent for Q2 had been murky at best since leaving the hospital, I guess you could say I'd been pensive. If I was indeed retired from the service, I would've liked my final kill to have been someone substantial in the criminal underworld. A big shot. A boss. Someone on a par with great fictional villains like The Joker, Doctor Doom, or Loki. Hell, how cool would it be to have a guy like Hans Gruber take my final bullet?

Instead, could I have closed out my illustrious crime-fighting career with the dimwitted Edwin Bolt? The only thing substantial about him had been his girth.

And yet perhaps that was exactly the way it should end. Offing a notable mastermind might only inflate my sense of heroic purpose, driving me onward to save the world again and again. With Edwin Bolt as my final act, the curtain could close and the play could quietly end. Yes, maybe it was time I quit killing people for the government. The bullet wound had mended; theoretically my psyche would heal with time.

For the moment, however, I pushed these heavy thoughts aside.

Christina and I strolled through the farmers market entrance to face an onslaught of people. The gorgeous weather had induced a thousand fellow shoppers to the large, open air bazaar, intent on finding seasonal produce and maybe a good deal on candles, jewelry, or homemade jam. The first tent to lure us in offered a variety of interesting salsas, which we sampled with small tortilla chips. They were incredible, and I said so to the woman behind the table.

"Thank you," she said, beaming. "I tweaked my mother's recipe." She lowered her voice. "She hates it, because it's not traditional, you know? I told her, you can't expect your children to always follow in your footsteps."

"So true."

The woman indicated Christina's pregnant belly. "Do you think your son or daughter will want to do what you do?"

I looked from Christina's stomach back to the lady. "Oh, that's not mine."

After we'd moved on, Christina said, "That will never get old for you, will it?"

"Never. Although I would've enjoyed the look on her face if I'd said, *Yes, I'm really hoping my daughter becomes a paid assassin.*"

She laughed. "I've got to pick up some things that will only bore you. Why don't you go wander around by yourself for a bit. Don't shoot anyone, babe."

"Not even packing," I said, patting my pockets. I gave her

a kiss and watched her move on to a vendor selling spices. Turning a full 360 degrees, I looked for anything interesting. Then I caught a whiff of something that had to be bad for you. I went on the hunt.

They turned out to be bourbon-roasted nuts. I mean, come on; they could charge any amount they wanted and I'd pull a muscle reaching for my wallet.

For the next ten minutes I drifted, weaving through a sea of people, dogs, and strollers. As an introvert that sort of crowd usually overloaded my senses. But after so much time cooped up, for now I didn't mind. The fresh air felt good and the people-watching was first-rate. Besides, I had my nuts to distract me. The day couldn't have started better.

Which is, of course, when things generally go to shit.

It began with the sound of a police siren, increasing in pitch and volume as it got closer. But a siren wasn't unusual, especially in D.C., so the farmers market crowd didn't look up.

Until a car—the object of the police chase, it turned out—roared into the vicinity. The dipshit driving it probably didn't count on so much traffic clustered in one place, and everyone was jolted to attention by the sound of a loud crash. Every person there must've immediately groaned, wondering if it was *their* car that had suffered the direct hit. Anxious to investigate, we all poked our heads up like the little rodents in a Whac-A-Mole game.

We needn't have bothered; the action came directly toward us.

Two men, now on foot following their crash, sprinted to the entrance, shoving people out of the way. An old man went flying, a couple of children went down and began wailing, and a general cry of alarm spread through the crowd like a virus. In situations like that people will generally move, even without a plan, so in a heartbeat the farmers market devolved into pure chaos, punctuated by the scream of the police siren as it arrived on the scene.

But the two perps were way ahead, and if they could maneuver through the horde, would likely escape. I watched them approach and noticed they got separated by the natural swirling eddies of crowd movement. One of them, a young man I gathered to be about 22, was heading right for me. He yelled to his buddy, with what sounded like "Dale." It might've been "Hale," or "Dell." And, in his haste, he shoved an older woman to the ground, eliciting a startled outburst from the people nearby. It didn't sit too well with me, either.

So as soon as he was close I laid into him with a shoulder. Seemed like the right call for an asshole like that. It was a solid block, and the only thing keeping him on his feet was the throng of people around us. Wide-eyed, and perhaps shocked that anyone dared to impede his exit, he charged at me, one arm rising to inflict damage on my skull.

I might've been sitting on my ass for six weeks, but years of training, including several in the employ of covert special ops programs, is like riding the proverbial bike. With two punches I dropped him, and this time the people around us cleared a space for him to hit the pavement. He wasn't out, but he was thoroughly dazed.

Two strapping young men stood nearby, as out of place at a farmers market as I was. "Do me a favor," I said. "Sit on this guy until the police get here. If he struggles, make him uncomfortable." They enthusiastically agreed.

Now I turned my attention to the other guy, who was older than his partner-in-crime. Dale, or whatever his name was, looked to be in his mid-30s, and carried the aura of someone who'd spent a lifetime being as bad as he could. He'd stopped running and now looked around for his buddy. I moved toward him, but before I could say anything the lone police officer who'd been in pursuit ran up, his weapon drawn. So Dale drew his own gun.

"Shit," I muttered. In situations like this someone often took a bullet, even if accidentally. Too many times it had been me. All I knew at the moment was that some dick named Dale was waving a gun around in a crowd of people that included my pregnant wife.

I stepped closer.

Dale and the cop made eye contact, and both raised their weapon. The cop yelled for the creep to drop his. But instead Dale fired. A hole sprouted in the cop's left leg and he went down.

Now the crowd's tension turned to absolute pandemonium. Some people dropped to the pavement, others tried bolting to safety, which was made more difficult by the dozens of people now lying on the ground. Screams filled the air.

Dale glanced around again for his partner, but couldn't spot him, probably because the guy currently rested beneath a couple of college beasts.

I wanted to make my move, but caution is always advised when approaching someone who's not afraid to shoot a cop. I'd closed within five feet when he whirled and saw me.

"What do you want, asshole?" he yelled, pointing the gun at my face.

I put up my hands, one still clutching the paper container of bourbon nuts, in the international sign of *I don't want any trouble*. From somewhere in the crowd I heard Christina's voice cry out, "Swan!" There was panic in her voice. Well, she'd never before seen me at work.

"I said what do you want?" Dale said, waving the gun, as if that somehow made it more menacing.

"I just don't want anyone else hurt," I said, my voice calm.

"Well take another step and you'll see hurt."

I stopped, my hands still raised, but by then I was within what I considered a semi-reasonable distance. Part of my brain calculated the next move, while another part chuckled over the phrase *you'll see hurt*.

Dumbass.

The hysteria of the crowd was bound to distract him sooner rather than later, and it did. As he looked back toward the cop, I shot my right foot out and up, connecting with his wrist, sending the gun flying. In the next moment I lunged toward him and, reluctantly dropping the nuts, landed a blow.

But this guy was big and certainly not ready to give up the fight. He was the kind who hit back.

We exchanged a couple of shots before he stepped back and brought out his next weapon. This time it was a knife.

"Christ," I said. "You're a goddamned walking arsenal."

I don't think he was used to opponents chatting him up. He took a swipe, and I managed to lean out of the way.

In my long experience of combat, having something to counteract the other guy's weapon is preferable to just using your hands and feet. A gun defeats a fist, and a knife has no respect for feet. I had nothing at my disposal at all.

But wait. I did. Beside me sat a vendor's table, stacked high with enormous zucchini and butternut squash. Hey, at least it was something. I grabbed one of the larger squashes just in time because he came in with another swing of his knife. I ducked that one and sidestepped another. When his next attempt was a slashing movement from top right to bottom left, I threw up my defensive tool and heard a loud thunk as the blade lodged in the vegetable. Without hesitating another second, I landed a kick to his gut which caused him to hunch over. Then, two quick blows with my free hand put him on his knees. From there it was a matter of one solid kick to his jaw.

Dale went down on his stomach.

I looked up. My left hand still held the squash aloft, the knife sticking out of it.

Before I knew what was happening, the crowd broke into thunderous cheering and applause. Two other police officers, just arriving on the scene, rushed up. One grabbed me, the other knelt over Dale. People in the crowd were still going out of their minds from the free matinee to which they'd been treated.

I told the police officer I was off-duty FBI, offered to show the ID I kept in my wallet, and also pointed out the second perp being detained by Joe and Jack College.

A moment later I turned around to find Christina standing beside me. "Oh, hey, babe," I said. "See? I didn't shoot anyone."

She shook her head and crossed her arms. "So now will you *please* go back to work?"

2

The way I looked at it, I never quit my job. I expressed extreme dissatisfaction, I let the boss know I was disillusioned, and the whole Q2 operation had left me disenchanted. And no doubt all of that could've led to me being disowned and the government disavowing my participation.

That's a lot of dis. But the words *I quit* or *You're fired* were never uttered. Quanta shook my hand the last time we spoke, and left me with the words *Let me know what you decide to do.* So I assumed I still had a job if I wanted it. The question was: Did I still want it?

Six weeks after taking a bullet from the organization's black sheep, a rogue agent named Butler, I still wasn't sure. But my little farmers market fiasco was rather eye-opening; I'd reacted on pure instinct, and that instinct was to take down shitheads. Whether they were trying to poison the entire country or simply wreak havoc in a Washington market, the response was the same. It was natural to me now. It's what I did.

Really, it's what I *was*. And a big part of me hated that. But although it's often easy to lie to others, it's damned hard to bullshit yourself. I'd probably been born with the gene to do the work, but years of Q2 training had driven it home.

So now I sat in my car, parked outside a home in a tranquil suburb of D.C., and prepared myself for an awkward meeting. For years these meetings with Quanta had begun with a significant workout, one that generally ended with me holding an ice pack to some part of my face or body. Today it would be all talk.

Her response to my text requesting a chat had been typical Quanta: *Tomorrow, 11 a.m.*

It was 10:58. There was no way I was going to play an amateur card by showing up late to make a statement. The statement was me walking in the door at all.

"Hello, Swan," she said. She sat at the round table in her kitchen, where we always discussed upcoming cases. As usual I'd just walked in. She had a glass on the table for me, filled with something pink.

"Quanta," I said in return, pulling out a chair and sitting down.

"Your timing is impeccable," she said.

"You said eleven. It's eleven."

"No, I mean the timing of your text yesterday. I have a case for you."

I stared back. She obviously wasn't going to talk about what had happened, what I'd done for the last few weeks, or whether or not I even wanted to come back to work. I glanced down and saw the usual manilla folder sitting between us.

I didn't know whether to be insulted that she automatically assumed I wanted to dive back in, or if I should be flattered that she couldn't live without me.

For the time being I chose B, and pulled the file over to my side of the table.

"This is another case that, on the surface, seems like something local law enforcement could handle. And they are. But there's a growing feeling that something bigger is underneath it all. And, since it involves an industry worth tens of billions of dollars and hundreds of thousands of farmers, we're starting an investigation."

"Farmers?"

"Yes."

Something clicked, reminding me of a conversation I'd had when I was laid up in the hospital, recuperating from the gunshot.

"This doesn't happen to involve a certain FBI agent we both know, does it?"

Quanta raised an eyebrow. "Why, Swan, you surprise me again. You've spoken with Agent Fife about this already?"

I shook my head. "No. Well, not really. He just mentioned a few weeks ago that he'd be looking into a case involving crops. Wheat, maybe?"

"Soybeans."

"Oh." I paused. "This is really a case for Q2? A problem with soybean farmers?

I began to wonder if this was Quanta's way of relegating me. To ostensibly allow me back into the program, but then to send me out on some silly case a sheriff's department out in the sticks could probably handle.

Her response was an exasperated sigh, as if six weeks hadn't been nearly enough of a break for her.

"All right," I said, holding up my hands in a make-peace gesture. "So am I getting details from you or from Fife?"

"Agent Fife will brief you. This—" She pointed to the file.

"—will provide you at least some baseline data so Fife doesn't have to do too much schooling."

I took a quick peek inside the folder. The first page was a bio, laid out in standard Q2 detail, including a large color photo. It was a woman, 38 years old, short blonde hair, and only the hint of a smile. Typical for a professional headshot: cordial and approachable, but businesslike. The name below the photo said Dr. Sarah Eklund. Undergrad degree from the University of Wisconsin, Masters and Ph.D. from Cal-Berkeley, specialist in plant physiology and bioagricultural sciences. Interests: Yoga, crochet, and target shooting.

I began singing the Sesame Street song in my head: *One of these things is not like the other.*

"Is she a good guy or a bad guy?" I asked.

"She contacted Fife," Quanta said. "Of course, that doesn't prove anything. You may have to make that determination when you get out there."

I closed the folder. "And where am I going on this latest field trip?"

"Why, the Heartland, of course."

"Of course. And although I'm sure I know the answer, I have to ask: Is everything up and running smoothly in the lab?"

"It is."

The lab was the basement laboratory at Q2 headquarters in Washington. It's where I ended up when I was invested into a new body. It had been ransacked two months earlier, which precipitated my last adventure. They'd had plenty of time to get everything back in working order, but it didn't hurt to check.

I waited a few moments, then added, "Is there anything

else we're talking about today, or is this the extent of our meeting?"

"I have another meeting to attend," she said. "Let's not discuss anything else for the time being. I'm sure we'd both like for you to get back up to speed and see how you feel about everything before we deconstruct the past. Would you agree?"

On some level I *didn't* agree, wondering if we needed a real clear-the-air confrontation. But, after a slight pause, I simply gave a curt nod. It would have to wait.

"Since you haven't uploaded in a while, you should probably do that tonight when you land in Iowa," Quanta said. "I'll make sure you have a complete set of digital files before you board the plane. I'll be in touch."

"This might've been our quickest meeting ever," I said, picking up the glass with the pink contents. "I didn't even get to find out what *this* was."

She laced her fingers. "It's not alcoholic, if that's what you were hoping for."

I took a sip, then another. "Goddamn, that's good." Then I set the glass down and stood up. "When does Poole have me flying out?"

THE ANSWER WAS 3:15. Just enough time to get home, pack a small bag, and head out. I left a note for Christina, but it wouldn't be a surprise for her. She'd kissed me goodbye in the morning, confident I'd be gone in a matter of hours. I assumed she'd be happy to know I was out of the house and back on the job. For all I knew she'd bribed Quanta to take me back by offering home delivery of five-star meals.

I called Poole on the drive to Dulles.

"Did you miss me?" I asked.

"Well, um," she said, and I could visualize her trying to assemble the proper response.

"The answer is yes, you missed me terribly," I said. "Sorry I didn't stop by and see you. Time sort of got away from me while I sat on the couch watching TV. You know how that goes." Then I added: "Actually, you probably don't. Poole, do you watch TV?"

"Documentaries," she said, in her usual dry tone. Poole was Quanta's assistant, working out of the drab, unremarkable building that housed Q2 headquarters. She was also officially the most humorless person I'd ever met, which only inspired me to do everything possible to ignite the fun torch. Try as I might, Poole never took the bait.

But, as much as I chafed over her dry, stoic demeanor, there was nothing I ever questioned professionally. Poole was a machine. The next time she let something fall through the cracks would be the first time. Put off initially by her complete lack of mirth, I quickly grew to appreciate the support she provided. She genuinely cared about the job.

"Listen," I said, "What are the chances of getting a bump to first class for this flight to Des Moines?"

"The flight you're on doesn't have first class."

"So you're saying that's zero chance."

"Um, correct."

"What about rental car? How about another Mercedes or Jag?"

"Also not available."

"Damn, Poole," I said. "You don't want me to have any fun in Iowa, do you? Or is that redundant?"

She paused. "I'm from Iowa."

I actually laughed. "No shit. What's a girl from Iowa doing working for a spy organization in the moral-decay capital of the country? Sick of corn, right? Miles and miles of it. Longed for the glamorous life of politics and sleaze."

She didn't answer, and again I imagined her wondering how to respond.

I saved her the trouble. "Poole, I'm kidding. I'd have said the same thing if you were from Oregon. Well, except for the corn part. Truth is, everyone I've ever met from Iowa is honest and genuine. Friendly. Salt of the Earth. Oddly attracted to heavy farm machinery. But friendly."

Her head must've been spinning, so I kept going.

"Listen, if you get a chance, reach out to Agent Fife and let him know I'll meet him at the hotel rather than the airport. And tell him the first round's on him. No, the first *two* rounds."

"I'll reach out to him as soon as we hang up."

"I'll check in with you when I get to the hotel."

IT WAS dark when I landed. While I'd secretly wished for a Mustang or something similar if no Mercedes was available, I understood the practicality of the mid-size SUV Poole had me in. I'm sure it made the most sense out in farm country.

I pulled away from the airport in Des Moines, whose marketing posters had greeted me with the slogan *Iowa to Anywhere*. The truth was, I'd spent some time during my childhood not far from this spot, and as a kid I'd have chosen *Anywhere*. Funny how when you're that age you can't wait to get out into the world. Then you realize the world has no interest in your dreams, and the small town you'd so desperately tried to escape begins looking better and better. I'd done my share of daydreaming in the last few years about leaving the big city and retreating back into the comfort of smaller-town life. I just couldn't be sure if that was the real me talking, or just the part terrified of what the big city was doing to me.

It didn't take long to reach the mid-level hotel. The clerk checked me in and told me a Mr. Fife had left a message to meet him at the sports bar across the street. That's exactly what I did after dropping my bag in the room. Fife was at a hightop, watching a Cubs game.

"Welcome to America's bread basket," he said, shaking my hand.

"I thought that was Kansas."

He shrugged. "Takes more than one state to feed us."

"Speaking of which." I picked up the skinny bar menu, looking for something filling and unhealthy. I wasn't disappointed. When the server stopped by I ordered a club sandwich, fries, and a beer. Fife asked for more of his scotch.

"You know," he said when the server walked away, "when I mentioned this crop thing in your hospital room I never really expected to see you out here."

"I never really expected to be doing *anything* for Q2 again."

Fife nodded, because he understood. A career law enforcement man, he'd worked on the second floor at Q2 before transferring to the FBI. There he acted almost as a secret liaison between the two organizations, although his fellow agents didn't know that. In fact, hardly anyone knew Q2 even existed. Having someone on the inside with the FBI, the CIA, Homeland Security, and others helped us get things done without messy involvement from nosy, inept politicians. Fife was our plant inside the J. Edgar Hoover Building on Pennsylvania Avenue.

"Well, I'm glad you're back," he said. "I'll bet you were bored off your ass sitting at home."

"Not nearly as much as you think."

"Then what made you come back?"

"A farmers market."

He had a good laugh as I told him most of the details—leaving out any mention of Christina. She was still a secret to everyone except Quanta.

"I might be too tired to glean much tonight," I said. "But at least give me a snapshot of what's going on here in Iowa."

"How much do you know about the soybean industry?"

"Before I got on the plane? Hardly anything. I mean, I like edamame, if that counts. By the time I landed here, though, I could write a term paper. More than I ever thought I'd learn about it, and I packed it all into three hours of travel. We can talk more about the industry tomorrow. I guess what I'm curious about is why the FBI—and now Q2—is out here in the cornfields."

"We're here because a few weeks ago someone expressed concern about a group of people who came out of nowhere and suddenly became active in the business side of soy farming. Extremely active."

The server showed up with my beer and Fife's scotch. We touched glasses, took a drink, and then I said, "And the person who expressed concern is Dr. Eklund, I'm assuming. What's she like?"

"Dynamic as hell."

"What does that mean?"

"It means I made a mistake by thinking she was only mildly concerned about what was going on. At first I didn't, uh, give it my full attention, you might say."

"Because it's a crop doctor out in the sticks," I said. "Not exactly ground zero for drug cartel murders or New York mob hits, right?"

"Well, two things taught me right away to not take her problem lightly."

I laughed. "One, she chewed your ass."

"That she did. I told you: dynamic."

I took another pull from my beer. "What was the other thing?"

"A New York mob hit."

3

———

It's naive to believe some areas of the country have all the crime, while other places are populated exclusively by angels. No matter where you go from coast to coast, when hundreds of millions of citizens are bumping into each other you're bound to have trouble. I don't care if it's the mean streets of New York or Chicago, or a suburb of Kalamazoo.

Or, it would seem, the farms of Iowa.

I went from drowsy to fully alert in an instant. Fife knew he had my attention and smiled.

"Yeah," he said. "We'll sit down tomorrow and go over the file, but here are the rough details. Man by the name of David Culbertson, 56 years old, a Criminal Investigator with the USDA, found dead 12 miles north of here. Two shots to the side of the head, execution style. His hands were tied behind his back with his own belt."

"Wait. Somebody executed an investigator from the USDA? As in the Department of Agriculture?"

"That's right."

"Not usually a department that handles violent crimes."

"Not usually, no."

I took another drink and eyed a couple of tough-looking farmhands I'd seen lumber up in a ridiculously-large and loud F-350. They leered at the young hostess as they passed by on their way to the bar. The bartender greeted them by name and tossed a couple of cardboard coasters in front of them. The decibel level in the place increased substantially.

"And this happened *after* you arrived?" I asked. "Then why were you here in the first place? You said you were talking to Dr. Eklund about people who were interested in the soybean industry. So I can see why the USDA was looking into it. But an *FBI* investigation?"

"A couple of reasons. The first has to do with the original allegation—the one I'd just heard about when I visited you in the hospital—which involves potential terrorism. We'll always look into those charges."

"But what was the target? I mean, no offense to the good people of Iowa, but this isn't exactly the first place that springs to mind when you think terrorist activities. Somebody threatening to bomb a silo?"

Fife gave me a wry smile. "Much more destruction than a single bomb. Instead of one silo, Dr. Eklund is afraid the target will be the *entire* soybean crop of the United States."

"Huh," was all I could think to say. "What's the other reason?"

"Our dynamic doctor is also well-connected. When you know someone in high places, you tend to get heard that much sooner."

"Who's her connection?" I asked.

"Her step-mother is Janet Halloran, and before you say *Who's that?* I'll tell you. She's the Deputy Secretary of Agriculture."

"*Deputy* Secretary? And that's high enough up to rattle cages?"

"She's still nominated by the President and approved by the Senate, so yeah, that's powerful enough to get some action from the people who rattle *my* cage. Halloran is also a former CEO of the American Soybean Association, so all of this is near and dear to her heart."

"So is this a legit concern," I asked, "or just a government agency playing politics and jumping when a politician speaks?"

We both looked up as the two loudmouths and the rest of the bar whooped at something going on in the Cubs game. The screen was too far away for me to see the score, but the fans at Wrigley Field seemed quite happy.

Fife turned back to me. "I was skeptical until Culbertson was murdered. And that could very easily be unconnected to Dr. Eklund's issue. I just started looking into that. Didn't know about his death until yesterday. But Eklund left me two messages this afternoon. She has no doubt they're connected."

I ran my finger down the pint glass of beer, sketching lines in the condensation. It was such an odd combination of factors, and in such an out-of-the-way location. First the USDA got involved, then the FBI. But now Q2. When a problem escalated through the alphabet soup of government agencies it meant more and more people were growing concerned, and the number of asses needing protective coverage grew exponentially. Landing in the lap of my particular department meant someone needed to get slapped down, and hard.

My sandwich arrived and I spun the plate so Fife could access the fries.

"All right. When do I meet her?"

"Tomorrow morning at seven-thirty."

Through a mouthful of club sandwich I moaned. "Seven-thirty? Why the hell so early? I've been traveling all day."

Fife put two fries into his mouth. "Quit your bitchin'. I talked her out of seven."

My hotel room was spartan, pretty much what I lived in during assignments. Five-star hotels and fancy suites were rare, reserved for the cases where I played the part of a high-roller.

That was not the case in Iowa. I was just Eric Swan, government agent on a budget.

Before crashing I left a voice mail for Christina. After putting up with my continual presence for weeks, she likely was relishing the alone time. I wouldn't be surprised if she had her phone off, with strawberries and champagne sitting on the edge of a hot, soapy tub.

Christina was carrying the child of a co-worker, acting as a surrogate for Antonio and his wife, Marissa. Life at this point hadn't changed much for her, but the time was approaching when I'd need to be back at the home front a little more regularly than my duties usually allowed. I wasn't sure how much help I'd be, but we'd find out when the time came. For now I was back in the field and Christina was enjoying the high-rise life.

I was tired and desperately wanting some sleep, but had promised Quanta I'd upload. From my small bag I gathered the usual tools, conveniently disguised as deodorant and a basic can of shaving cream. Inside, however, were the sort of electronics that allowed me to connect through wifi with the basement computers at Q2 headquarters.

There was also a pill, often called an adapter. The drug

basically calmed my mind and granted my neural circuits a clear pathway for digitizing thoughts and memories into a language that could be stored and later downloaded. Sort of widened the information superhighway. The actual science eluded me, but it worked.

My essence, condensed in this manner, lived in a special hard drive until I was killed, either accidentally or in the line of duty. Then, a volunteer body was rolled out and prepared to accept a download of my mind, a procedure we called investment.

As for where the bodies came from, well, that was another component of the Q2 investment program that either straddled the ethical line or stepped way over it, depending on your point of view. In a nutshell, the bodies came from felons serving life sentences without parole, men who did indeed volunteer to donate their bodies to science in exchange for monetarily setting up their families for life. All with no questions asked. Their own minds were uploaded and stored, leaving a hollow shell that I—or any other Q2 agent—could then inhabit.

How well? That was a question I'd brooded over for years, only to have some of my worst fears confirmed by the woman who'd created the process. Her name was Devya Nayar, but I called her God Maker, a nickname she detested. In a memorable exchange one evening she admitted that not everything with investment was perfect. But, she insisted, it was still very good, and improving.

Funny how it's easy to think something's *good enough* when you're not the guinea pig whose mind is being uploaded and downloaded. Despite assurances that things were state-of-the-art, I would always harbor a deep-seated feeling that each investment cycle robbed me of a tiny sliver of my soul. There was no way I was the same Eric Swan I'd been when I first took the job.

I popped the pill, set up the gear, and grabbed one of my favorite trashy celebrity magazines to pass the 90 minutes of uploading.

THE ALARM WOKE me at six. I showered, dressed, and stood waiting in the hotel lobby at seven when Fife pulled up in his rental. Sliding into the passenger seat I gratefully accepted the coffee he presented. The hotel's java had been horrendous.

"There's donut holes in the bag," he said, pulling onto the road, straight into a blinding attack of sunlight.

I passed on the little round mounds of dough and instead sipped the coffee, looking out the side window at the passing scenery. We were near the outskirts of Des Moines.

"Anything else you can tell me about our interview this morning?" I asked. "Are we walking into a hostile environment?"

Fife made a left turn and accelerated. "Let's just say the water's not boiling yet, but you can see those little bubbles forming on the bottom of the pan."

I turned from the window and looked at him. "Are you always this poetic in the morning?"

"Only before ten. By midday I'm all data and graphs." He helped himself to a donut hole. "Okay, here's what I know. Sarah Eklund is troubled, and from my lone face-to-face with her I gathered she's used to people jumping when she makes a request. Or a demand. Either that's part of her DNA or a result of growing up with a powerful step-parent. But the fact we can't just leap into action because of her concerns is frustrating."

"Any more pressure coming from the Deputy Secretary so far?" I asked.

He shook his head. "No. But I wouldn't be surprised if we got a strongly-worded suggestion from Washington before the week is out."

I went back to watching the scenery and absorbing the caffeine. Nobody in law enforcement, regardless of the level or the department, appreciated the not-so-gentle nudges that reeked of nepotism or cronyism. But it was an unfortunate aspect of a system where the shit not only rolled downhill, it gathered momentum. Like an avalanche, you understood that you wouldn't be able to outrun it, so just take cover and hope for the best.

Ten minutes later, in an area saturated with drab, aging office buildings, Fife pulled into a diagonal parking space in front of a surprisingly modern edifice.

"Fancy," I said, stowing my empty coffee cup and eyeing the glass structure.

"There's money in them beans," Fife said with a hick accent.

Once inside we stopped at a security desk and showed our badges to a young guard who directed us to the third floor. We took the stairs and came out into a suite of offices with an open floor plan. This early in the morning it was quiet and empty.

A woman of medium height and shoulder-length blond hair emerged from an office in the back. She began walking toward us with a determined stride, head high, shoulders back, her heels tapping out a cadence that echoed off the walls.

I recognized Sarah Eklund from the file I'd studied.

When she got close she extended a hand. "Agent Fife, thank you for agreeing to meet so early."

"No problem," he said. Then he indicated me with a nod.

"This is the fellow agent I mentioned. Eric Swan. He's here to help me continue our investigation."

"Mr. Swan," she said, shaking my hand. Her grip was strong, her eyes penetrating, as if she wanted to know everything about me in one look.

"Dr. Eklund," I said.

She turned to lead us back the way she'd come. "Can I get you coffee?"

We both declined the offer and followed her into an office featuring a desk piled with papers and folders. The credenza behind it was similarly busy. It all managed to come off as intense without being messy. The wall behind her desk was floor-to-ceiling glass, framing an early-morning view of the downtown Des Moines skyline. Hanging from the other walls were assorted plaques, photos, and awards of distinction. I lingered on the picture of Dr. Eklund with the Vice President of the United States, who had signed it, *Sarah, Keep fighting the good fight!*

I wondered what fight that might have been.

"So where are we with everything?" she asked, swiveling in her chair to focus on both of us.

"We're still in data collection mode," Fife said as we took our seats. "Although Eric's had a chance to look at the file during his flight from Washington, I thought you might start at the beginning and share your specific concerns with him."

She nodded and turned her attention to me. "For the last nine years I've devoted the bulk of my research to something called crop solvency. In its purest form it's a measure of how well a certain grain pays dividends on total investment. That investment includes everything from the acreage itself to the fertilization, irrigation, harvesting. It also factors in things like pest control, drought resistance, and how much it takes to reinvigorate the soil through rotation following a harvest."

"Sounds pretty complex," I said. "More than just watering a seed and plucking the fruit."

"Much more. A fractional difference here or there, when calculated across almost a billion acres, can mean profitability or bankruptcy for the farmers. My job, really, is to make sure they're getting the most bang for their buck when it comes to what they put into the ground."

"All right," I said.

"Factored into that," she continued, "the number of actual farms has been decreasing for a while now. Consolidation accounts for a lot of that. But the farmers who are left are increasingly battling larger conglomerates, who have plenty of resources behind them."

"So you're helping out the little guy," I said with a smile.

"I hope I'm helping everyone," she fired back. "But, yes, small farms in particular are very appreciative of the help."

I steepled my fingers in front of me. "From what I understand your biggest concern—the reason Agent Fife is here—has to do with soy. Correct?"

She nodded again. "The average person might believe that wheat makes up the largest percentage of farmland. That hasn't been true for a long time. Today it's corn and soybeans. They dominate, both agriculturally and financially."

"What kind of numbers are we talking?" I knew the answer, but wanted Dr. Eklund to feel like I was fully vested in the investigation.

"Tens of billions of dollars every year," she said. "So anything that poses a danger to those two crops should be considered a national emergency. I'd say it's no less a domestic security threat than a terrorist with multiple nuclear warheads."

I raised my eyebrows. "I see."

She gave a wry smile. "No, I'm sure you don't. But that's why I've reached out, so that you and Agent Fife—and ultimately the country in general—will sit up and take notice."

"Fair enough," I said. "Now that you've brought me up to speed on the dollars involved, why don't you tell me what set off the alarm for you."

"About three months ago I had a visit from a man named Jason Deele. He was bright, cordial, and very knowledgeable about the soybean industry. His mission, he said, was to help prevent a total loss of the nation's soybean crop to a malicious type of mold. That's a danger every farmer has to deal with: molds, fungi, pests. We rely on mother nature to provide the right amount of water and sunshine, but she's also capable of unleashing some pretty nasty bugs. So farmers play both offense and defense when producing their yields."

"And the country has become very keen on keeping pesticides out of the food," Fife added.

"Yes, and rightly so. But that doesn't mean we just sit around and hope the country's food supply can defend itself. Designing foods that can withstand a variety of harsh conditions and predators is very big business, too."

"So did you agree to work with Mr. Deele?" I asked.

"No."

"And why not?"

"Because he was selling a specific, very tightly-engineered new form of soybean, one that could withstand and actually flourish in the face of this mold. There was only one problem." She paused. "The mold he described had never been seen before. He essentially was selling a solution for a problem that didn't exist."

"Oh," I said, and looked from her to Fife and back again. "Then I don't understand. Why did you call the FBI?"

She sat back in her large leather chair. "Because two months ago that very mold—the one we'd never seen before —showed up."

4

———

We were told the wait for a table would be 20 minutes, but Sarah Eklund had insisted we go. No, she couldn't join us, she said, but we should invest the time to experience the best breakfast in that part of the state. I'm a pancake and waffle fanatic, so I was happy to indulge her recommendation. While waiting we killed time talking about current events, a bit of sports, and Fife raved about the streaming shows he'd been hooked on. After a while we got around to deconstructing our meeting with Dr. Eklund.

Following her announcement about the alien mold the discussion had continually returned to Eklund's assessment of the character—or lack thereof—of Jason Deele. It was apparent the man repulsed her, but I couldn't tell if her distaste was based on something personal, professional, or a combination of both. Her comments often criss-crossed between the two. At one point she'd said, "Mr. Deele's arrogance regarding his soy formula is wholly undeserved, given his lack of credible testing or peer review."

I'd quickly recalled a note in the files Poole had sent with me. "But his new strain is being grown in South America. Wouldn't that count as credible testing?"

"It's certainly a good baseline for testing," Eklund said, "but almost *any* new strain can find limited success in a short window of time. Real proof takes years of cultivating in a wide variety of environmental conditions. If we allowed any greenhouse hobbyist to pass themselves off as certified agricultural scientists it would be chaos."

Her use of the word *hobbyist* had struck me. I supposed that every field had its hierarchy, with a certain amount of snobbery and an entrenched old-school network, but I'd never thought it existed with the people who grew wheat and corn. And yet, why not? Again, with mind-popping amounts of money on the line, there would naturally be walls put up to protect against invaders, whether they were insects or competitors.

It was the money that kept me from dismissing her suspicions entirely. But I was still far from convinced as I stood now outside the restaurant.

"Yeah, it's fishy," I said to Fife. "Nobody would argue that. But the doctor's suggesting that Jason Deele blew into town, gave everyone his name and address while peddling his super soybean, then turned around and destroyed some crops with the very mold he was offering to defeat. Nobody's that stupid."

Fife examined a folded menu while we waited. "Sure, it sounds stupid. And fishy isn't enough to convict anyone. Deele's smart enough to know that. But why would he care if people *are* suspicious? All he has to claim is that he's a visionary, that he saw trouble coming, not that he created it."

"I don't know," I said. "This was a long way to come for something that doesn't sound like a conspiracy to me. It smacks more of professional jealousy than criminal intent."

"I might have agreed," Fife said, "until Culbertson took two rounds to the back of the head while trying to follow up Eklund's claim."

The hostess stepped outside to tell us they were bussing the table and it would only be another minute or so. After thanking her I said to Fife, "Okay, let's talk about this USDA agent. The only reason he was sent here to poke around in the first place was to placate a politician. But Poole's file included some background on Mr. Culbertson, and I perused it enough before drifting off last night to know he was into a lot of other shit besides investigating nefarious bean peddlers."

This brought a snort from Fife. "Do tell."

Before I could lay it all out the hostess was back, asking us to follow her. We wound our way through a maze of tables to a great spot near a window. After ordering hot tea and coffee, we were left to explore the full-sized version of the menu. Banana-walnut pancakes jumped out immediately so I set the laminated page aside.

"Agent Culbertson," I said, "was not a popular fellow. He was the subject of an internal investigation three years ago when a farming conglomerate accused him of extortion."

"Extortion?" Fife asked. "In what way?"

"Holding back a crucial report by a couple of months unless they ponied up some big bucks. The report meant a bottom-line difference of about $2 million, so I guess Culbertson figured that was worth a cool 50 grand. Anyway, that was the charge by the company's CEO, only there was no corroborating evidence. No emails, voice mails, nothing to confirm. So it was dropped."

"Could've been innocent," Fife said.

"Sure, could've been innocent then *and* the two other times it's been whispered by other companies."

Our server showed up with Fife's coffee and my tea. We ordered our food, then got to work doctoring our drinks.

"So you're saying he was a crooked USDA agent who never got officially caught," Fife said.

"Lots of smoke even if nobody ever found the fire. But that's just the beginning. I haven't gotten to the women or the gambling."

The FBI agent laughed. "I gotta get Poole's file."

"I'll send you a copy. Kept me up later than I'd planned. See, Culbertson was based in Chicago, and there's a *Mrs.* Culbertson there. Twice she filed for divorce on grounds of infidelity, and both times she withdrew the paperwork. The second time she did it after Culbertson took out a new life insurance policy on himself worth two million."

"With Mrs. Culbertson as the beneficiary."

"Naturally."

"You're not suggesting his wife had him executed, are you?"

I shook my head. "No. But the women he allegedly messed around with were the wives of some very important people in his territory. Oh, and one adult daughter."

Fife took a sip of his coffee. "Sounds like the beginning of a joke about the farmer's daughter."

"Yeah. And a punch line with two 9mm slugs. Anyway, all I'm saying is there were lots of people who cried no tears when he went face-down on that roadside."

"And the gambling?"

I blew on my hot tea then took a drink. "This one I actually have a connection with, believe it or not. Culbertson fancied himself a hotshot poker player. Loved to wiggle his way into some of those back-room/high-stakes games, the kind you see in movies."

"Like *Rounders*," Fife said.

"Exactly. And he was pretty good, too. But not always good enough."

"So he had debts."

"It's not so much the debt," I said, "but who he owed. And that's my thin connection to all this. Culbertson was rumored to be in deep with a Chicago-area gangster by the name of Vincent Volta."

"Vinnie Volta? You're making that name up."

"*Nobody* could make that up. Well, maybe Quentin Tarantino. Vincent Volta is a guy who came west from Philadelphia about twenty-five years ago and muscled his way into some extensive territory just outside the primary circle of influence of the Chicago mob."

"The suburban don, is that what you're saying?" Fife asked. "Why haven't I heard of him?"

"Because he's about as low-key as you'll find. Doesn't overplay his hand, doesn't squabble with other bosses, and keeps the body count to a minimum."

"And what's your connection?"

I took another sip of tea. "A few years ago I had a case that didn't actually involve the mob, but in a roundabout way the asshole I took out was on Volta's shit list. I have no idea how he knew where to find me, but he and a couple of his boys stopped by my hotel room as I was packing to leave. Vincent shook my hand. Said I did him a solid and he'd remember."

Fife laughed hard. "Oh, great. A Q2 agent helping out a gangster. I'll assume this is yet another chapter of your career that Quanta doesn't know about."

"Shit, I stopped thinking I could hide anything from her a long time ago," I said. "Let's just say it didn't make my official report. Besides, why bother reporting anything? That's a chip I may never cash in. It was more than ten bodies ago; Volta wouldn't recognize me today. I can't exactly waltz in and say I had a makeover."

"Good point."

Our food showed up and we spent the next five minutes making sounds of satisfaction. Dr. Eklund had been spot-on with her recommendation.

"All right," Fife said, savoring a piece of bacon. "So we have a strange combination of factors at play here. We have Dr. Eklund convinced that a guy named Jason Deele is intentionally killing off soybean crops. We have a USDA agent who investigated the claim and wound up murdered. But this same agent also had enemies because of extortion claims, infidelity accusations, and through crossing a Chicago gangster. Does that about sum it up?"

"Yes," I said. "Except it doesn't include the potential motives from Eklund. There could very well be more to her story, too. What's your status with all this? Are you in Des Moines for the duration?"

"I'm here for the next week, but I have another case I'm helping with in Dallas. So I'll be back and forth, juggling both assignments. What's your next move?"

"I'd like to sit down with the accused villain, Mr. Deele. Let's set that up."

Fife shook his head. "That'll have to wait a couple of days. He's in South America."

"Selling more of his magic beans?"

"That's right. He got the foothold in Paraguay and Argentina, now he wants more. He's making kissy-face with some of the outfits trying to take a bite out of Brazil's market share. His assistant says he may not be back in Iowa for some time."

"Where's his office?"

"Houston."

I pushed my plate away. "All right, then when he's back home I'll head down there. Maybe you can pop down from Dallas. In the meantime I'll start with two other angles. One more meeting with Dr. Eklund, this time outside her office. I'd like to get a gauge on her when she's not on home court. And probably a quick drive to Chicago just to eliminate the possibility of Volta having anything to do with this."

I checked the time on my phone. "Maybe I'll do that first. Drive out this afternoon, stop in and visit him in the morning, and get back here late tomorrow."

"Want company?"

"Sure, if you don't mind road trips. But I'll probably handle the actual meeting alone. It's going to be tough enough bullshitting my way in as just one guy."

"Since you can't tell Volta you're Swan, how are you gonna arrange a meeting?"

"I don't know. Haven't got that far yet." I waved a hand. "Probably a wasted trip, anyway. My gut says Volta's got nothing to do with this."

"I hope he doesn't," Fife said, reaching for the check.

"Why?"

He glanced at the breakfast total, then set the check back down with a credit card. "Because I'd hate for this to be just another mobster hit. That's boring. I'm pulling for the magic beans to spice things up."

A DRIVE SOUNDED GOOD. It would take five hours to reach Volta's stomping grounds in Illinois, and I wanted to use that time to let the preliminary facts simmer in the background. I did some of my best thinking behind the wheel. Not always focused on a case, of course, but good thinking nonetheless.

I threw a quick bag together and texted Fife that I'd pick him up in ten minutes. Then I walked to my SUV and called Poole, who said Quanta would be unavailable unless there were extreme emergencies. So I told Poole the plan.

"How do you know this Vincent Volta is even there?" she asked.

"As I recall he doesn't leave town very often. Doesn't do much of anything besides sit in the shadows and pull strings. That's what's kept him alive in a dirty business for so long."

She said she'd book two rooms near Volta's territory. "Anything else to report?"

"Not yet," I said, pulling up to Fife's hotel. "But since I'm going to be near Chicago, why don't you also see if you can set up a meeting for us with the widow of this USDA agent, Culbertson. Preferably tonight."

"Okay," she said before hanging up. "I'll let you know what I arrange."

The FBI agent threw his own small bag into the back seat and climbed in. I'd pulled up a favorite playlist on my phone and a song by Lenny Kravitz pulsed in the background.

As he buckled his seat belt I pulled out of the parking lot and headed toward I-80.

"I suppose you follow the rule of driver-decides-the-music," Fife said.

"Damned right."

He was quiet for a moment, then said, "This is pretty good, actually."

"*All* of it is good."

"We'll see." He pulled out his phone and scrolled. "I just

got the report on Culbertson's murder." Then he was quiet, until he added, "Hmm."

"Out with it," I said.

He read from his screen. "*Victim's hands were bound behind his back using a belt, presumed to belong to the victim. Lying on his side.*" Fife mumbled some technical details. Then: "*Victim appears to have been rolled over so that the entrance wounds were against the ground.*"

"Why would they shoot him and then roll him to the other side?" I asked.

"Hold on." He kept reading. "*Death caused by two gunshot wounds to the left side of the head, both shots having passed through the skull. No casings were found at the scene, nor were bullets recovered. Presumed that perpetrator or perpetrators retrieved the four items—two casings, two bullets.*"

It was my turn to grunt. "So they put his head against the ground, fired two rounds, then rolled him over and dug the remnants out of the soil. What about prints on the belt? Tire tracks, footprints?"

"Nothing on the belt other than a few smudges belonging to the victim. The car apparently stopped on the pavement, so no tracks in the dirt. And any tracks there alongside the road were kicked clean."

I shook my head. "Doesn't by itself spell professional, but implies someone was very cautious about evidence. And that *suggests* a pro."

Fife was quiet while he read a little more, then set his phone into one of the cup holders and adjusted his seat to lean back.

"I slept like shit last night," he said. "You don't mind if I nap for a few miles, do ya?"

"No problem. Want the music off?"

"A lot of times I sleep with a TV on. Sound doesn't bother me. Unsolved cases bother me."

Three minutes later he was lightly snoring. I turned the music down just a touch and settled in for a long drive to meet a mobster.

5

———

Against a background shuffle of songs—and an FBI agent's muted snores—I thought about Dr. Eklund and her concerns over Jason Deele. On one hand I wanted to dismiss her fears as either coincidence or, as I'd wondered before, professional jealousy.

But one thing had pierced the tough outer shell surrounding Sarah Eklund: A true passion for her studies. Her charge against Deele almost came across as a parent protecting her child against a bully. Or, to tap into an agricultural metaphor, Deele was an invading insect that needed to be stopped before he ravaged the country's heartland.

In many ways I envied the passion she brought to her job. I'd always taken pride in having similar drive and determination, whether it was a military operation in my younger days or a challenging case assigned by Quanta. But my recent education at the hands of the original Q2 agent and God Maker had my mind spinning. It wasn't that I didn't have the fire necessary to complete a task; it was more like the flames raged out of control, a fire unable to be contained, burning in a haphazard manner, threatening me as much as they threatened my targets.

This particular case in the heartland could be very important, but I was still surprised Quanta had sent me on the mission without insisting I first meet with Q2's resident psychiatrist. I'd felt sure my long layoff would've necessitated a mandatory session with the man known simply as Miller. And I wouldn't have complained. Miller and I had a long history of illuminating conversations; the fact that I hadn't spoken with him since the mind-shattering experience with Agent One was puzzling.

Or maybe Quanta and Miller had conferred, coming to an agreement that the great Eric Swan needed activity more than he needed analysis. At least for the time being. And part of me now questioned if this case in the cornfields—or soy fields, rather—wasn't more of a tune-up than anything else. A major league team taking on its Double-A affiliate. Just something to knock the rust off and get back into playing shape before the real brain-dissection began.

Was it possible this case was nothing more than that?

I tossed a quick glance at Sleeping Beauty next to me. That part didn't fit. Why involve more than one agency if this was merely a case of a philandering USDA agent who crossed a wiseguy and paid the price?

Then again, the FBI agent in my passenger seat was also a former Q2 employee, someone who'd worked with Quanta before being planted with the G-men. Was this just a favor to get me some work?

That would really piss me off. And it wasn't like Quanta and I needed any more bad blood between us at the moment.

For the time being I'd play it straight, assume that a vegetable version of *Jurassic Park*'s Henry Wu was designing both super soybeans and malicious molds, and do my job. But my bullshit detector would be set to sensitive.

Sixty miles passed before Fife woke up and stretched.

"Thanks for letting me sleep," he said, adjusting his seat to a more upright position. He looked at the track information on the screen. "Is *Imperial Drag* the name of the song or the band?"

"Band. Let me expose you to some good stuff and you'll thank me."

"Sure. But please don't make me a mix tape. We don't know each other well enough."

I pulled off the highway to pee and grab something to drink. When I got back to the SUV Fife was behind the wheel. He said, "Let me give you a break for a bit."

"Okay with me." I got into the passenger seat and handed him a bottled water. "But I still control the tunes."

He laughed and maneuvered us back onto I-80, heading east.

"Let me ask you something," I said, opening a can of Pringles and offering it to him. "Did you jump at the chance to leave Q2 to work for the FBI?"

He seemed to ponder his answer, and I realized he wasn't sure how much he could say. Then he said, "Well, technically, I still work for Q2. Or for both, I guess." He shrugged. "It's complicated. I don't communicate with Quanta nearly as much anymore, but she has access to me. That's about all I can say."

"Did she send you to visit me in the hospital?"

"What?" He turned to look at me with an expression that slowly faded into irritation. "No. I guess it might look that way now, but no. I went to see you because you're a friend. And to anticipate your next question, I was just as surprised as you when she assigned you to this case. I figured if Q2 got involved it would be another agent."

I didn't respond right away. During my last mission I'd discovered I was the only current field agent within the organization. Well, with the exception of a new recruit, a British agent I'd recommended named Parnell. But I had no idea if she was active at the moment. Even when there *were* other agents, we never knew each other's identity, nor anything else for that matter. The secret of a secret agent often began with their name.

I decided for the time being to let Fife assume there were several of us. "Okay," I said. "I had to ask. Sorry."

For a mile the only sound came from the music. Then Fife said, "I get it. You're in a much different position than I am, and I can't even imagine the shitty mind games you have to deal with. I've been a cop, then a data man for Q2, and now a quasi-agent for the feds. I don't blame you for wondering. But, honestly, I'm not keeping anything from you, Swan. All right?"

I nodded and let the matter drop. I liked Fife, and the last thing I wanted was friction between us. The fact that I had trust issues within the organization was my problem, not his.

"Let's talk about this Jason Deele character," I said, hoping a change of subject would break the sudden tension. "Poole's dossier on him is pretty black-and-white. Got any dirt?"

He reached for another Pringle. "I haven't met this guy yet. But I have to tell you, from the stuff I've read and the video clips I've watched, he creeps me the hell out."

I laughed. "Why?"

"I don't know. It's not like he's perfect. You saw that he had some minor issues in college, right? A bout of depression had him hospitalized for a couple days. No run-ins with the law. But he just doesn't . . . tick right."

"Did you say *tick right*?"

"Yeah. Like a good watch or clock goes *tick, tick, tick*. I have a feeling the watch version of Deele goes *tick, ticktick, tick, tickticktick*." He took a drink from his water bottle. "Like this one video I found. He's explaining some lab work and suddenly his eyes grow really wide and he freezes, like a thought was swelling inside his head, like a balloon. Then a second later he smiles, his eyes shrink down to normal size, and he slips back into his speech."

I laughed.

"No, I mean it," Fife said. "The dude is brilliant, but man, he's strange. Didn't Eklund get that across?"

"Hey," I said. "What she got across is that she hates the guy. I don't know if it's because of his soybean threat or his *tickticktick*, but she just does not like the man."

"Here's what bothers me. I get such an odd feeling about the guy that I wonder if he's mentally capable of doing what Eklund *thinks* he's doing. Not the brains, but the—what's the word? Maybe the capacity to pull that off. Does that make sense?"

"It does," I said. "And he wouldn't be the first person to get away with murder because everyone underestimated that capacity. So, yeah, I hear you."

"Then there's his daredevil side," Fife said. "You'll probably like this part."

"What kind of daredevil?"

"The jump-out-of-planes type. And bungee jumping, base jumping."

"Adrenaline junkie," I said. "Probably was the kid who

made a homemade cape out of a bath towel and jumped off the back of the couch."

"And more than just jumping. Paragliding, parasailing, cave diving."

"He's like a walking X-Games."

"The file says he spends a lot of his time doing something extreme. I wouldn't be surprised if he made his fortune just so he'd have the money to play hard."

We fell quiet again. I thought about what Fife had said when it came to ticking, and how for some people it was off just a bit. An adrenaline freak fit that profile perfectly. Fife might've been thinking the same thing. For the next ten miles we kept those thoughts to ourselves, listening to the music, and wondering if Jason Deele was the danger Sarah Eklund thought him to be.

CHICAGO ISN'T JUST A CITY. It's a hub, a sprawling mass of people and industry, a confluence of diverse backgrounds that somehow adopted an *us-against-the-world* personality. Its attitude extends from the lakefront and Michigan Avenue out through the North Side, the South Side, and the Westside, then seeps into the collective suburbs making up what's commonly known as Chicagoland.

Like many of the great cities of the world, it has a turbo-charged ego.

That's not a slight. Ego is a sense of self, and this Midwestern monster of a town swells with a healthy sense of self. It lies behind the city's catchy moniker, *the Windy City*, which may have begun as a nod to the bitter winds whipping off Lake Michigan, but soon came to represent the bellowing politicians and their propensity to blow loads of hot air.

When I was a kid it was a popular destination for my family, and I loved it even more the older I got. It culminated with one non-stop party in Chicago for the five days between leaving college and reporting to Fort Benning in Georgia.

Given my condition when I arrived for Army training, it wasn't the wisest decision I've ever made. But I wouldn't trade those five days for anything, even after all the puking.

Fife still piloted the SUV, so as we approached Naperville I became the navigator. Since it was late afternoon we drove straight to the hotel Poole had arranged. We agreed to meet in the lobby at six to hunt down dinner.

I collapsed on the bed, preparing to call Christina, when a text popped up from Poole. David Culbertson's wife would see us tonight at eight. Poole attached a phone number and the address of a house about 45 minutes from our hotel.

The call with Christina was quick. It was a rare day off for her, and she was preparing to go to dinner with an old college friend.

"Sounds fun," I said to her.

"Even better, she invited me and said everything's on her."

"Does she know you're eating for two? Could get expensive."

"With the way Antonio and Marissa have been on my ass, I feel like I'm eating for four."

I laughed. "You're not regretting this, are you?"

"Oh, no. Everything's good. Perfect, actually. I like to exaggerate how fussy they are—and it's mostly Antonio—because it's about the only thing I can find to complain about. You know, my mother always made it sound like carrying me around for nine months was a nightmare, so having this be a cake walk is just surprising. I was prepared to be miserable."

"Wasn't your mom generally miserable anyway?"

"Yes. But you're not allowed to say that; only *I* can say that. How's Iowa?"

"It was good, but now I'm in Chicago. Or right next door to it."

"Oh," she said. "Well, if you're near State Street have a slice of pizza for me from Pizano's."

"Doubt I'll get that far into town, but if I do I'll have two slices for you."

We talked another five minutes before she took off for dinner.

I had one more call to make before meeting Fife. I'd kept the number in my contacts for several years, just in case.

"Yeah," the voice said after four rings.

"Calling to set up a meeting with Mr. Volta."

There was silence on the other end, then: "And who are you?"

"All you have to tell him is that I was sent by Eric Swan. If he needs a memory refresher, just tell him it's about the favor Swan did for him in Grant Park four years ago."

Silence again.

"Have you got all that?" I asked. "Do you need me to spell Swan?"

"Do you need me to shove a swan up your ass?" the voice said.

"Maybe some other time. I've been driving all day. Just take down this number, give Volta my message, then we can all be friends again." I gave him the number. As soon as I said the last digit he hung up.

Fife was waiting in the lobby and had picked out a good brewpub within walking distance. By the time we got there and grabbed a high-top table I had another text message.

"What's the word?" Fife asked, perusing the beer list.

"The word is you only get one beer tonight. At least for now. We have a date with Tami Culbertson at eight o'clock."

"Then I'll get a 24 ounce."

"I'll join you. Plus the text just now was from the social organizer for a certain wise guy. I'm granted an audience tomorrow morning at ten."

"No shit. You already have a meeting set up? That didn't take long."

"You have to know how to sweet-talk the gatekeeper," I said.

6

Tami Culbertson was around 50, tall, dark hair, in excellent shape. She carried herself in the way you normally associate with confidence and determination.

She also carried a beer.

A 23-foot motor home was parked in front of the Culbertson house, and the now-widow of the USDA agent was cleaning it out. She'd offered us beers when we arrived, which we declined, then she pointed at a cooler near the RV's back door and told us to help ourselves if we changed our minds.

The inside of the Gulfstream wasn't huge, so Fife and I did our best to stay out of her way as she meticulously went through cabinets and drawers, pulling out things that either went into a large box or into one of those giant Hefty trash bags. From what I could tell, the bulk of the items ended up in the garbage. She did all of it with one hand while taking regular swigs from a bottle of Red Stripe.

"FBI, huh? Cops have already been here to talk to me," she said. "Twice. So I don't know what you can ask that I haven't already answered."

51

"Well," Fife said, "the police have their investigation, and we have ours. First, we'd like to express our condolences for your loss."

She grunted and took another drink. "Loss? I just made two million bucks."

Fife and I looked at each other, but before we could comment she continued.

"And on top of that I can finally get rid of this piece of shit RV, which I never wanted in the first place."

"David talked you into this?" I asked.

"No, he did not *talk me into it*. He just bought it. Said he wanted it to go hunting and camping. But see, Dave was not really a hunter or a camper, so it left the storage facility maybe twice a year. Soon as I get everything out of here it's getting sold. Cheap."

She stopped and pointed the beer at us. "Either of you want an RV with practically no miles on it?"

"No ma'am," said Fife. "But thank you."

She shrugged. "Don't blame you. So what do you want?"

"Uh," I said, not sure if we were witnessing a strange reaction to horrific news—people tend to respond to tragedy in very different ways—or if Tami Culbertson truly gave no shits that her husband had been murdered. "We're looking into an investigation your husband was involved with. It's possible it could explain what happened to him."

She moved toward the front of the motor home, speaking over her shoulder. "Oh, you don't need to investigate too much to find out what happened to Dave. I can tell you exactly what happened."

Fife and I exchanged another look. "Okay," I said. "We'd love to hear it."

She knelt down and began emptying a bottom drawer. I

noticed that now things weren't getting even a cursory inspection; all of the contents went straight into the trash.

"Karma. That's what happened to David P. Culbertson, asshole first class. Built up like magma under Mount St. Helens and blew the top off his world. Literally, from what I'm told. You can only shit on people for so long before the universe steps in and says *That's all for you, you son of a bitch. Good night.*" She stood back up. "So that should wrap up your investigation. Just fill in the paperwork with *Karma Is A Bitch.*" She spelled it out in the air with the hand holding the Red Stripe.

Okay. So this was *not* a strange reaction to grief. Tami Culbertson absolutely hated her husband and was about one step away from dancing on a table to celebrate his death. Not to be crude and insensitive, but in three minutes this had already become my favorite interview of all time. I could've talked with Tami for hours. For a split second the thought crossed my mind of taking her out for cocktails to see just how much she'd say once she really got wound up. But only if I could record it to play back whenever I was depressed about my work.

"I understand," Fife said to her. "But I hope you appreciate that we can't really log karma as a cause of death. As for the actual murder, we were hoping you might have some insight into who might've wanted him dead. And please, don't say *everybody.*"

She smiled. "Ah, you beat me to it. Well, I guess I should be Suspect Number One. I couldn't stand the bastard and I just made a shitload of money from his death. Trouble is, I didn't have anything to do with it."

"Did you think about doing it?" I asked, prodding her.

"Nope. Never had to."

"What does that mean?"

"It means somebody was bound to eventually shoot Dave. All I had to do was wait it out."

"But you tried to divorce him twice," Fife said.

"Oh, I never intended to divorce him. Never would've followed through. Because I knew he'd do anything to keep that from happening."

"Like bump up the life insurance," I said.

"Damn right. You thought I was kidding about knowing someone would kill him? That was no joke."

I leaned against the door frame. "So who would be most likely? Did he talk about the case he was working on in Iowa?"

"Nope. If you officers are not going to join me, would you reach into that cooler and hand me another?"

When Fife passed her a beer she said, "No, Dave didn't talk about his cases with me anymore. Used to, back when we first moved here. Thought I was interested in all the drama between the government and farmers, which I wasn't. Of course, he really wasn't, either. Just a way to make a living where he didn't have to work too hard and had enough free time and travel to screw around on his wife. I'm surprised he kept the job as long as he did. Wouldn't be surprised if his own bosses had him whacked. I'm sure the thought crossed their minds."

I asked, "So no one ever called or visited the house regarding any of his cases?"

She shook her head. "No. I did get an email from a woman about a year ago. Said she'd had an affair with my husband, thought I should know." She laughed. "Obviously he'd done her dirt and now she was trying to ruin his life. I wrote back to her and said, *Honey, you're like someone standing in line at the supermarket deli. Sorry to tell you, you're number 67. Try the smoked ham.*"

I didn't want to walk away empty-handed, but it didn't look like the merry widow had anything that could help. I tried another angle. "What about gambling problems? Did he ever say anything about that? Maybe somebody who he'd crossed?"

For the first time she paused in her frenetic cleaning. She sat down on the bench seat of the dining table, took a slow drink of the beer, and stared at us.

"You know," she finally said. "There was something going on there."

"Can you be more specific?" Fife asked.

She tapped a finger on the table, thinking. "He used to sit in on some big poker games. I only know because he bragged every time he came home a winner. Of course, he didn't say shit when he got cleaned out. Big ego when it came to poker, liked to think he was a Vegas kind of guy. But a few weeks ago he dragged in at six in the morning, after one of those all-nighters. And for the first time he seemed worried. I asked him what was wrong—not that I really cared, just, you know, making conversation."

"And what did he say?" I asked.

"He said, *I did something stupid.* It was all I could do to not say, *You've been doing stupid shit for years.* But I just acted curious, and he said he'd pissed off the wrong guy. Or something along those lines. But that was it. Seemed worried about it for an hour, then went right back to being his asshole self. Never said another word about it."

She set the beer down on the table and twisted the bottle, looking at it. "I forgot about that. Guess I should've told the police, but it didn't cross my mind until you brought it up."

"But he didn't mention any names? Any details?"

"No. Just said he'd screwed up. I figured he owed someone some big money, someone dangerous, but that it would blow over. I mean, the guy spent every dime the minute he made it. We have shit for savings, but he always found ways to pay his gambling debts." She looked up at us. "I didn't ask where he got the cash to do that, but it was pretty obvious it wasn't from his paycheck. Probably the same way he bought this piece of shit RV, and a golf membership, and expensive toys. Maybe blackmailing some of those married women he hooked up with. I don't know. I never asked."

If she was suddenly feeling a bit sad about things, those emotions expired in a flash. With a shake of her head and another swig of beer, she stood up again and grabbed the trash bag. "Sorry, but I didn't kill him. Anything else I can help with?"

"I don't think so," Fife said. "I'll leave a card right here. If you think of something later, maybe any names of people who may have been involved, please reach out."

"Will do," she said, not even looking at us. She'd gone back to work. We backed out of the piece of shit RV and walked back to my rental.

Once inside with the engine running, Fife and I both laughed.

"My lord," Fife said. "What just happened?"

"I am officially crossing Tami Culbertson off the list of possible suspects," I said. "If she'd done it, that lady would not only admit it to us, she'd probably go door to door in the neighborhood telling everyone. Most un-grief-stricken widow of all time."

"Very entertaining, but not too helpful."

"Oh, I don't know. In a way she corroborated the rumor that Culbertson was in debt to someone powerful. Could be

Volta. Could be someone else. Between that and Tami's phone call from the jilted lover, it's more evidence this murder might not have involved the soybean conspiracy at all."

"So this trip may not require the skills of the great Eric Swan," Fife said, pulling out of the neighborhood.

"Don't tell Quanta," I said. "But I'm having fun again."

As it turned out, Quanta was the one who wanted to talk. She sent a text, requesting a video call at ten o'clock.

That gave me enough time to get back to the hotel room, order some room service snacks, and get into comfortable clothes. At precisely ten my phone vibrated. Behind her I could see her kitchen.

"Poole tells me you're in Chicago."

"Naperville. Probably won't make it into the city. Which is too bad; the Cubbies are at Wrigley this week."

"And you met with Culbertson's wife?"

"Quanta, that is one straight-shooting woman. Well, not literally. She didn't gun down her husband or hire someone to do it. I'm sure of that."

"Did you get *anything* useful out of her?"

"So far I'm not seeing much to suggest that soybeans had anything to do with the murder. Dr. Eklund is convinced this guy Jason Deele is the antichrist. And who knows, he could turn out to be evil. But I won't get a chance to talk with him until he's back from South America. In the meantime I'm going to follow up some other angles around the murder."

Quanta narrowed her gaze. "The murder wasn't the reason you were sent out there. The Deputy Secretary wanted an investigation into Dr. Eklund's concerns."

"I get that. But let's say the murder of this USDA agent *is* connected to Deele. Eliminating the other possibilities strengthens that case, and might open more avenues to investigate. Right now we're basing everything on a bad feeling from someone who may be motivated personally rather than professionally."

"And a contaminated crop. That doesn't seem suspicious to you?"

"It does a little. But it's also an isolated incident. There are a lot of steps between one ruined crop and a plague on an entire industry."

She seemed to consider it. "All right. Now tell me about this person you're meeting with tomorrow."

"Hold on a sec," I said, and walked over to answer a knock at the door. A hotel employee had a cart with my late-night treats. I tipped him, rolled the cart over by the bed, and picked up the phone.

"Sorry, a quesadilla was calling my name. So, tomorrow. Vincent Volta could be a person of interest in the murder. It's maybe not crucial to what I'm doing in Iowa, but I'd like to know if Culbertson was killed because of soybeans or a gambling debt."

"And you expect a mobster to just come right out and tell you he had someone killed?"

"Actually, yes."

Quanta raised an eyebrow.

"Volta is proud and brutally honest," I said. "Believe me, if he had Culbertson shot he'll tell me in a way that won't incriminate him. That's all I'm looking for on this trip: crossing off possibilities. Tami Culbertson has been eliminated; tomorrow I'll see if we can scratch off another."

"I don't suppose I need to know how you arranged a meeting with the mob."

"Without going into too much detail, let's just say Vincent and I have crossed paths. Don't worry, nothing that would embarrass Q2 or put us at risk. And no, I haven't done anything illegal."

She didn't seem entirely mollified, but let it go for the time being.

"All right. Let me remind you that a deputy secretary has put pressure on the FBI and on us to figure out if there's a threat here. And this is someone with strong ties to Pennsylvania Avenue. Let's be sure to make her step-daughter feel she has our full attention."

I sighed. "Right. I'll kiss the appropriate ass at the appropriate times."

"Swan, bear in mind that it's possible Dr. Eklund is right, as outlandish as it may seem. I understand your skepticism. Just keep an open mind."

"Hey, I'm actually hoping Eklund's right. The case would be much more exciting if I stumbled onto a soybean mafia."

"In case Poole hasn't requested it," Quanta said, "I want you to upload tonight. And probably tomorrow after your meeting."

"Okay."

We signed off. But there was no way I was uploading twice within 18 hours.

For one thing, I didn't have enough good trash magazines with me.

7

———

F ife waited at the hotel while I made the 20-minute drive to Medinah, one of the ritzier private clubs in Illinois. My instructions were to check in with the security staff at the front gate, and from there to gather directions to The Oasis. Vincent Volta would be on the patio.

I had two lasting memories of Volta from my lone, brief encounter with him in a hotel room in Chicago four years earlier. One, he had movie star good looks. At the time he'd been in his mid-50s but looked 40, with perfect hair and a trim, athletic build. The only thing marring his appearance was the faint hint of a scar running vertically down his right cheek. He obviously used makeup to deflect attention from it, either out of pure vanity or to help facilitate his facade as a respectable businessman. Of course, he was a mobster, so I'd have been surprised if he didn't have mementos of a tough life displayed somewhere on his body.

The other memory involved his bass voice. Deep didn't begin to describe it. You couldn't help but imagine testicles the size of cantaloupes, which probably didn't hurt his image when dealing with fellow gangsters. When Vincent Volta spoke, you felt it as much as heard it, a rumble that caused your own balls to vibrate; I couldn't imagine what physical effect it had on women.

He'd be about 60 now, but he hadn't changed one bit.

He sat at a table in the sun, facing one of the club's three golf courses, his brown eyes obscured by a pair of Dior sunglasses that likely ran about 600 bucks. It was a cool day, but he wore a short-sleeved polo shirt, displaying toned arms. And, as expected, he wasn't alone. Volta had no idea who I was, and until he established some sort of comfort zone he'd have muscle right there—likely with a finger on the trigger of a concealed piece.

"Mr. Volta," I said, approaching the table. His associate, an imposing six-and-a-half footer, stood, sizing me up, wearing the face of a fighter at weigh-in. I reached to pull out the chair across from Volta, but the mob boss gave a slight shake of his head and his trained gorilla placed a hand on my wrist to stop me.

"I will need some information about you before I invite you to join me," Volta said, holding up a finger. Nothing had changed; shock waves like a car stereo with the bass on 10 made my balls shake.

I let go of the chair and tugged my arm out of the grip of his monster.

"Sure," I said. "My name is Griffin. Do I have permission to retrieve a card from my jacket pocket?"

He nodded once. I reached in delicately and pulled out one of my multiple cover cards, this one listing me as Special Agent D. Griffin from the FBI. I handed it to the gorilla who handed it to Volta. He glanced at it only briefly before tossing it on the table.

"That's a card. It's not exactly the identification I was looking for."

"Fair enough. I'm not a close friend of Eric Swan, but we're acquainted. I knew he'd worked a case in Chicago a few years ago where he might have crossed paths with you, so I got in touch. He said if I wanted to meet with you I should tell you one thing: *The bastard's cologne should've stopped the bullet.*"

For a moment there was no reaction. The cologne reference was something I'd said to Volta in that hotel room four years earlier, one of those comments that never goes into a filed report, but something Volta had found very funny at the time. His nemesis—the one I'd killed in the line of duty—doused himself regularly in some of the most foul fragrances I'd ever smelled on a man.

Finally a slight smile broke across the mobster's face, and he used a hand to indicate the chair facing him. I gave a *piss off* look to the bodyguard and sat down. The goon moved back a few steps but stood ready.

"I have only a few minutes to spare," Volta said.

"I appreciate that. I'm looking into the case of a murdered agent with the USDA."

Volta didn't answer, and, with the dark shades on, his eyes gave away nothing.

"The man's name was David Culbertson. He was investigating something across the border in Iowa when someone saw fit to put two bullets through his head and leave his corpse on the side of the road."

There was still no answer. Volta was a cool character, not anxious in any way to help me.

"The reason I'm here to see you," I said, "is because there are reports—strictly rumors, of course—that Culbertson had run into a bit of trouble with you."

Volta finally spoke, his words coming out slow. *"A bit of trouble?* Are you here, Special Agent Griffin, to question me about the murder of a government agent? You consider me a suspect?"

I shifted in my seat, an unconscious reaction to his voice. I resisted the urge to adjust the crotch of my pants.

"You're someone who's had recent dealings with the victim. Someone who, I understand, was owed a good sum of money by that victim. My visit is purely standard operating procedure in an overall investigation."

He was quiet a moment, then pushed his sunglasses up onto the top of his head. Those hard, brown eyes drilled right through me. Vincent Volta, between his eyes, his muscular physique, and that Darth Vader voice could scare the living shit out of anyone.

"It sounds, Mr. Griffin, like you're fishing for information to implicate me in a heinous crime, one I would never be involved with."

I smiled. "Mr. Volta. There's no wire here. I'm not recording you. I'm not trying to implicate you in anything. In fact, if you want to know the truth, I'm here to eliminate you as a suspect. But I *would* like to know a bit about David Culbertson's debt, to you and to others, and whether or not you know who *is* responsible for his death. Mr. Swan indicated that you would—if you'll pardon the pun—shoot straight with me. He didn't have to broker this meeting. But I can tell you that violating a trust with you would violate any trust I have with him, and I'm not going to do that."

A waiter stopped by the table and set down two glasses of water and two small metal bowls of snacks, a country club form of Chex Mix. When he'd walked away Volta picked up his water and took a drink, his eyes never leaving mine.

"All right," he said, wiping his mouth with a napkin. "I did know Mr. Culbertson. He was another guest at some gatherings I attended."

"Poker parties," I said.

He waved assent. "He was . . . not as skilled as he believed himself to be."

"I heard he had no business being in some of these high-stakes games," I said, dipping fingers into my snack bowl. "Liked the high-roller persona but couldn't back it up. Is that fair?"

"I find it distasteful to denigrate another person's abilities when they're not around to defend themselves."

"Lucky for us I have no qualms about that," I said. "So Culbertson was a shitty card player and owed you money. My information says one hundred grand. Would you describe that as accurate?"

Volta studied my face for a moment, maybe taken aback by my nonchalant style. "Yes, I would say that's accurate. Perhaps a bit more."

"Oh. Well, then you can see why it's important I talk to you. Many people would assume that $100,000 is sufficient motive for having a person killed. I'm guessing your threshold for that would be much higher."

He took another drink, and again dabbed at his mouth. "You're a somewhat vulgar man," he said. "In that respect you remind me quite a bit of Mr. Swan. In fact, your manner of speech is practically identical."

"We flunked out of the same charm school. You've had to deal with much cruder people than Swan or me, I'm sure."

It took a minute, but the same faint smile he'd displayed after the cologne comment reappeared.

"All right, Agent Griffin, if you want me to be up front

with you, I will. Yes, Culbertson owed me money, a great deal of money. But he's not the first person to be in debt to me, and I assure you he won't be the last. And as for having him killed over it? People only jump to that conclusion because they're amateurs or they listen to too many crime podcasts. There's a very good reason you don't kill someone who owes you a large sum."

"Yes?"

"A dead man can't repay his debt. Only a fool would let them off the hook that way."

"Right," I said, taking another dip into the snobby Chex Mix. "You'd be more likely to set up a payment plan."

"I *did* set up a payment plan."

"Oh. I was kidding."

"And I am not. I worked out an arrangement for Mr. Culbertson to pay off his debt over three months."

"Three months? That's it? To pay back a hundred grand?"

"Plus a little more."

I laughed. "Ah, yes. The juice."

Volta gave a small grimace, a sign he really had morphed into a gentleman mobster who disdained the old gangland terms.

"Three months may not seem like a lot," he said, "but Culbertson was confident that a rather large sum would be coming his way soon."

Now I sat forward, clasping my hands on the table. "Tell me about that."

He looked away, out across the golf course. "Obviously I have no details about the man's other associations."

"But as a businessman offering a loan, you'd naturally be interested in how a person would be able to repay it."

He didn't answer.

I took a long breath. "Look, Mr. Volta, I'm grateful not only for your time, but for your trust. The thing is, I've been tasked with looking into the same issue in Iowa that Culbertson was sent to investigate. I'm not interested in causing you any trouble. But I'd also prefer to avoid ending up face-down on the same country road. So if there's anything Culbertson said, anything at all that might prevent that from happening to me, I'd be very grateful."

There was a muffled buzzing sound, and the bodyguard reached into a pocket to retrieve a phone. After glancing at the screen, he walked over and showed it to Volta who studied it, then gave a quick nod.

"I'm afraid other business has arisen, Special Agent. I'm sorry if I don't have all the information you're requesting." He paused, then said, "But here's what I can share with you. During our discussion about his . . . obligations to me, he mentioned that the bulk of his debt would be taken care of by *squeezing someone*—his words— on one of his particular assignments. I assume now he was talking about the case you're investigating in Iowa."

I squinted in the bright sunshine. "He said he would squeeze someone?"

"What I took from his attitude and his confidence was that he would be able to make his repayment to me in a matter of weeks, rather than months. Now, is that helpful?"

My mind sifted through this development.

"I know you have to go," I said, sitting back again. "But was there anything else he said about it? Any name, or even a reference to what he was looking into?"

"I'm afraid not," Volta said. He pushed back his chair and gave one of his nods to the goon. "But his tone implied that squeezing people wasn't an unfamiliar tactic for him."

I recalled Tami Culbertson's comments about her husband's knack for paying off large gambling debts: *I didn't ask where he got the cash to do that, but it was pretty obvious it wasn't from his paycheck.*

Vincent Volta had provided additional evidence that Culbertson took his vacations and bought his RVs by blackmailing the very people he investigated. Could a jealous husband have had him killed? Maybe. But it was much more likely that the scumbag had finally crossed someone who didn't cotton to extortion. And the USDA agent was probably astonished to find that someone answered his extortion attempts with a couple of 9mm exclamation points.

Volta stood, and I did the same. Neither of us bothered to attempt to shake hands; we were transacting a much different brand of business, one that didn't conform to traditional etiquette. Instead we looked at each other with an odd form of respect.

"Please," Volta said, lowering the sunglasses back into position. "Stay as my guest. You'll find the menu here is remarkable." He pointed to the snack bowls. "Much more satisfying than those."

Then, with his bodyguard leading the way, he began walking toward the exit before stopping and looking back.

"And when you talk to Eric Swan again, let him know our ledgers are balanced. Have a pleasant stay in Chicagoland, Special Agent."

8

———————

The talk with Vincent Volta pissed me off.

Not at him. Myself. I always liked to believe my instincts were good, that I could solve a case in the first five minutes with brainpower alone. But solid-gold instincts, the kind that fueled Sherlock Holmes, Philip Marlowe, and Velma from the Scooby Gang, reside only within the realm of fiction. In real life, detectives and spies stumble their way through missteps, wrong turns, and dead ends until they reach an unhappy conclusion:

Our instincts are correct only as many times as it takes to keep us believing in them.

I have to continually remind myself that getting off track is fine as long as you wind up at the right destination. And on time.

What gnawed at me was the growing realization that the crop nerd probably did it. I'd wanted to believe Sarah Eklund's suspicions were motivated purely by jealousy, but my conversations with Tami Culbertson and the mobster forced me to once again consider Jason Deele.

Yeah, Volta was a criminal, responsible for way more deaths than Deele was. And lots of law-abiding citizens would be horrified to know that a representative of the country's top spy network accepted an offer of a free BLT and chips from a murderous dirtbag who sat around exclusive private clubs in his expensive clothes and designer sunglasses.

I looked at it like this: Volta certainly had people killed, but his victims were other criminals. That doesn't forgive the crime, but it's a lot like Dexter, from the TV show. He was a serial killer who only murdered other serial killers, and viewers cheered him on.

Or, if you want another analogy, I give you the Byers brothers.

Our family moved a lot when I was growing up, but I remember briefly living next door to this family with two brothers, about two years apart in age. They were constantly arguing and picking on each other, behaving exactly like brothers do. I was at their house the day their dad finally had enough of this nonsense. He ordered them to go outside and finally have *the* fight, just to get it out of their system. They couldn't come back inside until they'd settled it.

So they did. They went into the backyard and duked it out. And that was that.

Vincent Volta and his fellow gangsters were like the Byers boys. They stayed in their own yard and fought with each other. Again, he's scum, but he keeps his dirty business in his own yard. Through his long history of crime and his equally-slimy connections, he and his kind are sometimes able to provide useful information to help us nail other creeps.

Plus, his sunglasses really are bitchin'. And the BLT kicked ass.

I stopped at the the hotel long enough to grab my bag and

collect Fife. On the road to Des Moines I caught him up on everything I'd learned.

"So you think the squeeze Volta referenced was Jason Deele." It wasn't a question.

"Seems the most logical assumption," I said. "The bitter widow pretty much confirmed her husband used his position with the USDA to manipulate people and businesses into buying his toys. He made it a habit to lean on people, to the point that he began to count on it as a healthy portion of his income. Only a matter of time before he leaned on the wrong person."

Fife scrolled through messages on his phone as I steered us back onto I-80. "Right. The only other option with his murder would be an angry husband. That would be deliciously scandalous, but it doesn't sound likely anymore."

I just shook my head. "I want a longer chat with Dr. Eklund. We'll be back by five or five-thirty. Think she's game to talk with us tonight?"

"It'll have to be just the two of you," Fife said, holding up his phone. "I got summoned to Dallas early. I have to fly out tonight." He slipped the phone into a cup holder. "You're on your own for a few days. I'll try to meet you in Houston when Deele gets back to the country. That's looking like the day after tomorrow."

"All right." I set the cruise control for the five-hour drive and put the tunes on shuffle.

AS IT TURNED OUT, Sarah Eklund wasn't available until the following morning. That actually worked out okay because I needed 90 minutes to upload these last couple of days to Q2's basement hard drive. This time I made an effort to not think about the potential damage I'd be doing when I needed to download again into a new body. God Maker said the system had improved; I'd have to take her word for it.

Dr. Eklund and I met for breakfast at the same diner she'd recommended before. And because I'm that person who orders the same thing when I find a winner, I salivated over the thought of the pancakes.

"I intend to sit down with Jason Deele when he gets back from South America," I said to her while putting sweetener into my hot tea.

"That's it? Just sit down with him?"

"Well, I can't arrest him for anything at the moment."

"Not even murder?"

I took a sip of the tea. "Believe me, Dr. Eklund, the moment we have evidence he's responsible, he'll be in cuffs. Right now we don't have that evidence."

She let out a sigh. "I know. I'm just frustrated, that's all."

"Talk to me about the damage to the crops. What's the story with the mold?"

"How scientific do you want me to get?"

"It doesn't intimidate me; I find it interesting, even if I need training wheels for a lot of it."

This brought what seemed like a rare smile to her face. I wondered how often she smiled in her life. Was she always wound tight, or was the Deele Soybean War simply an exception?

"I wrote my doctoral dissertation on molds," she said, and gave another shy smile. "It's kinda my thing."

I returned the smile but kept quiet, encouraging her to continue.

"Specifically, I've always been interested in limiting the ability of insects to distribute molds from one crop to another.

That's a critical component to protecting the health of our food."

"And not all molds are bad, right?" I asked.

"That's right. Cheese makers rely on mold to help with many of their products. But the wrong kinds can be not only deadly to a crop, but deadly to humans, too. Something like aflatoxin, which is caused by certain fungi, can lead to liver cancer. And that's just one example."

"How many different molds are there?"

"Oh, god. Hundreds of thousands."

I gawked at her. "*Hundreds of thousands*? How can you possibly control all of them?"

"We'll never control *all* of them. But we've also come a long way. People take the quality of their food for granted, but your average farmer is a scientist in their own right, learning how to stay a step ahead of bugs and molds. That's why when you hear about an E. coli outbreak somewhere it's kinda big news, because we're spoiled by the consistently safe food we eat."

It was time to order. Sarah opted for yogurt and some fruit, and the server surprised me by saying, "You want the same pancakes you had yesterday?" I laughed and gave a hearty yes.

"Wow, two visits and I'm suddenly a regular," I said after the server walked away. "Her tip just went up to 30%."

"Now you know why there's always a line."

"All right," I said, "hundreds of thousands of molds, some of which kill crops *and* people. Tell me about Deele and his special blend of soybeans. I know we've already discussed some of it, but start at the beginning as if I know nothing. Sometimes I'll hear something in a second-telling that I missed before."

She sat back and draped an arm across the back of the

booth. "He first showed up several months ago. I didn't speak to him then, but I guess he was pushing a new strain of soybean that was resistant to a particularly nasty mold. The ag people he spoke with were a bit perplexed, because this was a new fungus he offered to protect against. They were courteous, but told him no thanks.

"Then, a soybean farm about sixty miles from here reported an entire storage bin was destroyed. Absolutely useless. It was a strange new mold."

I sat forward. "Wait. You said the beans were destroyed in a storage bin? So not while they were still in the field?"

"That's actually not uncommon," she said. "The plant might be exposed to the fungus while it's in the field, but sometimes it doesn't display any signs of disease until it's been harvested. Think about a pandemic caused by a specific virus. How it can spread so quickly because it often doesn't show symptoms for several days. This is similar, only with food crops."

"Shit," I said. "So how bad is this so far? Just the one crop?"

"For now. And that's a little suspicious, too."

"Because how would a disease like that be in one place, and one place only?"

"Exactly," she said. "The whole set-up is too perfect. Jason Deele rolls into town and warns people about a new strain of fungus that could potentially wipe out the country's entire soybean industry. And surprise, surprise, he has just the solution we'd all need. A super-soy that can resist the fungus. All we have to do is buy his product. Then, when nobody does, we all get a taste of what *could* happen."

I thought about all of it for a moment. Granted, it made sense, but I was still struck by the same doubts I'd had during the first meeting with Eklund. It seemed like the premise of a Marvel movie, or a sci-fi series on television. Deele had to be either the most audacious criminal ever, or just patently insane. Or both.

"What about Culbertson, the agent from the USDA?" I asked. "He shared your suspicions, probably."

She didn't answer right away, and turned to look out the window. Then she said, "Look, I don't want to speak ill of the dead."

I chuckled. "And I don't want to speak out of school here, but I'll tell you there's no shortage of people speaking ill of Agent Culbertson. That's just between you and me, by the way. But tell me what you know. He had to be giving you updates on his investigation."

She scoffed. "Investigation. Didn't seem like one. Seemed like he was on vacation."

I raised an eyebrow. "He didn't learn anything?"

"Maybe he did. We were supposed to meet the morning he was found murdered. But up to that point his investigation was pretty thin, at least the stuff he shared with me. I encouraged him to look into Jason Deele, and all I ever heard from him were glowing reports of a brilliant researcher." She lowered the tone of her voice, obviously to imitate Culbertson. "*This is a young man who's doing wonders in plant pathology and crop sciences.*"

In the back of my mind I began assembling some of the links in the chain. Culbertson, his propensity for blackmailing people and organizations for his own gain, and a potential bombshell of a case. He could've quickly grasped the enormity of it all and seen it as a ticket to not only paying off his mob debt, but funding a full retirement.

And in order to do that, he'd have to play everything

slowly, and certainly not let on to Sarah Eklund, her step-mother, or his own bosses at the USDA that something was afoot. At least not yet; not until he'd had time to squeeze his intended victim, to milk him for everything he could get.

Culbertson, I realized, could've seen Jason Deele as the biggest play of his career. And he may have been correct.

Right up until the first bullet entered his brain.

"So he didn't suspect anything at all?" I asked Sarah.

Eklund sighed. "Listen, Mr. Swan—"

"Eric."

"Eric. I think you might be starting to see how difficult it's been getting anyone outside of Iowa to take this seriously. First the USDA thought it might only be a limited, one-crop anomaly. Then my step-mother had to raise hell to get the FBI to show up. Then *you* were obviously skeptical in our meeting yesterday."

There was no sense playing dumb. "Yeah, you're right. I was. But I'm taking it seriously now."

"And I'm glad. I've got a feeling we're going to see another outbreak of this fungus somewhere, and soon. And it won't be long before it *does* start spreading."

The food showed up, and for the next minute we were quiet. The thoughts going through my mind were now scary enough to dampen my enthusiasm for the pancakes. Which takes a lot.

After getting a tea refill I wiped my hands on a napkin and looked at Eklund. "Suppose for a moment all of your fears are spot-on. Suppose that Deele—or someone—has created a mold requiring a special strain of soybean to survive. How bad could it get?"

She set her spoon down and considered the question.

"You've heard of the famous Irish potato famine, right?" she asked.

"Well, I've heard of it. I don't know details. Killed a lot of the potato crops, right?"

Her smile was a sad one. "Well, it did more than that. It wiped out crops to the point that things didn't recover for a decade. Starvation resulted. More than a *million* people died. More moved away just to survive. That was 1845, Eric, and to this day the population of Ireland *still* hasn't recovered to pre-famine levels."

I stared at her.

"If this fungus got out of control," she said, "it could potentially spread to other crops. Not just soybeans. It could wipe out the entire country's farm supplies." She paused, then added: "And we have way more people to feed than Ireland had in 1845."

9

I do some of my best thinking while I'm on a run. For years I did the usual earbud-and-music routine, which works quite well when you have sublime taste in music, which I do. I'll put my playlists up against anyone's.

But these days I save the music for my long drives. On a run I'll let my thoughts provide the soundtrack. There's something about the adrenaline kick and the fresh air that spins the rotors and provides a healthy boost to my frontal lobe. That's where all our deep thoughts, planning, and problem solving originate, so whatever you find to give it a turbo-boost, do it. For me it's running.

It was late afternoon and Sarah Eklund's grim vision of a nationwide blight on the food supply had me more than a little concerned. When I'd landed in Iowa I'd been a cocky, cynical secret agent. Now I had better data and I was nowhere near as cynical. Still cocky, but less cynical.

Even with the additional data, however, there was still the issue of confronting Jason Deele. Just walking into his office and saying, *Hey dude, what's up with the fungi?* didn't strike me as a winning formula. I needed a way to engage with the man without putting him on high alert. It meant using a badge was not the right play. I needed Deele to open up and gush about his project; he wouldn't do that unless he was anxious to sell me on his work. And there was only one way to do that:

Walk into his office as a prospective buyer, not someone looking to put him in a cell for 25 to life.

The brainiacs on the second floor at Q2 would need to get right on it. Of their numerous talents, creating fictional lives was my favorite.

You might think that meant coming up with a fake identity and supplying the necessary documents to go along with the new name. And sure, they do that—but so much more. In order to really fool people in this century, you need to have a digital history. Whether it's a job interviewee, a prospective blind date, or just naked curiosity, we look people up online all the time. If I waltzed into Deele's office and said my name was Little Boy Blue, I'd better have a substantial footprint on Google, including photos of me and my horn.

That's the kind of stuff coming out of the second floor. The only thing that chapped my ass about the whole procedure was they never let me pick my own fake name. It was probably for the best. They could, after all, sculpt a better profile when given free reign, whereas I'd probably clown around and pick something like Ty Mashieu. Don't think I haven't called an airport paging system and requested that Ty be summoned to a paging phone immediately.

By the time I'd finished four miles, I had a pretty good scenario laid out for my Houston trip. The only thing I needed now—besides the new identity—was for Mr. Deele to get his butt back into the country. Of course, if I represented myself as a potential customer, someone with big bucks to spend on a fancy new strain of soybean, he might even change his flight plans to accommodate me. People may not fly back from overseas for Cousin Ashley's wedding, but they'll damn sure fly back for a multimillion dollar contract.

Back in my room I showered and dressed, hungry after leaving more than half of my breakfast untouched. Just as I was getting ready to leave the room and hunt down some fish and chips, my phone hummed. It was a text from Fife.

May have caught a break on the Culbertson murder. Sending you security footage.

A minute later I got an email from him: *Hotel security camera, Culbertson.*

There was a video attachment.

I opened it on my tablet. The image was a little grainy, but otherwise of decent quality, and obviously lifted from a security camera in Culbertson's hotel parking lot. It was a night shot.

I watched a car pull into a space. The USDA agent emerged, but hadn't walked six feet before another man approached and got right up on him. I saw Culbertson glance down, and, although I couldn't make it out, I'm sure that meant a gun was poking him in the stomach. After a few seconds Culbertson climbed back in his car while the other man ducked into the passenger seat.

The car left the lot.

These would be the last images of David Culbertson alive.

Moments later I got a follow-up: *Visual ID.*

It was a different photo of the man from the parking lot. The FBI's lab people are pretty good. They'd zoomed in on the gunman, analyzed it, and found a matching photo in their database.

I studied the image. Average height and physically fit.

Maybe 35 years old. Dark hair, short and well-styled, no facial hair. Otherwise totally indistinguishable from any other face in the crowd.

At the bottom I clicked on the link, which opened a profile page on a man named Conor Wood. I sat down to take it all in.

Age turned out to be 36, former college track athlete, four-year stint in the Army, dishonorably discharged for insubordination.

Well, I couldn't hold that against him. I'd been insubordinate several times while in the special ops unit. You just have to be smart enough to know *who* you can mouth off to and who you can't.

A couple of minor scrapes with the law through age 32. And then nothing.

As in *nothing*. As in fell-off-the-face-of-the-Earth.

Until he turned up in a midwest town, four years later, kidnapping—and probably murdering—an agent from the USDA. Now wasn't *that* strange?

I texted back to Fife: *Whats his connection with everything?*

He immediately sent back: *Good question. Can you ask Poole for help?*

I responded with a thumbs-up, the laziest of the emojis.

Then I left the room and began my search for fish and chips.

By the time I returned, Poole and the crack squad on the second floor had all sorts of goodies for me. For starters, the fake identity I'd use for setting up a meeting with Deele was actually not too bad. Ryan Thomas. Q2 often used names that could overwhelm an online search, offering up thousands of people with the same name. It allowed me to almost get lost amongst the digital noise.

In this case, though, Ryan Thomas was an executive with agricultural giant D.M. Cash. This multinational organization, based in Europe but with a substantial presence in the U.S., was the perfect cover. They had their tentacles into everything from crop management and consulting, to farm equipment, to pesticide production. For the time being a nice bio and my history with the company lived on a detached web site that, from the outside, looked like it belonged to D.M. Cash, but was actually housed with the Q2 nerds. It was more than convincing to outside eyes.

It would take about 12 hours for everything to populate the Internet, but, when it did, the story of Mr. Ryan Thomas, of Alexandria, Virginia, would stretch back more than fifteen years. I especially liked the notice of an award from the South Dakota Farmers Union for "encouraging the healthy application of bio-sciences in grain production." Whatever that meant.

They'd even managed to create a photo of me shaking hands with some guy as I accepted my award.

What the second floor was capable of doing should scare the shit out of you.

Poole had been busy, too. On my tablet I now had an updated file on Jason Deele. I piled up the pillows on my bed, got comfortable, and dove into the abridged version of his life story.

Like me, he was a college dropout, but that's where the similarities ended. He'd left Stanford with only one semester to go. Started two different tech companies in the Silicon Valley area, both of which went belly-up within six months. But the third time was most definitely the charm.

Deele and a partner created a social media site that could

be highly refined so people with very specific interests could associate with fellow enthusiasts, hit on each other, then talk trash after it didn't work out. At least that's how I always looked at that particular site. His niche media, as opposed to mass media, struggled at first, and then exploded. Before his 30th birthday he unloaded his share in the company to a giant in the social apps world, pocketing more than a billion dollars.

Instead of retiring to a small island, he took his billion and launched another niche tech company, this time specializing in helping young entrepreneurs start their own companies. Having his name attached to it helped lure top talent, and the business competed well enough with the heavyweights in the industry that one of those Goliaths bought him out. That meant two successful start-ups, two acquisitions, and a shit-ton of money for a young man still in his mid-30s.

Jason Deele wasn't a household name, not to the degree of those tech icons people have worshipped through the years. But he wasn't entirely an unknown, either. He fell into a category that many of the world's super-wealthy appreciated the most: More money than God, but still relatively anonymous.

And now here he was . . . selling soybeans? I must've furrowed my brow trying to make the connection because I realized I was lying on my hotel bed, scowling. More than anything I wanted to meet with the guy just to ask him what inspired this startling deviation from his path, especially when he was not only set for life, his great-great-great grandchildren were set, too. I mean, I could do the math: Even with 'only' two billion dollars, his family could spend a million bucks a year for *two thousand years*. And Deele had way more than that.

Yet . . .

I didn't get to the good stuff about Deele until I scanned

Poole's later notes. Sure, all of it was rumor and innuendo, but it began to at least prop up some of the concerns Sarah Eklund had. And it might've even lent credence to the idea that Deele could be involved in Culbertson's murder.

The roaring success behind the companies he'd sold coincided with a change in his business style. During the early days, while struggling, he played nice. Then there were little things here and there—blog posts, magazine articles, social media posts—suggesting Jason Deele had turned cut-throat in his dealings. Poole found one source who claimed there was an investigation into the first start-up to find out why three different people with connections to the company had committed suicide. One was a senior executive within the walls, while two were CEOs of companies that Deele's organization later absorbed.

Coincidence? Possibly. Although the wife of one victim and the husband of another both insisted there was no way their spouses would've killed themselves. It was considered a tragic mystery, while some claimed it was merely evidence of the enormous pressure that comes with running a Silicon Valley business. Deele, for his part, publicly mourned.

But he also cleaned up on the deals.

I set down the tablet for a moment and thought about that. Could it be the college dropout tried to play nice and got humiliated in the process? And that experience led him to try an approach where he played dirty . . . and won.

Depending on the personality, it was certainly possible that it became a matter of cause and effect. Be a good boy, lose your shirt. Be an asshole, own the entire goddamned shirt factory.

There was no proof of any of this. But sitting in a hotel

room in Des Moines, trying to fit the jigsaw pieces together without a picture to go by, it didn't sound too farfetched.

Picking up the tablet again, I clicked on the notes Poole had left regarding Conor Wood, the parking lot gunman. He had no official records from the last few years—no employment data, no tax returns, no credit card information—which is suspicious by itself. But Poole ran his photo through the special ID program we use for mystery people like Wood. A handful of matches came up, only one of which seemed important or relevant.

It was a press report outlining the meteoric rise of a certain young tech wizard who'd profited nicely through another major acquisition. His personal net worth had swelled to more than six billion dollars. The accompanying candid photograph showed Jason Deele walking out of an office building, holding up a hand in a futile attempt to ward off the camera. But it was definitely him.

And trailing him, an expressionless look on his face, was Conor Wood.

No coincidence there. It was basically proof that Wood worked for Deele. But doing what? Company security? Bodyguard? Or did he carry out other deeper, darker assignments? Like maybe removing nuisance USDA agents who threatened blackmail?

I got up and paced the room. My next move was now clear: Go to Houston, meet with Deele, and get to the bottom of this bizarre case.

I sent a text to Fife, letting him know about the Deele-Wood connection. I also reached out to Poole, requesting a flight for the next day. The time had come to creep into the lion's den.

It was still fairly early and I felt like a walk. But I decided to do a quick upload of everything first; I'd be too tired later, and probably wouldn't have enough time in the morning.

I popped the horse pill, rearranged the pillows, grabbed my gear and a different magazine, and chilled out. This time it took only about 70 minutes. Maybe God Maker's improvements really *were* kicking in.

When I finished, I put everything away, put my shoes back on, and headed for the door. I debated whether or not to call Christina, but figured it was crunch time at the restaurant. I'd try later.

Outside it was dark, the air crisp and clean. I headed for the back of the parking lot and a path I'd noticed earlier. Looked like it led to a small park. As I strolled past the parked cars I thought about Culbertson, and how he must've been shocked to find a gun barrel sticking into his belly. Even with all of the dirty deals he'd been involved with, he still probably never thought things would go this bad.

What would've been going through his head as Wood forced him to drive out of town? True to his nature as a bullshit artist he probably tried to talk his way out. For that matter probably tried to *bribe* his way out.

Did Wood tell him anything? Did he at least let Culbertson know who had ordered his death?

My phone rang. It was Fife.

"Howdy. How's Big D?" I asked, reaching the path and starting toward the park.

"Spread out," he said. "Lots of pickup trucks and sweet tea."

"Nice work on the security footage. The confirmation I needed to stop looking at Chicago and start focusing on Houston. Which is where I'll be tomorrow."

"Got your cover?" he asked.

"I'll memorize it on the plane. They gave me two first names again. They know I hate that."

"Quit your whining. Try going through life with Fife."

"*Life with Fife*," I said. "Sounds like either reality TV or a PBS show for kids. Assuming I get the appointment with Deele, are you going to join me in Houston?"

"Can't get away for at least three more days. That's one reason I'm calling."

"So you drag me out of my pajama pants in Washington, fly me out to help with a job in corn country, and then abandon it? Why do I feel like I've been set up?"

"Man, all those years of uploads and downloads have turned you into a first-class crybaby," he said.

"Yeah, yeah. You said that's *one* reason you called. What's the other?"

"You'll probably be hearing from Sarah Eklund. Seems Mr. Deele reached out to her from South America."

"Yeah? What did he have to say?"

"Said he'd heard a rumor that some soybean fields took a hit in Iowa. Wanted to remind her that he could set up another meeting anytime. After he finishes his business down south."

"He's a ballsy bastard, I'll give him that."

"And a richer bastard than he was a few days ago. Just closed a deal to sell his super-soybeans in Argentina."

"Oh? Did he murder some of their crops down there, too?"

"As a matter of fact . . ."

10

———————

The call from Dr. Eklund didn't come until I was driving to the airport the next morning. I'm sure I sounded distracted.

"Is this a bad time?" she asked.

"No. I just dropped a hash brown nugget between the seats."

"Oh," she said, and then fell silent, apparently unsure how to follow up dreadful news. So I explained the tragedy to her.

"It was the last one in the bag. You know, there's something about dropping that last french fry or hash brown nugget that can wreck your whole day." Then, when there was still silence on the other end, I added, "Well, maybe you *don't* know."

"I can call you back if you need to pull over and effect a rescue."

"No, it's all good. There actually *was* one more in the bottom of the bag. So, I heard Mr. Deele called you from the Southern Hemisphere."

"The man has a lot of nerve, Mr. Swan." I noticed that with her irritation I was no longer Eric. "When he lands in this country please tell me your people will arrest him."

"I *can't* tell you that. We've been over this already. We don't have anything that would allow us to hold him."

"He's killing crops all over the world now."

"Well, let's talk about that," I said, wadding up a napkin and throwing it onto the passenger seat. "There's something I should've asked in our last meeting, but I'm just now learning enough to know what to ask. This crop here in Iowa that was infested. You said the mold was one of a kind and had never been seen before."

"That's right."

"But I got another report last night from Washington that says although it's *technically* new, it's a close relative to another fungus that's been around for years. In other words, it's a mutation."

She hesitated before answering. "It's a mutation that didn't exist until he showed up."

"But it's not entirely new. It's like a virus mutating over time. Correct?"

"Jesus," she said. "Are you defending him?"

"Not at all. My gut instinct is that he's guilty of a variety of things. But we're not allowed to show up and say *I arrest you in the name of my gut.* We have to be able to prove criminal activity. And, unfortunately, all Jason Deele has to do is claim this fungus mutated on its own and he was simply ahead of the game by preparing for that eventuality. Right place, right time."

"It's bullshit," she said.

"You're probably right." I softened my tone. "Listen,

Doctor, I'll let you in on something. An investigation like this is like a large, ocean-bound freighter. It doesn't move real fast, and it takes a long time to make turns. But it usually gets to where it needs to go. So don't think we're letting him get away with anything. We just have to put everything together properly."

She sighed. "Yeah, I get it."

"And," I added, "this case has all sorts of complications, not the least of which is a dead federal agent on the side of a road. Trust me, we want justice in this case just as much as you do. Now, tell me what you've heard about South America."

She spent a couple of minutes letting me know a fungus similar to the one that had poisoned the soybean field in Iowa took out several square miles of plants in the Pampas region of Argentina. And since that country is one of the world's largest exporters of biofuels made from soy, Deele managed to secure huge contracts.

"They weren't going to take any chances," she said. "Which he counted on."

I nodded, and turned toward the rental car lot at the airport.

"Okay," I said. "If things fall right, I'll sit down with Jason Deele in a day or two. And listen: No one is forgetting about you or the farmers in Iowa. We'll get to the bottom of this."

"I will hold you to that, Mr. Swan."

This came from a voice I didn't recognize. Someone else was on the line, by the sound of it an older woman.

"All right," I said. "And who is this on the party line?"

"This is Deputy Secretary Halloran. I'm the one who started this investigation."

"I see. And you've been secretly listening in for what reason? To make sure I'm not slacking on the job?"

"Agent Swan," Sarah Eklund cut in. "It's not like that. I—"

"Sarah didn't ask for this conference call, Mr. Swan," said Halloran. "I did. And yes, I wanted to remain silent at first to hear what you had to say without you coloring it because a politician was on the line."

"Did you catch that tale of woe regarding the lost hash brown? That's not part of the case, of course, but very important nonetheless. A good agent needs energy to get through the assignment, and a processed potato plug is packed with just the right amount of grease to last me through a late lunch."

Halloran sighed. "All right. You're angry. I don't care about that. What I care about is you taking this case seriously. I'm not convinced you are."

"Oh, but I am," I said with a placating tone. "I intend to do such a good job that you're sure to get bumped up from Deputy Secretary to Sheriff Secretary. You can count on me."

"I might need to make a phone call to someone about you, Mr. Swan. I don't like your attitude."

"No? Well, let me tell you what *I* don't like, Deputy Halloran. I don't like people secretly checking up on me. I don't like snoops on my phone calls. And I sure as hell don't like politicians threatening me. Now before you go and make a stink with your phone call you should know that I have a few friends myself inside the Beltway, and I'm willing to bet they're a lot more powerful than yours. The stink you make will be Chanel No. 5 compared to the retch-inducing funk I stir up."

"Yes, you're very tough," she said. "Just make sure you're giving this assignment 110 percent."

"Did you really just say *110 percent*? Here's a news flash for you, Deputy Secretary: A gallon jug with a gallon of water in it is doing the best it can. Understand what I'm saying?"

There was silence on the line. I could only imagine how horrified Sarah Eklund was at the moment.

"I started this investigation," Halloran finally said. "And I will check up on it as I see fit. If there's nothing else, I have a meeting to attend."

"Give my best to the sheriff," I said. That was answered with a click.

I waited a couple of seconds before I started to chuckle. "That was fun," I said.

"That was *fun*?" Eklund said with a sputter.

"Oh, God yes. You didn't like the show?"

"I wanted to throw up. Nobody has ever spoken to Janet that way. At least not that I've ever heard. You're insane."

I pulled up to the return lane at the rental car center. "People in power only respect other people in power. If you let them step on you at the beginning they'll never treat you with respect. You already know that in your line of work; you just think it's different when someone has an office in Washington."

There was another pause, then I could hear the tension in her voice let up. "Yeah. Okay." Then it was her turn to laugh. "Did you make up that gallon jug line yourself?"

"Stole it from a college professor. You're free to use it anytime."

"Not likely."

I shut off the engine. "I'll send you the hotel information in Houston in case you need to reach me in an emergency."

THE FIRST LEG of the flight found me sitting next to a man who talked on his phone right up until we were rolling down the runway for takeoff. People 15 rows away could've heard him.

You know the guy. In my head I had two dozen things I wanted to say to him. Instead I put on headphones and dominated the arm rest.

After that I closed my eyes and sifted through everything I'd learned in the past 48 hours. The idea that Jason Deele employed his own hitman fascinated me. Contract killing has been around for untold ages, and some reports say it's behind anywhere from two to five percent of all murders. In a way, *I'm* a contract killer; I just happen to be paid by Uncle Sam.

But generally we imagine it taking place in some seedy underworld, populated by shadowy mobsters carrying out their little gangland vendettas. Even with $3,500 suits, Vincent Volta couldn't disguise the fact he played in that sandbox. Sad to say, it's almost what we expect.

What we *don't* expect is a multi-billionaire in Silicon Valley pulling strings to murder people. Which, when you think about it, is probably naive on our part. Those could very well be some of the biggest players in the contract-killing industry and we just don't see it behind the walls of their estates. Money buys protection, influence, and really good attorneys. And when you're talking about that much cheddar, who knows how it warps the mind? At some point it becomes the ultimate scorecard, and some people need to win every game.

The difference between Volta and Deele was experience. Volta grew up in the world of blood-letting; Deele, as part of the vulgar *nouveau riche*, had probably seen it only in movies. Which made him, in my opinion, more dangerous. Sneer if you must, but at least Volta's type had a code, flimsy as it may be to a civilized mind. Deele and his crew practically flailed in comparison. Killing a USDA agent proved it.

And, I was sure, it would be his undoing.

By the time I changed planes—and rid myself of the gabber who'd jumped back on his phone the moment the wheels touched down in Dallas—I realized my vacation truly was over. Six weeks on the sidelines may have produced some rust, but now the challenge was on and my motor was revving.

THE SHORT HOP to Houston passed in no time. A message from Poole awaited, telling me the meeting with Deele was proving tough to arrange. His own gatekeepers were adept at putting off even big-money types from an organization like D.M. Cash. Another advantage when you already had billions in the bank. Poole said she'd keep working on it. Many people delighted in the power of being wooed a few times before saying yes.

That was just as true in business as it was in love.

This time my rental was a sporty Jaguar, a much better calling card in my role as executive Ryan Thomas. Not that tooling up in a mid-size SUV would've been horrible, but we operated under the assumption that looking the part was half the battle. To that end, I stopped on the way to my hotel and picked up an impressively modern business suit and shoes from a high-end shop. With an equally-impressive tip on the side I ensured the slight alterations would be finished by the following morning and the entire package delivered.

The hotel valet parked the Jag while I checked in and helped myself to a quick drink at the restaurant bar. That gave me a chance to call Christina.

"Houston?" she said. "Tired of the corn fields already?"

"Actually, those were enchanting. The bad guys just won't stay put. How's your belly? Everything still simmering the way it should?"

"As far as I can tell. I don't go back to the doctor for another two weeks. Marissa's coming with me."

"Good." Then, after a pause I asked, "I mean, is that good?"

She laughed. "Of course. She's been great." Then, lowering her voice, she added, "I did quietly ask her not to bring Antonio."

"Banned from the OB/GYN, eh?"

"Not for good; just this time. He's so wired about the whole thing that he makes me nervous. I told you, I can't even snack at work anymore without him giving me the look. Marissa's going to tell him we need some mother-surrogate bonding time."

We spent a few minutes talking about the restaurant before she got around to something she'd probably wondered since I left Washington.

"How does it feel to be back on the job? Are you officially in the groove?"

"I wasn't at first. Think I'm coming around, though. Always helps if there's an actual villain in the movie, you know?"

"Got a good one this time?"

"Won't know for sure till I meet him. Right now he just seems like a rich, spoiled asshole."

"But you're doing okay?"

I knew what her question was really about, but I still didn't have an answer. There was a distinct possibility my head would *never* be fully okay with the job.

Yet here I was. As Shakespeare's Henry V said, *Once more unto the breach, dear friends, once more.*

It seemed there was always another curtain call for Eric Swan. Always another fortification to storm.

Christina knew it, too. It was why she'd pulled me off the couch and pushed me out the door.

"I'm doing fine," I said, using the least-expressive and least-popular word to describe a condition. We both silently agreed to let it slide.

11

The room was unique, a suite done up in a Moroccan theme. I don't know why. My suitcase was propped on one of those folding luggage racks, and a bowl of fresh fruit sat next to a handwritten card from the hotel's general manager, welcoming me to *Houston, the city with no limits*—which was a focus-group slogan if I ever heard one. It's not as fun as Nederland, Colorado's *Home of The Frozen Dead Guy*, but not as embarrassing as Augusta's unofficial slogan, *The Asscrack of Georgia.*

After scouting the living arrangements, including the decadent bathroom, I plucked a handful of grapes and took in the view from the window. Staring out over the former capital of the Republic of Texas, it occurred to me I could easily manage a side-hustle as a travel writer. Over the years my assignments had taken me to 44 of the 50 states, as well as Mexico, Canada, and three separate islands in the Caribbean. I'd stayed in first-class joints like this one, but also spent more than a few nights in tents, cardboard shanties, and directly under the stars. My *nom de plume* could be Mr. Five-Star-to-No-Star.

Okay, so the name might need work.

The thing is, I mostly enjoyed the travel, and I was good at it. While some people get anxious just renting a car or finding their way around, to me it's much more fun getting lost in a strange city than making the same dull commute down the same clogged roads every single day. Granted, a break at home is always appreciated, and I sometimes find myself looking forward to three straight nights in my own bed. But living out of a suitcase is just one continuous adventure. Must be part of my wiring.

It was close to seven o'clock when Poole called. The fact that she didn't text, and actually wanted voice communication, told me something was up.

"Did you get me in to see Deele?"

She said, "Well, maybe. That's why I'm calling. I need to check on something with you before I confirm the meeting."

"This sounds good. Do they need blood and urine samples first?"

Poole hesitated, probably wondering if I was serious.

"Never mind," I said. "What's the story?"

"His personal assistant is Diana Capaldi. I'll send you a file on her, but it probably won't be ready until the morning. Ms. Capaldi says you can meet with Mr. Deele at 1 o'clock tomorrow if you don't mind driving out to a small private airstrip west of the city."

"To do what? Meet him as he arrives from South America?"

"No. He arrives in Houston tomorrow morning, has a quick meeting, and then he's going out to fly . . . something."

"*Something?*"

Poole sighed. "I didn't exactly understand everything she was saying, but I didn't want to appear unnerved. From what I gather, Mr. Deele enjoys piloting something known as experimental aircraft."

I gave a small laugh. "Well, that fits. Agent Fife told me the guy was a bit of a daredevil. I didn't peg him as Chuck Yeager, but whatever jacks up his adrenaline, I guess. All right, get back with Ms. Capaldi and let her know I'll be there. Then send me all the info on her and the airstrip."

At last I'd get the chance to meet the billionaire entrepreneur. He'd taken the bait.

The only question I had now was: Would I have to ride along in the toy airplane?

As promised, two new files from Poole arrived before I awoke. I downloaded them to my tablet, which I then brought to read in the lobby restaurant while sampling the fancy hotel's breakfast offerings.

Depending on how you looked at it, Diana Capaldi was either an underachiever or brilliant at career management. Holding a master's degree with exceptional transcripts and an impressive early resume, she'd launched a career in data science and became something of a star. One of the top journals in the industry featured her in their "Top 35 Under 35" edition, highlighting the best and brightest young executives.

Which is impressive, no doubt. Yet she left it all behind in order to take a position managing Jason Deele's calendar, among other things. Hey, there were worse jobs than booking lunches for your boss while jetting around the world, especially when the boss had a bank account with at least nine zeroes before the decimal point. Did she lie awake at night, worried that she'd jettisoned her career too soon, or did she laugh herself to sleep on Mulberry silk sheets?

Capaldi's photo wasn't your traditional, boring headshot; it featured the 34-year-old on the deck of a boat, wearing scuba gear, no doubt the adventurous image Deele preferred for his staff and his company.

Other than that, there wasn't much meat in this stew. She grew up in a middle-class family in a medium-sized Pennsylvania town, had no police record, never married—at least nothing filed—and had long since deleted all social media accounts. As I devoured my bowl of oatmeal I wondered if that last tidbit was a prerequisite for the job. Perhaps Deele insisted on plugging any and all holes leading inside his operation. If so, I had to admire that.

Still hungry, I went back for seconds and returned with a waffle they'd made in the shape of Texas, which was quite fun for those of us who, for our entire lives, had endured waffles shaped like Wyoming. It was just cute enough that it could've been an entry in my imaginary travel blog.

The next file included directions to the private airfield and Poole's standard counsel: *Be careful.*

Hey, I could control most of what took place on the ground, but if I found myself airborne, a reluctant passenger, there wouldn't be much I could do if things went sideways— literally or figuratively. Unless I fought my way to the plane's controls. Even then, my limited military training might bring *some* degree of comfort at the stick, but they don't call them *experimental* aircraft for nothing.

In fact, it had been almost three years since I last piloted an airplane, and even then *piloted* may be an exaggeration. An assignment had taken me to the wide open spaces of Montana, where a rancher insisted I take the controls of his beloved Beechcraft while he went back to take a piss. He thought it was damned funny as he left the cockpit and I nervously gripped the yoke. He didn't think it nearly as funny when I calculated how long it would take him to be in mid-stream and then jerked the plane sideways.

Nor did he find it humorous when later, on the ground, I shot him once in the chest and once in the head, in that order. Laugh at that, cowboy.

I LEFT the hotel at 11, allowing myself plenty of time to navigate the abominable Houston traffic and get outside the Beltway 8 loop. I also wanted time to stop and relieve my own bladder, just in case I found myself buckled into a flying death-trap. That's always a bad place to be when nature calls.

The airfield's security gate was manned by a guy who, no shit, wore aviator sunglasses. I stifled the urge to call him Maverick. He made a show of checking his clipboard—which I'm sure had a grand total of one name on it: mine—then directed me to a small hangar off in that direction. I'd know it, he drawled, because of the large numeral 9 painted on the side. I gave a small salute and motored through.

It was either a slow day, or they all were. I saw few people moving around, and no planes taxiing. Hard to believe an airstrip this close to a major metropolitan area wouldn't be jumping with activity, but maybe most of the big shots chose to fly their private jets out of IAH or Hobby.

The big 9 loomed just ahead. A corporate helicopter was parked to one side, along with a small collection of cars scattered near the hangar's door. I noted at least two of them that ran six figures, not counting options. My Jag was so bourgeois.

A man sat perched on a stool just outside a doorway to the hangar. He wasn't overly muscle-bound, but one glance told me he was tough enough. I figured a clone would be stationed inside. When you were worth millions you might have a body-guard. When you were worth billions you kept a unit of them.

I strolled as nonchalantly as I could from the car, and had my ID out before I got there.

"Ryan Thomas, here to see Jason Deele," I said.

The man didn't smile, but also didn't scowl. With a cool, professional demeanor he took the ID, studied it, looked at me, then back to the ID. Keying a mic on his lapel he announced my presence to someone inside. I couldn't hear what came over his earpiece, but he handed back my identification and said, "Someone will be here in just a minute. Will you please raise your arms?"

I pocketed the card and did as he said. As he patted me down, quickly but efficiently, I acted indifferent to the whole process.

"You ever pilot anything?" I asked.

"No. Turn around, please."

"I tried it a few years ago," I said. "Never really mastered the landing. They say that's an important part of the process."

He finished the search, then resumed his place on the stool, looking off in another direction. It was clear we'd never be in a bowling league together, so I gave up and stood there, pretending to study the horizon.

It was five minutes until the door opened, and a tall, smartly-dressed woman emerged, shielding her eyes from the sun. I recognized her as Diana Capaldi. Unlike the bouncer at the door, she turned on a megawatt smile and extended her hand.

"So sorry to keep you waiting, Mr. Thomas. Diana Capaldi. Won't you come in?"

I followed her inside, the tap-tap of her heels echoing in the large space. Two small planes were parked near a far corner, one of them in the process of maintenance, an overalled man poking around underneath. Ahead of us and up a flight of stairs, lights were on in an office, and that appeared to be our destination. As predicted, another stout, serious gentleman stood near the bottom of the stairs. He sized me up in a professional manner, his hands in front of him, one lightly resting over the other wrist.

"Did you enjoy your night in Houston?" Capaldi asked. "Are you enjoying the ZaZa?"

I hadn't mentioned where I was staying. Had Poole? I wouldn't think so.

"It's my kind of place," I said. "I prefer boutique hotels. You?"

"Oh, absolutely. Quirky but upscale is the only way to go."

I doubted she stayed anywhere these days that wasn't upscale.

We took the stairs while she continued to make pleasant small talk. She didn't even acknowledge the security beef as we walked past, so I smiled at him and said "Hello." He responded with a slight nod, while his face radiated distrust and barely-repressed anger.

Inside the office Capaldi indicated a comfortable chair for me and offered something to drink. I declined, and she sat facing me on a fashionable love seat.

"Mr. Deele is looking forward to speaking with you," she said. "Your timing is perfect. Things are going so well with the business that in another few days we may not have been able to fit you in so quickly."

"Business picking up domestically?" I asked. "Or mostly from South America?"

"Both, actually," she said, flashing the smile. "But

Paraguay and Argentina are definitely taking off right now. Mr. Deele will be happy to fill you in."

In other words, she deferred to the boss when it came to business particulars.

"What's your background, Ms. Capaldi?" I asked, feigning ignorance.

"Please, call me Diana. Well, I'm a small-town girl who couldn't wait to get to the big city. Happens a lot, these days. I'm afraid small towns are getting smaller each year."

"I don't know if Houston can squeeze in any more people," I said with a smile.

"Isn't that the truth? Some of us feel like it's growing so fast it'll eventually merge with Dallas."

"Does Mr. Deele fly the helicopter himself to visit the airfield?"

"He detests traffic," she said in lieu of a direct answer. "Tell me about your work with D.M. Cash. Your specialty is bio-science, is that right?"

And so the pre-interview began. It would be Capaldi's job to engage me in business chit-chat, to casually pry into my story to see if I really was someone worthy of valuable minutes in the day of the billionaire. Fortunately I'd done my homework on the plane.

"Well, when I enrolled at Duke my passion was evolutionary biology, but pretty soon I realized my calling was more along the lines of biosciences as they pertained to crop management."

Capaldi nodded as if that was the most natural pivot a biologist could make. I was tempted to make up some totally extraneous bullshit, just to entertain myself, but decided that could come back to bite me later. Better to stick with the *prepared* bullshit.

"When DMC came calling, I put them off for a year to do some traveling. I trusted they'd still be interested when I got back."

"You took a gap year?" she asked, laughing.

"A little sabbatical. Eighteen months, actually. I have a tendency to go above and beyond, especially when I'm having fun."

"Good for you," she said.

"But it wasn't all horsing around and wasting my parents' money. I spent a lot of that time studying crop management in other countries, mostly Central and South America. Experiential learning, they call it. Well, that made DMC even more interested in hiring me, so my playtime was beneficial, both personally and professionally."

"And now you're interested in our work. May I ask what put us on your radar?"

It would've been funny to see her reaction if I said, *A dead agent with the USDA*. Instead I said, "I've always been intrigued by alternative approaches, whether it's alternative energy sources or alternative management techniques. But especially alternative methods of food production." I chuckled. "When I was finishing up my studies I fancied myself a bit of a granular superhero. You know, solving the world hunger problem with super grains."

Her smile increased. "The Superman of seeds?"

"Something like that."

She sat back and draped a long arm across the back of the love seat. "Normally someone with that type of vision strikes out on their own. But you ended up with a mega-corporation. They're not usually known for radical thinking."

I fought the urge to fidget. Mostly because she made a

good point. But I kept perfectly poised, gave a boyish grin, and dipped into my bag of bullshit.

"Very true. But they also have the resources to make a difference. Rather than stand outside the gate, shaking my fist, I chose to embed myself within the system, then worm my way into a position where I could effect change."

"And are you?" she asked.

"Slowly but surely. That's why I'm interested in what Jason Deele is doing with his modified soy. I think something along those lines is the future in preventing global famine."

Diana Capaldi didn't respond right away. Instead, she seemed to study my face. Had I overplayed the hand?

Finally she gave a slow nod. "Well, it sounds like you share much of Mr. Deele's vision. You two should get along quite well." She stood up. "If you'll wait here, please, I'll be back shortly. There are plenty of refreshments right over there, so please help yourself."

With that she left the room. I imagined she'd be filing her initial report on Ryan Thomas, offering an opinion on whether or not he was a legitimate potential partner.

After a few minutes alone I stood and wandered over to the small alcove functioning as a makeshift kitchen. I filled a glass with ice and poured some ginger ale, picked through a basket with assorted snacks, mostly out of curiosity, but satisfied myself with just the soda.

As I took a second sip the door opened and a rich, baritone voice called out: "If you think I'm doing business with you, you're crazy."

I turned, holding my glass of ginger ale, and looked into the face of Jason Deele.

12

———

Of all the greetings I could've received, this one I never anticipated.

I stood still, looking first into the face of the young lion, this billionaire who may or may not have been a cold-blooded killer. Deele's gaze was one of the steeliest I'd seen. He stood with hands on hips, his feet spread in a challenging stance. Glancing to his left, I studied the glamorous Ms. Capaldi. She gave away nothing.

Had I made a gross miscalculation? Had I flown to Houston only to get rejected before even getting a chance? In a split second I replayed in my head the brief conversation with Capaldi, looking for something I may have said that slammed the door. Or was it something I *hadn't* said?

Quickly recovering from the shock, I did what came naturally to me.

I took a sip of my ginger ale and shrugged. Then said, "Crazy? Well, my ex-fiancé would agree. But then, she put milk into the bowl *before* the cereal. So who's the crazy one?"

After a pause, Deele walked toward me, stopping two feet away. He continued to glare.

I took another sip.

Then he spoke again. "I grew up a fan of the Tar Heels, Mr. Thomas. You think I'm going to work with a Blue Devil?"

He was talking about the University of North Carolina, and my alleged alma mater, Duke.

After a few tense seconds a smile broke across his face. He stuck out his hand.

"Nice to meet you, Ryan. I suppose I can let your horrific choice of matriculation slide this time."

After releasing my hand he slapped me on the shoulder and walked over to the kitchen area. "Get you a refill?"

I hid the surge of relief by shaking my head and holding up the half-empty glass. "I'm good, thank you."

Deele filled a glass from a bottle of sparkling water, then pointed to the sitting area where I'd met with Capaldi.

"How was your flight?" I asked, sitting down.

"Oh, haven't taken it yet. Just going over a few things with Benjamin first. He designed most of it, and I wanted to have a look before taking off."

"And it checks out?"

He made a shrugging gesture with his glass. "As far as I can tell. But his last plane crashed on takeoff."

"When will you come back and fly? I'd love to see it," I said.

"Come back? No, I'm going up as soon as you and I have finished our little talk. Benjamin's going with me."

He took a long drink and set his glass on the coffee table. "You know," he said, "this particular beauty seats six. How'd you like to be part of a maiden voyage?"

I grunted. "This is another joke, right? Because it's much funnier than your Tar Heel/Blue Devil schtick."

"All you have to do is sign some papers saying you don't hold me or my company responsible, that you understand the risk, that sort of stuff. And we can take off in about twenty minutes."

Multiple questions ran through my mind. Was he bluffing, just trying to fluster me? Was this some sort of game, a way of challenging anyone who dared to deal with him as an equal? And, perhaps the most important: Was it a test, an initiation into his bubble, a way for him to spot fellow daredevils who might take financial risks with him after they'd conquered personal ones?

If that was the case, how could I say no? I could hear Quanta's reaction when she discovered I'd missed an opportunity to connect with the target because I didn't want to go for a ride.

And what did I have to fear? If the plane went down, it would be game over for Deele and this guy Benjamin while I would simply dial up a new body.

Besides, part of my nature—the part that had landed me in trouble too many times to count—is a childish inability to shy away from a dare. It served me well in Special Ops, but also got my ass kicked a few times. Or killed.

All of these thoughts were considered and catalogued to Deele's great amusement. I'm sure he knew the little tussle going on in my head and loved the power of provoking such a dilemma.

"Yeah, what the hell," I said. "The blood of Charles Lindbergh flows through my veins."

His eyes grew wide. "No shit."

"*Total* shit," I said. "My ancestors always took the train."

He laughed and stood up, preparing to leave the room.

I looked up at him. "I was hoping we'd be able to talk some business, too."

"The only way I was going to talk shop with you was if you agreed to go for this joy ride. So put in the time cloud-hopping with me, and I'll be delighted to chat about the wonderful world of soybeans." He walked toward the door and called back to me: "Diana will have you sign some things. I'll see you on the tarmac."

I turned my gaze to his assistant. "Should I call my family and tell them I love them, just in case?"

She took a deep breath. "I've always told Mr. Deele that some day he's going to be too bold for his own good."

I grunted. "Just not today, okay?"

OBVIOUSLY I WASN'T the first guest Jason Deele had lured into the sky. They had prepared documents ready for me to sign, all stating I understood the significant risk of death or severe injury, and I waived claims of any kind against Jason Deele or his company, his associate Benjamin Hughes and his company, and basically anyone else who'd ever had anything to do with Deele, Hughes, or the airfield. It would've been funny trying to find the tiniest detail they could've possibly overlooked, but I probably signed away my chance to even sue the guy who filled the vending machine.

Or we could just not crash and call it a day.

Fifteen minutes later I walked back down the stairs to find the large sliding doors to the hangar thrown open, and a sparkling new machine parked right outside. The guy with the overalls had turned his attention to this craft, and was getting help from a wiry dude with a straight-out-of-the-70s mustache.

This Burt Reynolds look-alike appeared to be schooling the mechanic on some detail near the tail section. I assumed the teacher was Benjamin Hughes.

It was. Deele walked over and made the introductions. Hughes shook my hand but seemed to be as uninterested in me as a person could be. My snap assessment was that he cared about his machines way more than he cared about people.

"What do you think of the *Amy Leigh*?" Deele asked with a smile, nodding toward the airplane.

"Well, it looks like an airplane," I said, walking around it. "I guess when I heard *experimental aircraft* I expected something really bizarre."

Deele joined me on the far side of the aircraft. "Well, they'll pretty much always look like a plane on the outside. I mean, they need to follow the laws of aerodynamics, so you can't very well put something in the air that looks like a backyard shed. This one has some classic lines with just a few tweaks for style."

He stepped up and unlatched the cabin door on the co-pilot's side. "Here's where you get a lot of the experimentation. Inner controls, cockpit arrangement, things of that nature." With a wink he added, "And maybe a few adjustments to the engine."

I didn't want him to see the effect that last part had on me. The limited time I'd spent in the cockpit of small planes during my military stint was enough to teach me you don't stay airborne if your engine goes out. At least not for long. And if you weren't somewhere that accommodated a smooth landing, things got broken. And by *things* I mean humans.

After peeking around the cockpit I decided it didn't look too unusual. But then, I didn't really know what I was looking for, other than the mayday button and a parachute. Then I turned my attention to the good-sized rear compartment. Back here it held four additional passengers, two facing the front, two facing the rear. A second glance told me it was relatively stripped down inside, but I imagined they eliminated a lot of weight for early test flights. Best to make sure the damned thing could get off the ground first.

"Who's *Amy Leigh*?" I asked.

Deele leaned close to my ear and lowered his voice. "She's Benjamin's soon-to-be ex-wife. He thought naming his newest creation after her would win her back."

"No go?"

"Well, since spending all his time working on airplanes is what caused the split in the first place, not even close. I think it pissed her off even more."

I chuckled. "Speaking purely from a selfish standpoint, I'm glad he spent a lot of time working on it."

He gave me another clap on the shoulder. "Nothing to worry about. We've only ditched our toys twice this year. Here, climb in."

"Do I need a helmet or something?"

"Would you feel more comfortable with one?"

I pulled myself up into the rear compartment. "Just going for the Red Baron look."

Deele pulled himself into the co-pilot's seat and slammed the door shut. A minute later Benjamin joined us, slipping into the pilot's seat. I sat quietly, watching the two of them go through a pre-flight checklist, throwing switches, checking gauges, at least *looking* like they knew exactly what they were doing.

And of course they did. It was an alien landscape to me, but they lived for this kind of stuff.

Of course, others had died for this kind of stuff.

I was out to win Deele's trust, though, and that wouldn't happen if I was a frightened passenger. I'd already earned a black mark just for requesting a helmet. I assumed a relaxed position, stretching out to the extent the harness system allowed.

Shit, I thought. *Might as well have fun.*

The engine fired up, incredibly loud in the small space. Deele turned around and pointed to a headset hanging from a low hook. He and Ben were in the process of putting on their own. A few seconds later I heard Deele's voice in my ear. "All set? You comfortable?"

I responded with the pilot's thumbs-up, and he returned the gesture.

Ben, satisfied with his inspection, slowly began taxiing the plane away from the hangar. I had to admit, if it wasn't for the experimental aspect of what we were doing, I'd be enjoying the hell out of it. Getting a feel for the controls would be a kick in the pants, too, but I was in no position to make such a request.

We trundled down to the end of the taxiway where we stopped, awaiting clearance from the tower. It seemed we waited an inordinate amount of time, but that could've just been a slight case of nerves. It all made sense when another plane glided in to land on the sole strip of runway. Once it was clear, we got the okay to go.

The engine roared to life as we shot down the runway, and soon Ben had the nose up. We climbed quickly.

I'd been holding my breath and now relaxed a bit. Looking out the side window, I watched the ground fall away before we banked to the left. Within another minute Ben relinquished control of the plane to Deele.

For a few minutes he made some basic turns, staying in

touch with the tower. He took us higher, he dropped down, and he even tried some banking that had all the earmarks of showing off. But after a few minutes I'd lost all my trepidation and simply basked in the experience.

Until Deele glanced back and spoke to me through the intercom.

"We're gonna try some stuff now. Don't be alarmed if the engine shuts off."

"What?" I asked, not sure I'd heard what I *thought* I'd heard.

He didn't respond. Instead, he and Ben discussed something I didn't understand. The result, however, was that Ben killed the engine.

My rational mind knew this wasn't necessarily a problem, that pilots train for it all the time.

But try telling your monkey mind that when you're ten thousand feet above the plains of South Texas and your aircraft's engine dies. I threw a nervous glance out the window as we began settling toward the ground. My stomach lurched.

Thirty seconds passed that felt like thirty minutes. While I certainly was interested in the activities up front, I couldn't tear my gaze from the view outside. The brown landscape below, which moments earlier had been merely a pleasant patch of scenery, now threatened to kill me. I found that with the engines off we'd popped into a surreal environment, more terrifying than if we'd plunged earthward with the engines screaming in protest. There's something about hurtling to your death in absolute silence that your mind can't or won't process.

Through my headset I heard another quick discussion between the pilots. I finally turned my attention away from the window in time to see Ben pointing vaguely at the instrument panel. Deele triggered something and the engine kicked back to life.

Then died again.

The two geniuses in the front seat chattered for a moment before Ben did something else.

The engine tried to start, but didn't catch. Then it happened again.

The plane's descent accelerated. My fingernails dug into my palms. The situation was obviously not ideal up front and I was powerless to do anything to help. So I resorted to my customary response: Laughing in the face of death.

"Hey," I said. "When do you start the drink service back here?"

No reaction from the pilot, but Jason Deele offered a quick laugh. "You've earned a drink, I think," he said. "No worries, we'll be fine."

I started to give another thumbs-up, but decided that would be ridiculous. Instead I looked out the window again. Well, at least the view was pretty. Even if it was going to be my last view for a few days.

More chatter from the Wright brothers, who, I had to admit, sounded remarkably calm. After we'd dropped another few hundred feet I saw Deele throw a different combination of switches. A moment later the engine roared back to life.

And kept roaring.

There are deep breaths, and there are deep breaths when you realize you're not going to die in a horrific fireball. That's the deep breath I took.

After that excitement the rest of the trial flight held no further drama. We stayed up about forty minutes, and then Deele brought the plane in for a landing. Smoothly, I might add, like a total pro. Which I suppose he was. I paid close attention from my perch in the back seat, genuinely curious about how the operation of this plane differed from others I'd flown.

We taxied back to the hangar where Diana Capaldi waited outside, her own look of relief visible. She'd no doubt witnessed plenty of dangerous stunts pulled off by her boss. I wondered if she'd ever had a front row seat, too.

The engine shut down, we removed our headsets, and a minute later I stood on terra firma.

Deele spoke briefly with Ben, then walked over to me with a big smile.

"Fun?" he asked.

"Loads," I said. "Especially the ol' run-out-of-gas routine."

He laughed. "There was never any danger. We were trying some unique ways to restart, some method Ben thinks could work if he does a little tinkering. But the standard restart—which we eventually did—was never in question."

"Thanks for the heads-up beforehand," I said.

"Oh, but you would've missed out on that shot of adrenaline," he said. "The one you felt when it wouldn't start up. Then, of course, you lived more when it finally *did* start than you have at any other time this year. Maybe the last several years. I'm sure of that."

The thing is, he believed it. That was his mantra. Squeeze every drop of excitement you could out of life's thrill ride. Savor as many intoxicating moments as possible. All the way to the end.

And, apparently, indoctrinate others along the way.

"I have to get back to the office pretty soon," he said, leading me toward the large hangar door. "But Diana has arranged a late lunch for us. Let's talk about soybeans before I have to go, shall we?"

13

The lunch was more of a snack, a modest spread of salad and fruit, delivered while we'd been airborne. It occupied a six-foot banquet table set up in the hangar. Some of the workers stood around, obviously instructed to wait until the boss had helped himself before they could dive in. Three round tables had also been hastily arranged for dining. Assembling an on-the-go cafeteria on a whim beat the hell out of your typical drive-thru, and was easy when you had the money and a platoon of helpers. I wondered if Jason Deele ever wanted for anything in his life.

Of course, we always imagine the supremely-wealthy living carefree, glamorous lives, with everything perfect. Movies and television had warped our perception until we naturally assumed these people never experienced a moment of unhappiness.

Now this is where you expect me to tell you it's all baloney. That billionaires live sad, lonely, stress-filled lives. That they can never develop satisfying personal relationships because their own view of normal, day-to-day living has been sublimated by layers of phantasmagorical excess. That deep down they're miserable.

Ha! That's complete bullshit. They're not miserable; they're having the time of their lives. They love every glorious moment of their gilded existence, and can't wait for one day to end so they can experience another one tomorrow that's just as fabulous, if not more so.

In fact, I think the rumor that they're unhappy is spread—probably by these very same wealthy people we're talking about—to make the rest of us feel not so envious. If we can say, *Yeah, they're super rich, but they have problems, too*, then we don't covet their $20 million mansions and their $300,000 cars nearly as much because the money has darkened their souls and they're suffering.

Nope. You and I get stressed and angry if our car breaks down because it means a couple weeks of hassle and an inconvenient expense. Billionaires have someone pick them up in another spectacular car, if not a helicopter, and they have *people* to clean up the messy details while they jet away to the Caribbean, Europe, or a sun-dappled island in the South Pacific. Hell, by the time they get back they've probably forgotten they ever even *had* the broken-down car.

They have a billion dollars. Even if they get a toothache, I promise you it will never hurt nearly as much as the one you get.

For now it was interesting watching Jason Deele interact with the people around him. I hung back for a minute and observed him talking to some of those airport workers. As smooth as he was, you could see it was still an effort for him to converse with the *hoi polloi*, his awkward forced interest and their clumsy nervous laughter a dead giveaway. I gave him brownie points for valiantly attempting to relate to the common folk when he knew they were bending over backwards for even the *opportunity* to kiss his ass. Neither side was comfortable in the exchange, although the players all tried their best to make it appear that way.

As I watched, I realized this was the avenue I'd been looking for. My calm, unaffected reaction in the office to Deele's aggressive opening comment had earned me the airplane ride; that same unimpressed attitude would perhaps get me even further along.

I filled a plate with a smidge of salad and some pineapple and breezed over to the table where Deele sat with Diana. He pointed to the chair across from him.

"Is Ben joining us?" I asked, looking around. The private security man who'd been stationed at the stairwell now stood nearby, his arms crossed. He gave me a glance before scanning the rest of the room.

Deele shook his head. "Benjamin wouldn't be caught dead eating salad. I'm sure he's off to get a burger somewhere before he spends the rest of the day under the hood of that beast." He nodded toward his assistant. "I told Diana you earned your wings today. Did you have fun?"

"Oh, I figured you'd do something to spook me, but killing the engine was an A-plus prank. The only way you could top it would be with a surprise ejector seat."

He grinned and leaned toward Diana. "Make a note to ask Benjamin about an ejector seat."

I pushed some leafy greens around my plate. "It would seem you're a certified adrenaline junkie. Have you always danced around fear?"

Deele wiped his mouth with a napkin, then sat back. "When I was a kid I remember my father being terrified of spiders. So when I was seven I got my first deadly specimen, a red widow."

"Not a black widow?"

"Oh, much too pedestrian. From there I worked my way up until at 11 I got my first *Atrax robustus*: the Funnel-web spider from Australia. My parents hated it, but as long as I kept the spiders contained they put up with it. You know, one of my favorite pastimes was to bring a classmate home from school and, when their back was turned, place one of my lovely critters beside them." He laughed. "God, they all pissed their pants. I don't know why it was so funny to me, but I couldn't resist. Sadly, it wasn't long before the word got around and suddenly nobody would accept my invitation to come over."

It was a little thing, but I noted that he referred to them as classmates. Not friends.

His eyes sparkled as he continued. "I branched out to snakes, and was satisfied with creepy-crawly things until I was a teen. Then I discovered physical rushes. Bungee jumping, skydiving, underwater cave diving. Some call it a type of sickness, but I figure why go to the trouble of living if you're not pushing the needle to the max? So that's what I do, with my hobbies, and with my business."

I smiled. "Yes, business. Now that we're safely on the ground I'd like to hear about your work with soy."

His brow wrinkled. "How did you hear about it? I'm always curious what brings people to our modest outfit, especially when those people represent a sizable organization like D.M. Cash."

I took a gamble. "Oh, let's just say you've caused a stink with some of your claims. Word gets around."

"Would this stink emanate from Iowa?" he asked.

"It would." I placed a bite of pineapple in my mouth and said no more.

After a pause, he smiled again. "I'm offering something new, something different. It makes some people uncomfortable. But I never expect the forces currently in power to hop on board right away. They're much too complacent. Success breeds intractable laziness."

He sat back, and for the first time I witnessed what Fife had described as Deele's *ticktick* problem. He became quite still, almost frozen in his seat, while his eyes grew wide. Fife had claimed it was like a balloon swelling, and I had to admit he was spot on.

It lasted only a few seconds, then Deele's eyes returned to normal and he grinned. "Do you know, Mr. Thomas, what the New York Times had to say when they first heard about this new invention called the telephone? They called it, quote, *a device of the enemies of the Republic.* They were convinced it would be our undoing."

I decided to poke him. "And you're the Alexander Graham Bell of farming, I take it."

At first he just stared at me. Without looking in her direction, I could feel Diana Capaldi fidgeting. I stabbed another piece of fruit and ate it.

Finally, Deele laughed. "All right. I'll say yes. I *am* the Alexander Graham Bell of farming. I've showed up with a new spin on the recipes and techniques that many of these traditional communities find, at the best, unnecessary or, at the worst, dangerous. It's neither."

I wanted to say, *Well, it was dangerous for David Culbertson.* Instead I pushed forward.

"There's talk you're offering a solution to a problem that doesn't exist."

"Which is ridiculous. There are always threats to the world's food supplies. The problems we faced yesterday are nothing like the ones we'll face tomorrow. And the day after that they'll be different still. Only a fool bets on the status quo."

One of the catering people stopped by, offering glasses of tea or ice water. The drinks we'd discussed in the air were nowhere to be found. I thanked her and took a long drink of water. Then I sat back and crossed one leg over another.

"Jason, I represent people who aren't afraid to bet on tomorrow. If you've looked at our history—if you've looked at *my* history—then you understand why I'm here talking to you. You may have even *expected* a visit from DCM."

He assumed his own casual, relaxed pose. "Well, let's say I'm not surprised. Your company has a reputation for innovation. But you're right, I do my research, Mr. Thomas. I know D.M. Cash plays the part of serious suitor even when they have no intention of marriage. So if you're here for just a few dates, then I'm afraid I won't be able to accommodate you. To be quite straight-forward, I don't have time for an individual, personalized sales pitch if it's only meant to entertain. As high-end realtors are fond of saying, serious buyers only."

I pursed my lip. "Suppose I'm serious. How would I go about finding more information on your magic beans? It wouldn't require another joy ride, would it?"

"Before I answer that," he said, "tell me what else you've heard from your sources."

The question caught me off-guard. Was he asking what I'd heard about the actual soybeans? Or was he fishing for a sign that I'd heard about serious trouble in Iowa? A lesson that had served me well through the years was simply this: Don't jump to the conclusion that your enemy knows that you know. That has short-circuited a good number of assignments. Better to give an innocent answer and force your opponent to be more transparent in their enquiries.

"I feel like I'm gossiping on the playground," I said. "But okay. I've heard your product has promise, but that you personally are difficult to deal with. That your brash approach hasn't been earned yet through experience and success. And, if you want all of my intel, you've ruffled a few feathers because your attitude doesn't mesh with your background, which isn't in agriculture at all, but in technology. One person labeled you the *Silicon Valley Farmer*. I don't think they meant it in an endearing fashion."

Now, from the corner of my eye, Diana's restless worry was fully evident. I may have been the first potential customer who'd ever spoken to the billionaire boy wonder this way, and *she'd* set up the appointment.

Rather than let the wound sit there and fester, however, I followed it up with the salve.

"But frankly, Jason, I have no respect for people who let fear of the unknown impede progress. It's why I climbed into your experimental airplane for one of its first flights, and it's why I investigate new opportunities in traditional fields. In this case, literal fields. You see, I really don't give a shit if your background is in technology or in Tinkertoys. I care about one thing: Planning for the future of agriculture and farming. And making a healthy profit through that planning. Now, if you have a product geared more for tomorrow than for today, I'm interested in learning about it. And, as you already know, when my company gets serious they make healthy investments."

I punctuated the speech by finishing the pineapple.

Diana looked from me to her boss, probably as curious as I was to see how he'd react to the one-two punch I'd delivered.

I wasn't sure he *knew* how to react. I'd cuffed him across the face and followed it up with a kiss on the cheek. Not the kind of formula one normally associated with wooing, but, if my hunch was correct, it was the right tactic for this particular chase. Use force against force, with a sprinkle of investment talk.

Deele kept his expression neutral for the longest time, but finally another smile spread across his face. "I may have to get business cards printed that say *Silicon Valley Farmer*. I rather like the sound of that."

I held my ground. "So about that additional information . . ."

He leaned forward. "I'll tell you what. I'm giving a small presentation tomorrow to some representatives with a rather large co-op, and one or two other interested parties. Normally that would be closed to anyone else. But why don't you join us and you can meet the person who knows more about the science of it all than I do. I assume your calendar is open?"

"That's why I'm in Texas, Jason."

"Very good," he said, pushing back from the table. "I have to run. Diana will set you up with all the details regarding the presentation."

Standing with him, I shook his hand. "Thanks for the ride today. It was . . . memorable."

"I hope we can do it again sometime," he said. "Maybe even let you handle the controls for a bit?"

"I'll bring my helmet," I said.

He gave a sarcastic thumbs up and began to walk away. Then, pausing, he looked back.

"By the way," he said. "What are Tinkertoys?"

I felt pretty puffed up on the long drive back into town. I'd made contact with our shady billionaire and finagled an invitation to one of his closed presentations. Not to mention surviving a white-knuckle ride in his dodgy airplane without soiling myself.

Of course, all of that was worthless if it didn't produce credible information tying Jason Deele to a nefarious scheme involving the country's farmland. The idea of the presentation intrigued me, especially with his quick reference to a person who knew *more about the science of it all*. The nerd in me looked forward to it.

My job required I make snap judgments on people, and in one hour I'd done that with two of the players. Deele was easy; he tried to camouflage his cutthroat demeanor with an easy laugh and somewhat-gregarious manner around staff and strangers, but I've encountered enough psychopaths to practically sniff them out.

Or so I thought. That subject was at the root of a fascinating session I'd once had with Q2's psychiatrist, Miller. He'd asked me to describe a villain I'd recently dispatched, a particularly nasty character one might describe using Quanta's term for the worst of the worst: a *knave*. In fact, I did; but Miller had wanted more.

"The guy was a psychopath," I'd said. "Or am I using the wrong term? Maybe a sociopath?" I shrugged. "It's been a few years since I took *Introduction to Psychology*. Refresh me on the differences."

"Sociopath and psychopath are just pop culture labels," Miller said. "You won't find them in many of the mental health textbooks; the psychiatry profession prefers the term *antisocial personality disorder*. Sort of an umbrella diagnosis, maybe, but an apt description."

"But come on, you know I love pop culture," I said. "Humor me."

Miller set down the tablet he'd been using for notes. "Okay. Well, the two have similarities and differences. Both are rooted in antisocial tendencies. But it's often believed that psychopathic behavior is something you're born with, while sociopathic tendencies are more likely induced by your environment."

"A psychopath is born and a sociopath is made," I said.

He nodded. "Also, a psychopath is more of a planner, the sociopath more impulsive. Of course, neither takes into account the harm they're causing others. They're generally incapable of feeling guilt, although some experts will tell you sociopaths have a tiny sliver of conscience. Just not enough to stop their actions. Perhaps they'll feel bad about it later, but they'll get over it."

"No conscience. That explains a lot," I said.

"Bear in mind that a psychopath is capable of *pretending* to have a conscience, but it's usually a smokescreen to hide his motives. They'll even pretend to fall in love and form strong emotional attachments, but that's an act, too. A tool to get something else they want."

I absorbed this for a moment, mentally tagging the various villains I'd dealt with in my Q2 adventures.

Miller kept going. "What makes it difficult to peg a true psychopath is the fact that they're often quite charming. I'm sure you've encountered more than one like that on your assignments. But, again, it's just another tool. They're master manipulators, right? And the charming personality just makes their job easier."

"I'm assuming one is more dangerous than the other," I said.

He raised an eyebrow. "Oh, they'll both kill you. In your case they probably have. The difference is one of them might feel *slightly* bad about it. For a few minutes. So if you're forcing me to pick one that would be more dangerous, I'd go with the psychopath. Only because they're able to dissociate from their actions."

Miller wrapped up the discussion by assuring me not all psychopaths or sociopaths were dangerous.

But we both silently understood that this particular disclaimer had little relevance with my job. I only dealt with the dangerous ones.

Specifically, the *deadly* ones.

Now, behind the wheel of my Jag, I thought about the easy smile Jason Deele had dispensed at the airfield. The annoying tendency to clap me on the shoulder and flash his teeth, the manufactured laughter.

Was it all an evil facade? Did a psychopath lurk behind the smile? Had Deele ordered the murder of a federal agent without hesitation and with no trace of remorse? And was there something truly sinister at the heart of his newfound fascination with the business of food? Sarah Eklund was convinced his plan could ultimately be catastrophic for one of the country's most important cash crops. And, assuming his scheme eventually encompassed more than just soybeans, it wasn't out of the question, the scientist said, for dominoes to tip over until starvation became a real possibility.

While Jason Deele smiled and contemplated his next move.

Miller had been spot on: Over the years I'd come up against my share of charming killers. Only weeks earlier I'd personally battled a man who displayed all the classic traits of a psychopath. He'd spent years meticulously planning his crime. He was a complete loner, with no messy attachments; in fact, even his closest ally was on his scheduled hit list. On top of it all, he'd been the most intelligent and the most charming knave I'd ever faced.

What disturbed me was the chilling realization that he'd also been the person—other than my wife—with whom I felt the closest connection. It was this fraternal bond that scared the living hell out of me. What does it say when the person you're most simpatico with has a murderous, vindictive streak dominating their personality?

Much of my six-week convalescence was spent rolling around that darkness. Not a place you wanna spend too much time. I never came to any rock-solid conclusions about it, other than the fact that—so far—I'd used my powers for the greater good. That would have to pacify me until I fully deconstructed everything.

Assuming that was possible.

· · ·

NORMALLY I'D UPLOAD JUST before bed, backing up all my head's data at the natural conclusion of a day. But the meeting with Deele, including the flight and the lunch chatter, was too important to lose in case a bus jumped a curb and flattened me on my walk to dinner. I owed it to Future Swan to archive it all, and finished by six o'clock.

After packing away the upload gear I checked my phone, surprised to see a text message from Dr. Eklund. It read: *Call me when you get a moment.*

I did.

"What are you doing for dinner?" she asked.

"I'm in Texas, so I suppose I should either do a steak or something chicken-fried. Although I have no idea how one chicken-fries anything. Why do you ask? Are you worried about my cholesterol?"

"Not particularly," she said. "I thought I might buy you dinner and we could talk some more about the case."

I sat motionless, staring at the wallpaper as the words sank in.

"You're in Houston?"

"I'm in Houston. In fact, I'm in the lobby of your hotel. Are you here, or out somewhere?"

I sighed. "I'm at the hotel. I just don't understand why you are."

"A last-minute thing. I can explain. So, are you joining me or not?"

"I guess I am. Give me twenty minutes. I've got some calls to make."

POOLE WAS HAVING her own dinner at her desk, which is where I think she took the majority of her meals. On one hand I felt guilty that she worked an unseemly number of hours and subsisted on Tupperware-packaged leftovers while I was heading out for a hot meal of something smothered in jalapeño gravy. On the other hand, her manner led me to believe she wouldn't have it any other way.

She was excited to hear about the presentation I'd be attending the next day. Well, *excited* might be overstating it; I'd never really heard Poole excited in the way most people associate with the word. Let's say she was optimistic that the presentation would provide helpful intel for the assignment.

When I asked if there was any news from the boss, the answer was no. Quanta, she said, had been called to a meeting in London and wouldn't return for three days. This piqued my curiosity.

"Gimme the dirt," I said.

"What dirt?"

"The meeting in London. She's not quitting and going back to a job in Europe, is she?"

"She hasn't mentioned anything like that," Poole said.

I grunted. "She wouldn't. I thought you might have a feeling."

There was a pause while Quanta's assistant thought about it. In the silence something else occurred to me.

"Does this trip have anything to do with Parnell?" I asked.

"I don't know what the meeting's about."

"Yeah, all right, never mind. Listen, I downloaded already, and in a few minutes I'll be meeting with Sarah Eklund. She's in town for some reason. I'll check in with you tomorrow before the meeting with Deele."

We hung up. Before my next call I sat quietly, thinking about Quanta and her sudden mysterious trip to the UK. Perhaps it was just coincidence that our latest addition to the

Q2 roster of agents included the former British intelligence officer.

Parnell had worked with me on my last assignment. It didn't end well for her. She'd been killed right in front of me, which meant she'd now experienced the agency's investment program for the first time. While agents in our department are discouraged from communicating with each other, I couldn't help but be curious how she was handling everything. I was, after all, responsible not only for bringing her into the fold, but also for the bullet which had ended her previous life.

Maybe things were working out so splendidly with her that Quanta had taken a recruiting trip across the pond. She could be hunting down more European players to replace the agents Q2 had lost.

I shook my head. It wasn't worth worrying over at the moment.

The next call was to Fife. He expressed a bit more enthusiasm than Poole regarding the next day's meeting.

"How the hell did you con your way into that?" he asked.

"No conning necessary. Well, unless you count my fake identity and bullshit agenda. Otherwise you can chalk it up to my innate charm and captivating wit. Oh, and, as it turns out, my iron stomach."

"I have no idea what that means. But color me impressed," he said.

"I'd invite you to join, but they specifically said no Elvis impersonators, art history majors, or FBI agents allowed."

"Damn, I'm screwed on two counts."

"I'm not surprised. How's your cute little assignment going in Dallas?"

"*Cute little assignment*? You mean the one with major national security ramifications? It's going well. But never mind that; tell me about Jason Deele. Wish I'd been there when you met him. Was it like meeting a rock star?"

I chuckled. "You're not too far off. He definitely parades around with the air of a celebrity, has the usual sycophants orbiting him, and a two-man muscle detail. The guy loves being rich."

"What about Eklund's read on him? Did you get any kind of feeling that she may be right?"

"Maybe. But it's funny you mentioned the plant professor. She's down in the hotel lobby right now."

"Swan, you sly dog. I didn't figure you for the type."

"Oh, hush."

"All right, so what's she doing there?"

I scratched the stubble on my chin. "There's no way this is a coincidence, like visiting family or anything. She's obviously here because of Deele."

"Maybe she doesn't think much of your detective work and she's come to make a citizen's arrest."

"I wouldn't stop her. I'd love to see that some time."

"You already have," Fife said. "Remember your excitement at the farmers market? You and those college dudes who sat on the perps until the cops arrived? That's a form of citizen's arrest."

"This is why I hang out with FBI dweebs," I said. "You're so damned knowledgeable. In case I need a little smarty-pants backup, are you almost finished in Dallas?"

"Getting there. But if I don't make it before all hell breaks loose on your end, I'll be sure to visit you in the hospital. Again."

"Wow, smart *and* funny. Anything else to report before I go meet the doctor?"

"I heard through the grapevine you pissed off Eklund's step-mother, the deputy secretary."

"How did you hear this?" I asked.

"She thinks you're connected with the FBI, so she made a strongly-worded complaint. Something about a *lack of respect*. That's when I knew she'd talked with you."

I laughed. "Normally it's Quanta who tells me to play nice."

"Oh, I'm not telling you to play nice. Where's the fun in that?"

15

───────

In the elevator on my way down to the lobby I remembered something Fife had said to me on my first night in Iowa. When I'd asked him to describe Dr. Sarah Eklund, he'd used three words:

Dynamic as hell.

There were two kinds of people you could pin that description on. One was the sharp, detail-oriented self-starter, the person who'd lead a charge up the hill and you'd follow because you were caught up in the wake of their strength of will. They were born leaders, people you admired. There have been presidents, prime ministers, civil rights leaders, and entrepreneurs who embodied this spirit, oozing confidence in themselves while inspiring others to achieve results they'd never imagined.

The other was just the common, everyday pain in the ass.

I'd been around both types of dynamic personalities. You never forgot either one, for drastically different reasons.

I hoped to God that Sarah Eklund was version number one. Something told me I'd know before the night was over.

She stood near the front door, relaxed. Most people would be engrossed in something on their phone; Eklund seemed comfortable without a distraction.

"This is quite a surprise," I said.

"Sorry to spring the visit on you," she said. "But I felt like our first few talks didn't go so well."

"You came a long way just to start over."

She gave an easy smile. "Would you believe I was in the neighborhood?"

"I can't wait to find out why. Where are we going?"

She nodded toward the door. "There's a great cafe nearby. I can't promise they'll chicken-fry anything for you, but the reviews are good. Come on, my treat."

We walked into a relatively crisp evening by Houston standards. I knew the humidity would crank up in the next month, but this night was pleasant. The cafe she'd picked out was eight blocks away, and the walk felt good. We made small talk, first about Texas in general, then about Houston, and finally about the area we were in, the Museum District. She told me she'd once attended a conference at Rice University, less than a mile away. That explained her familiarity with the area.

"Well, you called this meeting," I finally said. "What's on your mind?"

"Like I said, I probably didn't get things off to the best start with you. You're on this case to investigate, and instead of being patient I kept insisting you charge after Jason Deele. I'm sorry about that."

I waited a few moments before responding, measuring my words. "I can tell how passionate you are about your work. And I don't blame you for being concerned."

"Well, I thought having dinner together might give me a

chance to slow down and explain how the passion and the concern are connected."

"Sounds good," I said. "Why don't you start by telling me why you're in Houston?"

"I'm going to a presentation Jason Deele is giving tomorrow."

I laughed. "You're kidding. *I'm* going to that presentation. I didn't know you were invited."

She pointed across the street, indicating we should cross.

"He understands I'm a threat to his plan," she said. "He sent me a message last night, asking if I'd come down and hear him out, one more time. I think *he* thinks a formal presentation, rather than just an impromptu meeting in my office, will impress me. Sway me, I guess."

"Apologies if this sounds rude, but you haven't come across so far as someone who could be swayed on this case."

She shrugged. "I was this close to telling him to shove his presentation. But then I remembered the old saying about keeping your friends close but your enemies closer." She paused. "I don't know who originally said that."

"Michael Corleone. *The Godfather* movies. Paraphrasing an old Indian poet, I believe. But pure gangster. Which is interesting. You've now reduced your conflict with Mr. Deele to the level of the mob."

Which immediately reminded me of Vincent Volta, who'd worked so hard in pursuit of the exact opposite effect, trying to elevate his own brand of thuggery to the level of respected businessman.

Seemed nobody was happy staying in their own lane.

"Well," I added, "just remember, when I see you there tomorrow, you don't know me. Right?"

"Understood," she said. "Did you meet Deele yet?"

"I did."

"I'm curious about your first impression. Do you mind sharing?"

We waited at an intersection for traffic to pass. "He's almost exactly what I expected, and in some ways that has *me* concerned."

She gave me a quizzical look. "What do you mean?"

"I know it sounds odd, but let me see if I can explain. In my business I come across a lot of people who do bad things. I almost always have a dossier on them before I go to work, so I don't go into a meeting blind. You learn about their past, their connections, their motivations. You think you know almost everything about them. But when you meet them there are always a few things you don't expect."

The light turned green and we began walking again.

"And that's completely natural," I said. "People have their own quirks, their own peculiarities that aren't the kind of things you get in a report. I think of it as accessorizing a personality. Make sense?"

Sarah nodded.

"But when I met Jason Deele, he behaved almost entirely the way I expected. Of course, he did a few things that surprised me just because I wasn't ready for them. But he didn't display anything I wasn't briefed on."

"I still don't understand why that's concerning," she said.

"Well, because to me, at least, it means he's playing a part. Full tilt. He's not doing anything, or saying anything, that I couldn't get through a background report. It's as if he knows what his file says, and he's reciting the proper lines to fit that file."

Sarah seemed to contemplate that. "So he's not giving you anything."

"Not a damned thing. He lives behind a facade. And that concerns me because it means he's extremely clever. And I don't like going up against clever bad guys. I much prefer they be morons."

She laughed, a light, pleasant sound that belied the gruff demeanor I'd experienced in our first conversations. "Do you come across many of these morons?"

"Not often enough, but it's a treat when I do. Makes my job so much easier."

What I didn't say—but what certainly crossed my mind—was that I'd lately encountered two of the most intelligent, crafty opponents I'd ever faced. Perhaps I was secretly hoping this case would give me a break, like the college football champions scheduling a game against a Division II school to start the season. A tune-up game; that's what I'd hoped for after my short sabbatical.

Things rarely were that convenient.

"This is the place," Sarah said, pointing to the colorful cafe on our left. "Maybe we'll be lucky and snag a table on the patio."

We were and we did. After quickly settling on drinks and entrees from the menu touting American fare, we got back down to business.

"All right," I said, taking a sip from the one beer I'd allow myself. "Tell me more about your plant passion. How did it start?"

She laced her fingers together on the table and leaned forward.

"When I was seven we moved to a new neighborhood. I didn't know anybody, I was the new kid in school, and I was kinda shy anyway. My mother got tired of me spending all my time outside of school hours just hanging out in my room or in front of the TV. She forced me to go outside and explore. I was pissed. So at first I stayed in our yard, just sitting on the grass."

"What a rebel," I said.

"Right. I'm sure my mom saw me through the window and got a good laugh. But after a few minutes I stood up and looked around. There was an alley running behind our house, and on the other side of it I saw an older woman going into this strange shed, made entirely out of glass. I was intrigued."

I furrowed my brow, then said, "Oh. A greenhouse."

"I'd never seen one. Didn't even know they existed. There I was standing on an old tree stump to get a better view over the fence, when she saw me and waved. Then she came to her fence and asked if I'd like to see the inside of the greenhouse.

"Well, my mom would probably be angry that I trusted some stranger, but hell, she'd told me to go explore. And this was another way to rebel, right? So without asking permission I left the yard, crossed the alley, and walked into paradise."

She took a drink of her white wine. "Her name was Mrs. Krock. At the time she seemed so old to me; looking back now she was probably in her 50s or early 60s. But the sweetest woman in the world. She could tell I was interested in her greenhouse, and when she opened the door I probably gaped.

"To this day I remember every detail. The rows of tables with the most colorful, exotic forms of life I'd ever seen. The hanging plants. The gardening utensils everywhere. She grew flowers, she grew vegetables, she grew mushrooms. The air was warm and thick, but not uncomfortable. And there was this . . . scent. It was nothing I'd ever smelled before. This wonderful mixture of soil and nutrients and love."

I laughed, and she did, too.

"No, I mean it," she said. "That's what it seemed like to me. Like I'd wandered into someone's complete labor of love.

And I think that's exactly what attracted me to botany: the intimate relationship a grower has with everything blooming under her care. And it's not like the feelings we have for pets; I think with a dog or cat we love them for their companionship and for their personality.

"But when we grow flowers or plants or food crops, we're subconsciously feeling the connection to life itself. Not just the life of the plant, but the life it provides *us*. The sustenance it gives, from the food it bears all the way down to the oxygen it produces. It's the plant life on our planet that provides almost everything we need to live."

I couldn't help but smile at the way she painted the picture, the way she described it in terms of a love story. But at the same time she was right. We took it for granted, but without the generosity of plant life around the globe the human species wouldn't even be around. People like Sarah Eklund got it.

"So you made them your life's work," I said, prodding her forward.

"It's almost pitiful," she said with a guilty smile. "I don't really even have hobbies, other than running. And I do that outdoors, in nature."

I took another sip of my beer. "All right. I understand the passion. Now tell me about your concern."

She studied the wine glass, twisting it between her fingers. A somber look settled over her face.

"Working on my graduate degree I was touched for the first time by the notion of not just producing, but preserving. I began researching the dangers we face around the world, studying the history of catastrophic destruction of food crops. Untold millions of deaths throughout the years, and many of those deaths preventable. Sometimes it's unavoidable, you know, a natural disaster. But people would be shocked to learn how many times it's man-made destruction, either through negligence or sabotage."

"I'm assuming the negligence is from, what? Poor farming skills?"

"Some of it. Also things like toxic waste, irresponsible water management."

"Tell me about the sabotage," I said, understanding that this was the reason she'd reached out for help in the first place.

"It goes back thousands of years," she said. "Ancient armies began a process known as scorched earth."

"Destroying the crops and fouling water sources, right?"

She nodded. "It's against the Geneva Convention these days. Doesn't stop it from happening in isolated incidents."

The server arrived with our food, and I dove into my burger.

"Are you familiar with the global seed vault in Norway?" Sarah asked.

"No. A seed vault? Literally seeds, like plant seeds?"

"Yes. Individual countries have had them in the past, but those wouldn't do much good in the event of a crisis in a particular country, either a natural disaster or invaders. So in 2008 a special vault was built into an arctic mountain in Norway. Countries from around the world store the seeds of plants, providing a safe haven against what could be a total loss.

"When I first heard about it I nearly cried," she said. "A few years ago I was able to visit. For someone like me it was a pilgrimage. And it reinforced my purpose in life: to protect one of the most vital resources we have." She paused, looking down at her salad. "See? We take this for granted, don't we?"

I felt like a caveman, my hands wrapped around a burger,

dripping juices onto my plate. Hey, at least I had some lettuce and tomato on it.

"Of course you're right," I said. "And I didn't know about the seed vault. That's very cool." I set down the burger, wiped my mouth, and reached for the beer. "But let's tie all of this together with Jason Deele."

She pushed her salad around the plate for a moment, but I could tell she had no appetite.

"When a drought or a flood damages a nation's food supply, I'm concerned," she said. "I'll do everything I can to help. And although I'm furious to hear about armies poisoning the fields and water sources, I recognize it's part of our primitive DNA, maybe one of the ugliest parts.

"But if Jason Deele is manipulating the world's food supply, and in the process destroying millions of acres of life-sustaining nutrition for millions of people—and he's doing it simply for personal profit?"

She didn't finish the thought for a long time. Just sat there, holding her fork, looking down at her plate.

Then she turned her gaze back to me.

"In my opinion it makes him one of the most evil people in the world. And one of the most dangerous. If you won't stop him, I promise you I will. Somehow."

Dynamic as hell.

16

———————

The instructions gave an address, which brought me to a thoroughly modern office building two miles from my hotel. At the front desk sat a uniformed security man who must've pumped iron twice a day. His shirt practically cried out from the strain, and you just knew he intentionally wore them a half-size too small for that very reason.

His name badge said M. Dick. I secretly hoped the M stood for Moby, but, really, what were the chances? Regardless, the man had no doubt turned to physical fitness in order to overcome the trauma of having all of his high school sports jerseys say *Dick* on the back.

He asked for my ID, checked a list on his screen, and found the mythical Ryan Thomas representing D.M. Cash. I felt he overdid the intense studying of my ID photo, looking back and forth between it and me. When he glanced up for the third time, I opened my eyes wide and gave him my best zombie stare.

He found no humor in it whatsoever, but it brought me immense joy.

Instead of an elevator I was directed to an escalator. Someone would be waiting at the top to check me in.

Let me explain something. I've served tours of duty in deserts and jungles, and been face to face with plenty of people out to kill me. I've been balls-deep in gun fights, knife fights, and brutal hand-to-hand combat. I even had a leg wound stitched up without pain-killing medication.

And yet none of that ever creeped me out as much as riding an escalator. Can't explain it. Just one of those things. I lose every thread of a conversation as I climb aboard because it takes all of my concentration. I'm mostly okay for the ride itself, but then tense up again at the end, where I invariably look awkward. I either step too soon and look like an idiot, gliding along with one foot in the air, or I step too late and come close to stumbling. Maybe it's an inner-ear thing. I don't know. What I *do* know is that it's become a mind game with me now.

Trips to London are fun, I enjoy the people and the life-style; but when I'm forced to take the Tube I get decidedly worked up. Many of the stations in the London Underground have ridiculously long, steep escalators, and my anxiety is compounded by the fact they're generally packed. The only thing worse than falling on your face in public is taking down total strangers with you.

The dread is real and it goes back as far as I can remember. There must be some horrible escalator incident buried deep within my early childhood, a tale that might come screaming out of me under hypnosis. It's the one embarrassing compo-nent I wish would get lost during the process of investment.

No such luck. It follows me around like a shadow from body to body.

This particular escalator was quite long as well, but at least

I had it to myself. Approaching the top I inwardly groaned to see my escort waiting for me, hands behind her back, and a headset keeping her updated on the approaching guests. A large Texas smile played across her face. Well, great. Nothing worse than having a witness to my transportation troubles. I smiled back, then turned all my concentration to the dismount.

It didn't help.

"Whoa, careful," the woman said with an accent like Dolly Parton.

"That'll teach me to be drunk before lunch," I said, one of my go-to comments every time I stumbled. She laughed, but probably wasn't sure if I was joking or not.

"You're Mr. Thomas," she said, handing me a name tag. It wasn't one of those Hello-My-Name-Is stickers with *Ryan Thomas / D.M. Cash* scrawled in Sharpie. This puppy was engraved in metal, as if I'd been a valuable employee for years. Oh, the things your company can do when it has billions to play with.

"I am indeed," I said, pinning the name plate on my sport jacket. Then I glanced at her tag. "Where's the party, Alma?"

She pointed toward the nearest door. "Before you go in, though, I have to ask you to please leave any and all cell phones here." She held out a small, reinforced pouch. "You can pick it up after the presentation."

I pulled out my phone and dropped it in the bag. "But Alma, how am I supposed to secretly record everything?"

She flashed the big Texas smile again. "You don't look like a spy to me."

"You should've seen me a few months ago. You wouldn't have recognized me."

I waved goodbye to her and to my phone and walked away.

The room wasn't large, and didn't need to be. About thirty

chairs were set up, and not the typical hotel banquet type. These were large and cushy. A catering team finished arranging an impressive fruit, appetizer, and beverage station along the side wall. A bartender stood at attention nearby, just in case the guests preferred something more stimulating than a strawberry smoothie.

Some of those guests were already in attendance, standing in a small knot near the front of the room. Two of them threw a brief glance my way, then, having decided I was no one of importance, went back to impressing each other.

There was no sign of Jason Deele or Diana Capaldi.

I passed by the bartender and gave a nod of sympathy that she had to work such a lame—and unprofitable—gig, then helped myself to a glass of cranberry juice at the snack table. I was anxious for something—anything—to happen. On the list of life's most awkward moments you'd have to include standing alone in a semi-professional setting, waiting for a meeting to begin. I didn't even have a phone to distract me.

A few minutes later Sarah Eklund walked in.

Her gaze fell on me, she gave a simple nod, then, without acknowledging anyone else in the room, took one of the seats in front. I liked her style; she intended to be right in Deele's face.

A man and a woman entered, looked around, then made their way to the snack table. After filling small plates with fruit and mixed nuts, they meandered over to me. The man's name tag read Rob Byzinski / Tepperran Inc. I'd never heard of them.

"Hello, Ryan," Rob said after reading my badge. "How are things at DMC?"

Poole and the team at Q2 had made the right call in going with D.M. Cash; it was well known, which would get you in the door, and populated by enough people for my Ryan Thomas character to be anonymous.

"Business is growing," I said with a wink. I hoped he got the joke.

He gave a serious nod and took a bit of pineapple. "Well, good to know."

He didn't get it.

I think the woman must've, however. She gave a sly smile. Her name badge read Kate Hall. Probably hated attending meetings and having to cover for the company hotshot who was dense as a board.

"Kate," I said, "have you met Jason Deele before?"

She shook her head. "No, I haven't. You?"

"He tried to kill me yesterday," I said, and took a sip of cranberry juice.

Before either could respond, Diana Capaldi walked in, talking with a man. I recognized him from the Iowa hotel security footage.

Conor Wood. The most likely suspect in the shooting of Agent Culbertson. I sized him up as best I could without appearing too interested. He still had the body of an athlete, perhaps a little bulkier in the shoulders. His suit was well-tailored and expensive, his skin tanned, but his hair looked like it got the most attention. I pictured his house having lots of mirrors.

The conversation didn't last long, and Wood stalked back out, looking angry. Or maybe that was his everyday look.

Diana came over, putting on her professional face. "Ms. Hall. Mr. Byzkinski. Mr. Ryan. Thank you so much for being here today."

"Thanks for having us," said Byzinski. "Looking forward to it."

God, he was a bore.

A couple more attendees entered the room, and right behind them a tall woman with long, brown hair, carrying a leather bag over her shoulder. Diana got her attention and she joined our small group.

"Let me introduce one of our speakers today," Diana said. "This is Dr. Jaclyn Stone."

This would be the scientist Deele had described as the brainchild behind his new process.

Like Capaldi, Stone could apply the artificial business smile, but on her it was less believable. The handshake was firm but cold, and through her fashionable glasses I noticed dark eyes appraising me, like an adversary. That was odd, and I catalogued it. First impressions were important in my work, and this initial read signaled that Jaclyn Stone was an academic who would probably kick your ass if given the right provocation. I found the combination fascinating and, if I wasn't happily married, attractive as hell.

Byzinski rolled out another *looking forward to it*. Kate Hall merely nodded. It was up to me to say something witty.

"I haven't heard about magic beans since my mother read Jack and The Beanstalk. I'm guessing your story has an equally unhappy ending for the giant."

It was clear she didn't appreciate the snarky comment, and her phony smile faltered a bit. Then, recovering, she said, "Somebody once claimed that truly advanced technology is indistinguishable from magic."

I nodded. "Arthur C. Clarke, the writer. I also liked what Leigh Brackett said: *To the ignorant, science is like witchcraft.* Or something like that." I raised my glass of cranberry juice in a mock toast. "I assume your presentation today does not include a bubbling cauldron."

The other three people in our circle were quiet, not sure what to make of this exchange. But Jaclyn Stone finally unleashed a real smile, albeit a small one. She still didn't like me, for whatever reason, but probably appreciated the verbal jousting. It beat the hell out of anything that would spill out of Byzinski's mouth all day.

"Mr. Deele will be here any minute," Diana said, attempting to re-establish control of the situation. "If you'd like to top up your refreshments, we should probably take our seats."

Stone gave me one more sharp glance, then shifted the bag across her shoulder and walked to a lectern at the front of the room. Thoroughly satisfied with myself, I set down my glass, nodded at Kate and Rob, and wandered over to the lonely bartender. Ryan Thomas, I'd decided, was the guy who'd buck convention and take advantage of free booze.

I ordered a whiskey-diet, tipped the grateful bartender five bucks, and headed over to the chairs.

They'd filled up. I found an empty seat behind and to the side of Sarah Eklund so I could see the speakers and her reaction.

Diana began the presentation, adjusting the microphone and welcoming everyone. While she went through this perfunctory greeting I scanned the seats, wondering what it took to receive a golden ticket. I figured every organization represented around me likely had a business war chest fat enough to write Jason Deele an eight- or nine-figure check. Thus the cushy chairs and fancy metal name tags.

But where was the elusive billionaire? Out paragliding somewhere? Bungee jumping? Scaling the side of the Chase Tower a few blocks away?

Diana finished her comments and the lights actually

dimmed, like a concert getting underway. Fife's reference to Deele as a rock star began to seem apropos. Contemporary electronic music from a high-end sound system pulsed, at first very low, gradually increasing in volume and tempo. Two large screens deployed from above, one on each side of the lectern. And then the show really began.

A true multimedia presentation lit up the room. Visuals, including a combination of agricultural images mixed with laboratory shots, splashed back and forth on the two screens. Scenes of lush, golden fields, swaying in the breeze. Pictures of scientists, complete with the requisite microscopes and test tubes. Farmers and their families, all smiling, of course. It was all synced to the music, and must've cost a fortune to produce.

I began to see why Deele had voiced his reluctance to do an individualized sales job in that airplane hangar. Nothing could've compared to the stunning display going on before a room full of captivated buyers. The production lasted nearly two minutes, with no narration, for good reason: It wasn't needed. The producers had done a marvelous job of telling their story, explaining with images alone exactly what we'd soon hear about.

Two images remained frozen on the huge screens. On the left, a majestic crop of tall, vibrant plants basking in bright sunshine, while in the background a happy, smiling farmer, sitting up high in a gleaming combine that must've cost half-a-million dollars. The implied message was pretty clear: We deal in success.

The image on the right was pure tech. A scientist, exhibiting her own smile, looked intently at a glass beaker she held aloft.

Successful crop management aided by the highest degree

of scientific study. That was the message. Now it was up to Jason Deele to sell it.

And just like that, out of the darkness between the two screens, he appeared. Now he *was* the rock star, emerging from back stage after the band warmed up the audience with an instrumental jam. In fact, there was even a smattering of applause, undoubtedly started by Deele's employees, and the assembled crowd felt obligated to politely join in. He walked to the lectern, smiling, even offering a quick wave to someone he knew in the crowd. I couldn't help but chuckle at the silliness of it all.

Then the Q2 agent in me snapped back to reality. This glitzy, high-tech display merely cloaked a potentially wicked criminal enterprise, one that had already taken lives and was poised to chalk up many more. I couldn't be sure Jason Deele was psychotic, but I wouldn't have bet against it, either. This might look like an innocent, run-of-the-mill sales presentation, but underneath loomed a plot threatening to devastate the agricultural foundation of countries worldwide, and conceivably lead to the starvation of millions.

I set my half-finished whiskey on the floor beneath my chair.

Deele didn't bother with a cheesy introduction or welcome. He got right down to business.

"I've been involved with several startup companies. In my business life I've succeeded far beyond anything I ever dreamed, but I've also crashed and burned. Some of those failures made a few headlines, didn't they? And always with the most unflattering photos they could possibly attach to them."

This brought a small ripple of laughter in the room.

"What all of it taught me was this: I won't hire anyone on my team who hasn't had both victory *and* defeat. People who claim they've never failed in life are either lying or of no practical use to me. In fact, I'd rather work with someone who has clawed their way up from the ashes than someone who's lived a charmed life.

"I want people who've had their ass kicked. People who've been insulted and ignored. But also people who've had enough of a taste of victory that they can contrast and compare the two. Who know what it's like on the top *and* on the bottom. Those are the fighters. Those are the ones who work harder, work longer, and produce the most dazzling results."

It was an interesting speech. I couldn't disagree with him, but I wondered where this was leading.

"I was fortunate to meet a woman four years ago who embodies this particular spirit. In a minute you're going to hear from Dr. Jaclyn Stone. She's brilliant, and I've known more than a few brilliant minds after many years in Silicon Valley. She's determined, and I cherish that as much as any other quality in a person."

Here he paused, looked down for a moment, then slowly returned his gaze to the crowd.

"But what makes Dr. Stone so valuable, not just to me personally but to the technology world, is the drive. The passion. It's a passion fueled by exactly what I described to you.

"We like to think science is a quiet, gentle pursuit. Men and women in pristine lab coats, toiling for years on experiments, supporting one another. Encouraging their peers. Celebrating their successes.

"But that's not always the case. There are times when the scientific community aligns itself against you and your work. Not just to criticize you, but to discredit you."

Another pause. The room was dead silent.

And in the midst of this silence an odd feeling washed over me. Something I couldn't put my finger on. Something familiar. But it wasn't a pleasant familiarity. What *was* it? For the moment, at least, it wasn't setting off massive alarm bells, but rather producing a mild sensation of dread. Something buried within Jason Deele's speech tickled a memory. A memory of an earlier case.

Since my cases always involved vile people and nasty outcomes, it couldn't be good.

Now Deele smiled, lifting the audience out of the gloom he'd intentionally created.

"Why would I tell you all this? Because Jaclyn Stone has enjoyed the sweet taste of victory, and she's battled against the petty jealousies and vindictive motives of former colleagues. But at no time did she wilt, or lose her focus. She fought back. And, with her presentation today, you'll see that she has triumphed. Because of her work, *your* lives will be remarkably changed for the better."

He held out a hand toward the side of the room. "Please welcome Dr. Jaclyn Stone."

There was another polite round of applause, the room's occupants sizing up the elegant woman who now approached the microphone. Deele welcomed her with a somewhat awkward hug, then moved to the side of the room to stand beside Diana Capaldi.

I threw a glance at Sarah Eklund. She was not applauding, choosing instead to sit still with her arms crossed.

When I looked back at Dr. Stone I blinked.

It hit me. I remembered.

And my dread now sent an ice-cold shudder through me.

17

———

Growing up I had a next-door neighbor who was bat-shit crazy. His name was Raymond Poke, and for the 18 months we lived in that house I was terrified he'd grab me and toss me into some sort of dungeon he'd dug beneath his basement. The first time I saw *Silence of The Lambs* I actually trembled at the scene where the senator's daughter is down in that hole. It was exactly the kind of thing I expected of Crazy Raymond.

My fear was based on a total of two encounters I'd had with him. Once, when my Frisbee accidentally sailed over the fence into his yard—because Frisbees have a mind of their own and will always adopt a flight path you didn't think was possible. I'd scaled the fence to retrieve it, unaware of the old guy sitting in the shade of his back patio. He barked something at me in the angriest voice I'd ever heard, and I scrambled back over the fence so fast I spent days pulling splinters out of my hands and knees.

The second time I was tearing up and down the sidewalk

on my bike, seeing how long of a black skid mark I could lay by slamming on my brakes. It's one of those things kids do.

Of course, I'd made the mistake of leaving one of these skid marks on the sidewalk in front of the nutty next-door neighbor's house. He charged out his front door, waving a fist, telling me I better come back with a bucket of hot, soapy water and clean up his property.

And I actually did. Probably one of the lowest moments of my life, outside on a beautiful, sunny day with a bucket and sponge, trying to clean burned rubber off cement. But I was afraid that if I left it I'd wake up in the middle of the night to find Raymond leaning over my bed with a rusty butcher knife at my throat.

One day my dad asked me to return a hacksaw he'd borrowed from the guy, and I think my blood froze. How could my own father ask me to risk my life by returning a goddamned saw? Didn't he know Crazy Raymond would probably use it to slice off my limbs?

Of course, nobody else in my family feared our neighbor. Just me. My dad told me to quit dragging my ass, and pushed me out the door.

We lived in one of those neighborhoods where the houses were practically on top of each other, but it still took me an eternity to make the walk. As I approached the dark porch—of course the porch light was off—I had a notion of tossing the saw up by the door and running back to safety as fast as I could. But my dad had said to ring the bell, hand it to the man, and tell him thank you.

I was nine years old and convinced I'd never see ten.

Practically in tears, I climbed the steps, paused for a full fifteen seconds, then tapped on the screen door. The heavy wooden door was open, and from inside I heard the old man holler to come in.

Oh, shit. Go in? Alone?

Well, at least my family knew where I'd gone, so they could send a hearse directly to the scene of the crime.

I pulled the door open and walked toward the lamplight emanating from Raymond's living room around the corner. He sat in a recliner facing a TV playing something incredibly loud, a dead cat sprawled on the ground beside him. *He'd murdered a poor cat?*

Of course he hadn't. When I walked in the cat woke up, stretched, and rolled onto its other side.

I was quickly losing my nine-year-old mind.

"Well, bring it over here," Raymond said, holding out his hand.

For a split second I thought about being proactive, and rushing the old man with the saw extended, slicing his head off before he had the chance to kill me.

But I wasn't a trained killer at that point. I was a trembling little pissant, scared to death of an old man in a La-Z-Boy. I held out the saw, handle toward him, and hoped I wouldn't pee my pants.

He looked at it, perhaps making sure I hadn't somehow damaged it during the walk, then grunted and set it on the end table beside him. His eyes narrowed to slits as he examined me.

"What's your name?"

My mouth was dry but I managed to tell him.

"Eric," he repeated, as if trying it on, seeing how it fit with the names of all the other bodies he'd buried out back. "Sit down, Eric."

What the hell was this? But I found the edge of the couch beside him and leaned my narrow ass on it.

Raymond pointed his remote at the TV and muted the sound.

"You ever watch anything besides cartoons?" he asked. "Ever watch anything to expand your mind?"

I shook my head no, partly because I didn't fully understand the question and partly because I didn't want to have to rattle off names of shows I *did* watch.

"This one here," he said, gesturing with the remote, "is about the moon landing. You know we supposedly landed on the moon, right? Tell me you at least know that."

"Yes, sir," I said.

"Do you believe it?"

Again, I didn't understand him. "Uh . . ."

He waved the remote in disgust. "Don't you believe it, young man. Nobody landed on the goddamned moon. This show *proves* it was fake."

I turned to look at the television. A very earnest man seemed to be pleading a case into the camera, with a still shot in the background of a full moon with a red line through it.

"You quit watching those cartoons, which will only pollute your mind," Raymond growled at me. "Start watching shows that'll teach you something. I can tell you which ones to start with."

When I looked back at him, I saw someone entirely different than the monster I'd always seen before. As young as I was, still in elementary school, I was perceptive enough to recognize something about Raymond:

He was a lonely old guy. He yelled at neighbor kids because he had no one to talk to. And if he could educate me somehow, it would bring him a bit of contentment. It might make him feel useful again. Someone to be listened to.

For the next ten minutes he lectured me about the moon landing, how it was all a big con, and how the world had been fooled. He talked about other major events, too, how they were complete bullshit.

Crazy Raymond, it turned out, was my first experience with a conspiracy theorist. He was practically a poster child— or poster old man—for the demo. Over the next few months, until we moved again, I'd occasionally wander over and bring him some of Mom's baked goods, and he'd tell me how the CIA had murdered JFK, and how New Coke was a giant ploy by the soft drink giant to double their grocery store shelf space. As a kid I had no idea what that meant, but it sounded really important and he struck me as an authority.

And, in all that time, he never once tried to murder me.

HERE'S why I dredged up that story. No, I don't believe the moon landing was a hoax, I'm agnostic about the Kennedy assassination, and I've never even tasted New Coke.

But my eccentric neighbor did have an effect on me. From that point on I never automatically dismissed tales that might, on the surface, seem nuts. Conspiracy theories are sometimes so zany that all you can do is laugh. And yet I'll at least mull them over for a moment before writing them off completely. Taking into account the law of averages, Ray had to be right once or twice.

Now, as I sat in a hotel ballroom in Houston, listening to the introduction of a noted scientist, one particular account bubbled up from my recent past. On the surface it was crazy, but I'd become a believer. All it lacked was official verification, and therein lay the problem: verifying the existence of shadowy plots or obscure organizations rarely came with an official stamp.

If it was true, however, it had just turned this entire assignment on its ear. And, in a flash, it may have validated every one of Sarah Eklund's fears.

What I needed to do was talk with someone about it. I glanced at Sarah, but ruled her out. It wasn't necessarily a security-clearance issue, but I couldn't rope a civilian into it, no matter how personally invested she might be.

Fife. That's who I needed to share this with, to see if he agreed with my assessment. I trusted the combination Q2-FBI agent.

And there was one other person who might hold valuable information.

To have *that* talk would require visiting a federal prison.

I reached back down for the whiskey, which I decided I wanted after all.

JACLYN STONE WASN'T the greatest speaker, certainly not on the level of Jason Deele, but the stunning visual accompaniment made up for her shortcomings. They'd even invested in professional lighting to bathe her in a warm, soft halo that stood in fine contrast to the bright, dazzling display on the screens.

The key points of her thirty-minute presentation could be condensed into a relatively-short summation. But the whole purpose of the meeting was to engage the hearts and minds of people with very deep pockets. These were hearts and minds used to being wooed; they'd built up a wall of skepticism that a traditional PowerPoint display could never assail.

What the people in the seats most wanted to see and hear was that their money would finance an operation guaranteed to return the investment many times over.

Stone began her talk by laying out a brief history of the soybean, from its domestication in ancient China to its spread around the world, and to its eventual explosion as a top export. Videos showed a few graphs to drive home her data, but mostly concentrated on the people involved in the cultivating and harvesting of the crops.

She spent several minutes exploring the connection between science and soybeans, tracing the plant's earliest breeding all the way forward to the modern laboratory. Genetically-modified versions helped catapult the product into one of the world's most valuable commodities. By the end of that portion of her talk Stone had pretty well established not only the history of soy's market value, but had clearly defined what the future of the market looked like.

And it was sizable. I knew the numbers were big, but her estimates for future growth were eye-popping.

This is where she paused, as if letting the numbers settle in the minds of the audience. When she spoke again, her tone—and the images flashing behind her—were considerably more grim.

Pictures of wilted crops, dying fields, and destitute farms. They were like modern images inspired by scenes from the Great Depression of the 1930s.

I saw the silhouette of Sarah Eklund in the row in front of me. She shook her head, agitated by the scare tactics, I was sure.

"So what's the answer?" Jaclyn Stone asked. "You might say we need better forms of pest control. Or we need better ways of managing our water tables. Or we need updated methods of crop management. And all of that is true. Those things *can* help.”

She stepped to the side of the lectern, removing the microphone from its stand and carrying it with her. It seemed like a well-rehearsed stage move.

“But the truth is, we need much more. Because no matter how we try to predict what type of parasite might do harm, something could easily slip past us. And as you’ve seen, the fallout would be utterly disastrous. Supplies for livestock could vanish, and what would that do for the overall food market? Supplies for fuel oil could dry up, and I think you know what that means for markets globally. When food and natural resources become scarce, desperate people have been known to do desperate things.”

I couldn’t believe what I was hearing. She was predicting global chaos. And she wasn’t through.

“No. The answer doesn’t lie in simply trying to swat flies. The answer is to genetically stay ahead of the problem, not to react after it happens. Science does have the capability to modify the way our crops are produced, engineering the growth process itself to do two things.”

She held up a finger for each of these.

“One, to create a design impervious to the natural diseases that could inflict the worst possible damage on this incredibly valuable commodity. And two, to build into that product a defense against a much different risk, one that doesn’t come from insects or fungus.” She paused, a look of concern on her face. “I’m talking about risks from the human species itself, from our blatant disregard for protecting our natural environment. I’m talking about designing a new, modern form of soy —and perhaps other species as well—able to withstand anything nature *and* the human species can throw at it.”

The room was silent, sobered by the weight of the presentation.

Then Stone moved back over to the lectern. And she smiled.

"Fortunately, we've thought ahead. And our new, fortified soybean is here."

I noted the subtle use of the word *our*, creating a subliminal sense of family within the room.

On both screens simultaneously, a single image of a soybean plant, basking in sunshine, swaying gently in a breeze. The camera pulled back to reveal row after row of the healthy pods, and a farmer, walking through the field, caressing the plants as he passed by.

The view pulled up and away, until the blur of green dissolved into a scene from a sparkling laboratory, with a woman in her spotless lab coat smiling into the camera. That image, in turn, dissolved again, leaving the company logo.

There was a short stretch of silence before a smattering of applause rippled through the room. I looked around to see if I could read the expressions on the guests, and they did indeed seem impressed, murmuring to each other and nodding toward the screen.

When I turned back around I caught a glimpse of Sarah Eklund, sitting still, arms crossed in front of her. Staring toward Jason Deele as he walked toward Jaclyn Stone, grinning and applauding. After warmly shaking her hand, then pulling her in for a quick hug, he announced to the crowd that he and Dr. Stone would join them in the foyer to personally answer any and all questions.

I glanced down. My drink was empty.

The guests stood and made their way to the side of the

room. When the seats were about empty I leaned forward and tapped on Sarah's shoulder.

"Listen, I need you to do me a big favor," I said when she turned around. "I need you to graciously thank them for the presentation, but tell them an emergency has come up and you must run."

Her face contorted into a mixture of disbelief and anger. "What? I came all the way here—"

"Yes," I said, glancing around. "You did. And I need you to leave without stirring up anything right now."

She scoffed. "I'm sorry, but you don't get to order me around."

I sighed. "Dr. Eklund. My job is to get to the bottom of this. It's a job you requested. The best way you can help right now is to not put Jason Deele on alert in any way. It could compromise what I have to do."

Now she looked over my shoulder at the assembled group of people. "So are you saying you finally believe me?"

"I believe something is very wrong. What it is, I can't say for sure. But it's possible it's connected to something much bigger than what you might think. So I need to ask you, respectfully, to let me do my job."

Her eyes narrowed. "I'm supposed to sit here and listen to their bullshit, then just smile and walk away?"

"That would help me more than you know."

She glared at me. Then, without a word, she grabbed her bag, stood, and walked down the aisle. A moment later she bypassed the swarm of people gathered in the lobby, and left.

I wandered through the double doors in time to see her disappear down the escalator without a look back.

Just outside the ballroom, Jason Deele and Jaclyn Stone stood side by side, greeting the attendees, thanking them, and answering as many questions as they could, given the setting and time constraints. I caught sight of Conor Wood nearby, as well as the two other goons I'd seen at the airport. Everyone was calm and unobtrusive, like Secret Service agents quietly keeping an eye on things.

A few feet away, Diana Capaldi also watched her boss carefully, a digital planner in her hand. At a slight nod from him, she'd intercept the people he'd just spoken with and arrange a follow-up discussion. Those who weren't worthy of the nod were simply thanked and handed an expensive packet of information.

During his superstar days in high tech Deele had plenty of experience in soliciting investors. He'd no doubt learned how to size up how serious someone might be in less than a minute. Time was one of the most valuable commodities, and couldn't be wasted on fringe believers.

When the last of the potential investors had finished their audition, I sauntered up to Deele.

He smiled and I anticipated his signature clap on the shoulder. When it didn't come I wondered if I'd somehow lost favor.

But then he said exactly what I'd wanted to hear.

"I won't ask what you thought of the presentation, Mr. Thomas. You were dazzled, of course."

"You spent a lot to give me that reaction," I said. "And it succeeded."

"Good." Now I got the shoulder slap. "Rather than stand here and gab about it, what would you say to having dinner at my home with Dr. Stone and me? Unless you've made other plans."

"I'll look forward to it."

Oh shit, now I sounded like Byzinski.

"Excellent. Why don't we say seven o'clock. Diana will make sure you have the address. Now I've got to run. See you tonight."

I thanked him, then turned to compliment Stone on her presentation.

She was already walking away without a word.

18

———

Three o'clock found me in Hermann Park near my hotel. I had time for a nice sweat before needing to shower and change for dinner. Running felt good, and this particular body handled it well.

And that's not a given. There are times I've inhabited bodies that *looked* to be in great shape, but you never really found out until you took them for a test ride. Or test run.

In the early days I made a typical rookie mistake. I obsessed over getting each new body into the condition I'd been used to. If it couldn't handle the seven-minute-mile pace I expected for a 10k, I'd work my ass off until it could.

That is, until two things dawned on me. One, every body was simply built differently, and to expect Body A to match the abilities of Body B was foolish. Some people are born with naturally-adept athletic forms, and some definitely aren't. Sure, with enough training I could get it close.

But that led to the second thing: Why torture myself when the expiration date might be rapidly approaching? Get myself into badass shape, only to be offed the next day? What a waste.

I eventually came to the conclusion that the bodies Q2 selected were generally in good condition, and any maintenance I applied to them could be nominal.

As someone once put it: Nobody washes a rental car.

These days I ran because I enjoyed it, and because it helped me think. On this particular day my brain had absorbed a revelation or two along with a pretty strong hypothesis. I needed time to process all the thoughts cascading through my head. It was the hypothesis that worried me the most. I was counting on dinner to help me determine whether or not it was worthy of such concern.

If things were still vague after tonight, I'd likely be on a plane tomorrow. There was one person, a thousand miles away, who could be helpful. Hostile, I'm sure, but helpful.

At the two-mile mark I felt a familiar ache in my right heel. This convict either had lousy joints or had jacked up his foot at some point. I slowed to a walk for the next half-mile, watching parents and their kids streaming out of the Houston Zoo.

I contemplated how to handle the icy Dr. Stone.

IF I WAS WALKING into the lion's den, it was one of the swankiest dens I'd ever seen.

Deele's temporary residence in Houston was a gated estate built with old money. It loomed large over its neighbors; my quick estimation from the outside was about 20,000 square feet. I tried to imagine what the air conditioning bill was like in August. Of course, if you bought a home like this you didn't fret over piddling things like utility bills.

A valet service had been engaged for the evening, so it was clear I wasn't special enough to rate a private dinner with

Deele and Stone. That was a little deflating, as I'd hoped to monopolize their time.

It turned out, however, to be a small dinner party. Jason and Jaclyn were the star hosts, while I was one of seven guests deemed important enough for the private affair. Not surprisingly, Byzinski had not made the cut. I did not grieve.

For a moment I worried that my simple sport coat without a tie would be slumming it, but fortunately the host was even more casual. Deele welcomed everyone in dress jeans and a T-shirt. How very start-up-ish.

During the cocktail portion of the evening Jaclyn was caught up in a lengthy conversation with another guest, a man named Abbott. At first I thought he was pumping her for trade secrets; then I realized the horndog was hitting on her.

Deele took me and three other guests on a quick tour of the estate, showing off the home theater, the library, the indoor/outdoor pool, and the basketball court. He slapped my shoulder, of course, and told me I'd have to stop by sometime and play a game of Horse.

It was apparent why Deele had rented this particular home. Although huge, the interior updates were contemporary and comfortable, eschewing the usual stuffiness associated with mansions. It had a lived-in feel, which I appreciated, rather than a museum vibe.

When I buy my $20 million home I'll do it the same way.

"Is this your office?" I asked outside a room with a modern desk and several bookshelves. Large windows revealed the soft mood lighting surrounding the pool area out back.

"Oh, I spend a few minutes in there," he said, scowling. "I'm not much of an office guy. I probably get way more done in the back of a car than I ever do in there."

I held up a business card. "You don't want to carry this

around. I'll plop it on your desk." He opened his mouth to object, but I'd already scampered into the room. I was back in the hallway in seconds, but he looked concerned I might've seen something. I changed the subject and we moved on with the tour.

It was a long shot and I knew it. But it also never hurt to try. The business card was a goofy little gadget we called the series-8. Inside its thick stock was a listening device that allowed us to snoop. They worked fine, but the vast majority didn't survive long. *No* business card ever did.

When dinner was announced, the group moved into an impressive dining room. The table sat up to 18, so we clustered near one end. I was surprised when Jaclyn Stone took a seat beside Deele and gestured that I should sit across from her. I nodded thanks and settled in.

As expected, each guest was asked to share a bit about themselves. It was standard dinner-party practice, engineered to spark lively conversation.

When my turn rolled around, I was ready.

"I was the guy who was bored throughout high school and college. Not because I thought I already knew it all, but because I was ready to do grown-up work. The problem was, every job for people that age assumes you're an idiot. I jumped around from position to position, looking for a business—or a boss—who did things a little differently."

"Did you find one?" Deele asked.

"Nope," I said right away, which elicited some laughter around the table. "At 21 I got the usual stern talking-to from my dad, worried I'd never connect with anything. But I tried explaining to him: It's not the job itself I care about; it's how the company *does* the job. I've always been drawn to people and organizations finding new ways of doing traditional things."

I made brief eye contact with Stone, then went on.

"No offense, Jason, but it's not actually start-ups that interest me. I think too often they're focused on entirely new markets, sometimes pushing products nobody's really looking for. What gets me hot and bothered are the disruptors in old sectors." Now I looked directly at Deele. "And not to sound like a total suck-up, but that's what has me interested in what you're doing. Farming isn't new. *How* we farm, though? Using more high-tech than ever? Show me new ways to do it and I'll be interested enough to put money behind it. And that's why I'm in Houston."

I may have been overplaying my hand, but I didn't care. And I certainly didn't give a rat's ass what the other stiffs around the table thought. I needed Deele's attention, and Jaclyn's. More importantly, I needed to draw her out.

Poole had come through again, of course. When I'd stepped out of the shower this afternoon she'd had a dossier on the scientist waiting for me. It was time now to see how much of it she confirmed, and how much she glossed over.

"So Jaclyn," I said. "I understand you did your undergrad work not far from here, at A&M. Are you originally from Texas?"

"No," she said. "I grew up on the West Coast. I had no intention of doing this kind of work when I was young. I was naive, a computer nerd, and didn't even realize the potential of high-tech in agriculture. It was a high school science teacher who opened my eyes."

One of the other guests spoke up. "How did you happen to choose to work with soybeans?"

"It chose me. I did some preliminary work with a colleague

and just happened to discover that some of the techniques worked best with that plant."

I remained silent, but compared this to the file Poole had sent to me. The colleague she casually referenced was a woman who later filed suit against Dr. Stone. It was eventually settled, with both sides agreeing to a non-disclosure agreement. Almost immediately, Stone lost her seat on the board of another biotech firm and a big chunk of grant money. Coincidence? I didn't think so.

I noticed none of that was included in the press releases Diana Capaldi had distributed.

"Crops have been engineered for years to withstand pests and disease," I said, swirling the wine in my glass. "What makes your formula any different?"

She was ready for this one. "Biotech is almost always geared with the past in mind: Thinking about the problems we've always faced and how we can eliminate them. What we don't do enough is anticipate the future. And with enough data accumulated, we can run simulations to tell us what problems we *will* be facing. That way we're not working from behind, scrambling to solve a problem already devastating our food supplies. We'll be prepared."

"Brilliant," I said, and took a drink of the wine.

"And," said Deele, jumping in, "by saving time, we save lives and money."

Even while he spoke, Stone kept her gaze on me. From the very beginning she'd been sizing me up, as if searching for my motives or for a weakness. I couldn't be sure which.

The flirt, Abbott, spoke up, addressing Deele. "Your inventive strain of soybean is not just more expensive than anything on the market right now, it's *considerably* more expensive. How are you justifying that?"

Our host sat back, holding his own glass of wine. "Well, for one thing I would question the word *considerably*. True, it costs more. But weigh that against the price of ruined crops. What would it cost to suffer a year, or more, of barren fields? If you look at it that way, Mr. Abbott, our development actually saves your company *considerably*. Would you agree?"

Abbott shrugged. I wasn't an expert, but I was sure his chief objection matched what other skeptics said: You're asking us to gamble. Gamble that some nasty fungus will wipe out our money crop, when a fungus of that type has never been seen.

If Sarah Eklund was right, Jason Deele already had an answer for that objection.

He'd created the killer fungus in advance.

For years companies in almost every industry had learned that you create sales by creating the demand. Often it's done with marketing and the use of well-placed influencers. When people are taught they can't live without something, they're sure a lot easier to sell.

In this case, the one-two punch was more insidious than someone pimping the demand for a new video game app.

What I really needed was a peek inside their lab, to see if Eklund's fears were warranted. It didn't look like an invitation was forthcoming. Well, there was no harm in asking.

"What's the chance I could stop by and see your work?" I asked. "I may not fully understand what I see, but I'd love to get a tour."

It was the brief, nervous glance Stone flashed toward her boss that excited me.

Deele, for his part, was cool. He raised his eyebrows, feigning excitement.

"That would be excellent, Ryan. Some people have no

interest in how the kitchen works; they only want to see what comes out on the plate. I'm sure Dr. Stone would be more than happy to show you."

"Great. When could we make it happen?"

"Well, if it's okay with you, I'd like to be there, too. I'm ultimately responsible, you know. I may not have done the experiments, but it's still my baby. Sadly, however, I'm leaving in the morning again for South America. May not be back for a week or two."

"You're logging a lot of air miles these days," I said. "Things must be going quite well down there."

"Don't be surprised when Paraguay triples its exports within the next five years. And I'm not too modest to say our product will be one of the reasons."

"Then I definitely want to see the factory," I said, saluting him with my glass. "I'm patient. Is it in the Houston area?"

"Not far," he said. The look he included was either one of gratitude that someone in the States was taking a serious interest in his product.

Or one of sudden distrust.

When the dessert plates had been picked up, it was obvious the social gathering was over. It was Deele's habit, I noticed, to cut almost everything short of normal. There would be no after-dinner drinks in the parlor.

I was the last guest to leave. Jason Deele shook my hand, then, for good measure, clapped me on the shoulder.

"Thank you for joining us," he said. "I look forward to giving you that tour. Stay in touch with Diana, will you, please?"

"Of course. Thanks for a lovely evening."

I nodded thanks to Jaclyn Stone, but she surprised me for the second time.

"I'll walk Mr. Thomas to his car," she said.

The valet had it waiting, so it wasn't much of a walk. But I was dying to know why the ice-cold scientist had thawed during the evening. The obvious warning bell in my head was that Deele was curious to find out something about me, and he'd instructed Dr. Stone to cozy up.

I tipped the valet and accepted the fob from him. Turning to Stone, I said, "It's a beautiful night. Let's walk around the property for a minute before I have to leave."

We strolled toward the gate, which had been left open for the evening. It was her move, so I remained quiet.

"I'm curious about something," she finally said. "You came to the presentation today, and you were a charming guest at dinner."

"Why, thank you, Doctor."

"But you're not really interested in my product, are you?"

It was important I not react visibly. I hadn't expected this.

"Why would you say that?" I asked.

"It's my business, Mr. Thomas. I know when someone's interested and when they're bullshitting."

"Perhaps you've just had bad experiences with the wrong people. I can assure you there's nobody more interested in your work than I am."

She stopped and took me by the arm.

"I may have misspoken. I'm sure you're interested; I'm just not sure *how* you're interested."

I smiled. "You think I'm a spy for a rival company, is that it? You know my background, and you certainly know the track record of my company. D.M. Cash isn't prepared to even begin the process of competing with your product. It would take years for us to develop anything close. By that time you'd have already cornered the market."

She shook her head. "No, I don't think you're a spy, necessarily. But I saw you talking with Sarah Eklund at the end of the presentation today. And Dr. Eklund is the most outspoken of our critics. I just wanted to get you alone, away from Jason, and ask you to your face: Are you working with us, or against us?"

I put on my best look of confusion. "I don't know a Dr. Eklund. If you mean the woman who sat in front of me today, I simply wanted to know what she thought of your presentation. A tiny bit of market research. She was in no mood to discuss it, really. And now that you've told me she's a critic, I understand."

Her eyes looked back and forth between mine, as if they were some biological polygraph test. "Okay. Well, your request to see the laboratory struck me as a bit clumsy, too. Just wanted a minute to talk with you, that's all."

"I'm glad you did. You've been pretty insulated up until now. So insulated, in fact, that it's prompted a few questions of my own."

"Questions about me? Like what, for instance?"

"Like why someone of your training and capabilities would suddenly begin working with Jason Deele, a man with no background in this field whatsoever. It can't possibly be simply for the bankroll. Or could it?"

She crossed her arms, the classic defensive posture. "That seems unusual to you? Really? Science has relied on patrons for thousands of years, just like the art world."

"But the patrons generally feel a connection with the work they support. Are you telling me Jason goes to bed at night dreaming of soybeans?"

"I won't deny he's dreaming of making a fortune when this takes off. But is there anything wrong with profiting from something that also does the world good? Besides, isn't that what you and your company are trying to do?"

I put my hands in my pockets and looked up at the stars. Or tried to. The city glare allowed only a few to pass through. I made a quick decision to stop playing nice with Stone. Poking the bear could be dangerous, but sometimes it was necessary.

"Look, Doctor," I said, still gazing upward. "I'm in Houston with the express purpose of deciding whether or not to invest a shit-ton of money into an experimental new product. Now, it's either a product that could revolutionize an entire industry—and do the world good, as you say—or it might be a complete train wreck."

I slowly lowered my face to hers. "For someone who's supposedly eager to make a big splash, and to perhaps atone for a few career missteps in the past, you strike me as desperate when you partner with someone who shares none of your passion. Someone who truly believes in her research and her outcomes would wait for another benefactor, one who may not have the deepest pockets, but at least shares her enthusiasm for the work, not just the payday."

I watched her bristle at the mention of her past, and the anger simmered the more I spoke. This may have been an error in judgment on my part, but I couldn't resist. Assholes bring out the asshole in me. Besides, knocking your opponent out of their comfortable space often paid dividends later.

Before she could respond, I continued. "Look, I've been known to rub some people the wrong way. You may be one of them. If you'd prefer I communicate exclusively with Jason moving forward, that's fine with me."

Now she appeared to measure her words before speaking. After a long intake of breath, she said, "No, I'll be happy to answer any of your questions, Mr. Thomas. Thank you for setting me straight about Dr. Eklund and your *keen* interest. I'll see you when Mr. Deele returns from his trip. Have a good night."

She turned and walked back toward the house. A moment later, my hands still thrust into my pockets, I strolled toward the Jag.

Apparently Sarah Eklund—and Michael Corleone—weren't the only people who believed in keeping a close eye on their enemies.

Now I knew for certain who my next appointment would be.

19

"You're going where?" Quanta asked. She was on a plane, returning from London. She offered no details about her trip, and, although curious, I didn't ask.

"Colorado," I said. "On my way to the airport now."

"What does this have to do with the Deele case?"

"Maybe nothing. But there's someone in Colorado who may be able to answer questions I have concerning one of Deele's associates."

"And you can't just make a call?"

"Oh, this guy doesn't have a phone anymore. He has a cell, but not a cell phone."

She let out a long breath. "All right. Who is this knowledgeable person in a Colorado prison?"

"Steffan Parks."

There was silence on her end for a long time. When she finally asked me what possible connection Parks could have with the assignment, I told her. It took a while. When I finished, she was silent again.

Then: "You've done a thorough upload, I take it?"

"Before I checked out of the hotel. If I get shanked at the prison everything's been saved for posterity. Oh, and Agent Fife is flying from Dallas. He's meeting me at the Denver airport and we'll drive down together."

"All right. Keep Poole informed." She broke the connection.

I made a quick call to Christina, got her voicemail, and left a sufficiently sappy message. I missed her.

My plane was delayed leaving Houston, so Fife beat me to the Mile High City by almost two hours. He immediately let me know how much I'd put him out.

I pointed to the nearly-empty plate of nachos before him. "Not *too* put out, though."

Our rental car was a Mustang, and Fife took delight in zipping onto the toll road that eventually would get us to I-25 and the 100 mile jaunt south to the supermax prison facility near the town of Florence. Lots of really bad people spent their days and nights confined to the cells in this particular prison, specially built to house the worst of the worst.

Some were international terrorists, some were domestic terrorists, most were deemed insidious threats to either the general public or to the staff of a traditional corrections facility. They were kept in their cells for up to 23 hours each day, and granted a single hour for exercise. The man I wanted to see fell under the domestic terror umbrella.

"You pulled your FBI strings, right?" I asked Fife when we were southbound.

"No. But I called someone who did. You'll get your hour to talk with the prisoner. Now do you wanna let me know why this Steffan Parks guy is important to the case?"

"Don't play coy with me," I said. "I'm sure you pulled his file before you got on the plane. You know who he is."

"I know you put him away for trying to poison an entire town in Arizona."

"Including a congresswoman's family. You probably didn't peek through all the backstory, though, did you?"

"I skimmed enough to see there wasn't any mention of agriculture. So what's the connection?"

Sitting in the passenger seat of the Mustang, I gazed at the mountains of the Front Range.

"Steffan Parks was dangerous enough on his own. He had more than one axe to grind with society, and he held grudges. We're talking major league grudges. But he didn't work alone. He was part of a secret organization."

Fife grunted. "I like it. Sounds like one of those thriller novels."

"Scarier than that. In this case the organization is a group of scientists, each of whom feels slighted or punished unfairly. And some of them have gone beyond just bitching about it."

"Like Parks."

"Exactly."

"What are they called?" he asked.

"They're known as the Arcetri." I spelled it for him. "Looks like Ar-set-tree, but it's Ar-chet-tree."

"And where do you find them?"

I shrugged. "That's just it. It's not as if they have a club-house somewhere, or scheduled meetings. From what I gathered they're about as informal as you can get, mostly for their own protection."

We passed two large semi-trucks just before a construction zone forced us to slow down. Fife seemed to be digesting this latest intel.

After a minute he said, "So you think Deele is being helped by this group of scientists? This Arcetri bunch?"

"It was the way he introduced Jaclyn Stone. He made a point of talking about how she was disrespected by the corporate world and by many of her peers. I don't know, but the way he said it reminded me of the way Parks and his cohorts talked about their own poor treatment. And since the Arcetri's style is to exact revenge, to make people pay for their sins, it all tied together very neatly. Stone, if she really is connected in some way with this group, has been offered a platform for horrific revenge."

"And a very large bankroll to fund it, courtesy of Jason Deele," Fife said.

I nodded. "Those two could have the same goal in mind, but for very different reasons. Probably do, in fact."

Another four miles passed in tight highway traffic, the corridor between Denver and Colorado Springs its usual congested mess. The cone zone didn't help. When things loosened up again, Fife said, "If all of this is true—I mean about the Arcetri—then this is a bigger issue than just Sarah Eklund's crop problem. If you don't even know how many people are in the group . . ." He left the sentence unfinished.

But it was something I'd contemplated from the moment I'd heard about the enigmatic organization. Who knew how many members waited for their own chance to strike back against their perceived injustice? How many more were being recruited each year?

I counted on Steffan Parks to enlighten me.

And he had no reason whatsoever to play ball.

•   •   •

Storm clouds draped low as we pulled into the prison parking lot. The day had a flat, gray look about it. This part of the state already appeared nothing like the picturesque image one normally associated with colorful Colorado. It was brown and bleak. When an inmate managed a glimpse outside it was nothing to swoon over. Even the nearby mountains failed to lend beauty to the scene; they more or less played the role of simply another wall.

I let Fife do the talking as we checked in. The entire process took quite a while. There are maximum security prisons, and then there's supermax. You're not waltzing inside quickly.

Eventually we wound up in a drab room that held a table and four chairs. We waited another fifteen minutes. When the lock clanged in the door again, I looked up to see the grizzled face of Steffan Parks.

Bound in heavy restraints, he shuffled into the room in front of a beefy guard. A second officer stood right outside the door. While Parks was seated at one of the chairs and his chain attached to a hook on the table, I studied his face. The long hair and the goatee he'd sported during his arrest were gone. His head was now buzz-cut and his face smooth. He remained impassive, doubtless at a complete loss as to why he'd been removed from his cell. But I'm sure he didn't care, either; at least it provided a break in the monotony.

The guard took up his post near the door. Fife gestured at me as if to say, *He's all yours.*

I was the guy who'd captured Parks, and yet he wouldn't recognize me. I'd occupied a different body at the time. To him I was just another no-name fed sent to make his life uncomfortable.

He stared across the table, first at me, then Fife, then back to me. He said nothing.

"Professor Parks," I said. "I'm Agent Crown. This is Agent Fife. I appreciate you meeting with us."

He blinked, but still said nothing.

"I'd like to talk with you about an organization you were a part of. The Arcetri."

Still not a word. The man didn't even blink. I hoped I hadn't come all the way across the country for nothing.

Nothing to do but keep plowing away.

"Of course, we can have you taken back to your cell if you'd prefer to keep to your one-hour time limit outside." After letting that sink in a moment, I added: "Specifically, Professor, I'm hoping you can shed a bit of light on one of your fellow scientists. Dr. Jaclyn Stone."

This finally delivered a reaction. Not much of one, but at least I'd earned a raised eyebrow.

"What can you tell me about her?" I asked.

He didn't respond, but I didn't either. I could play the stare-down game as well as he. The quiet treatment was a tired old game often played by inmates. They felt it was a display of power. Which, if you think about it, was ridiculous. It never came across as anything but childish. But they still did it.

When the silence grew uncomfortably long, he shifted in his seat, cleared his throat, and asked, "Has Dr. Stone found herself in hot water?"

"I'm not sure. That's why I'm here, talking to you. Is the good doctor prone to getting into hot water?"

Now he chuckled. "Jaclyn is prone to expensive suits, sloppy research, and fudging figures."

"Does that disgust you? Not the outfits, but the sloppiness?"

"I never worked with her. If I had, it would've pissed me off." He shot a glance at Fife, who seemed content to sit back and listen. Then, looking back at me, he said, "And since our paths never crossed in the laboratory, there's not much else I can help you with."

I tapped a finger on the table. "You can help me with the Arcetri."

He smiled. "Which is what? A type of cheese?"

I returned the smile. "I feel like we should let you go back to your cell and feel important. Sit and bask in the glory of wasting our time. That'll give you a big warm feeling that'll last about as long as it takes us to get to a decent restaurant, order a steak dinner and a couple of drinks. Then catch a ballgame, and finally drift off to sleep in a comfy, 4-star room with Egyptian cotton sheets and a view of the mountains. Pretty nice. Of course, you'll have won because you wasted our time and can feel all superior about it as your curl up in your six-by-eleven-foot cage. Congratulations. You're a powerful man."

I leaned on the table. "Now stop being a dick. We're the last two people on the planet you'll ever be able to impress with your self-importance. I've spoken to you respectfully, and asked simple, easy questions."

He stared at me for a while.

"Seven by twelve," he finally said. "My cage is seven by twelve."

I sat back in my chair. "Oh. What do you do with all the extra space?"

After another spell of silence he shrugged. "You can't possibly expect to come here and have me spill everything I know. There are two problems with that.

"One, there's not much *anyone* knows. This organization you reference, the Arcetri; it's not even a real organization. It's an informal club, and a name tossed around by a few people who thought of it as a foundation for fighting back."

"Against what, exactly?" I asked. "Disrespect?"

He paused, and then grunted a laugh. "And that sounds preposterous to you? Probably because you've never known what it's like to watch your entire life's work thrown out like garbage. All of your dreams and passions dismissed as nonsense, while people whose work was actually built on the back of *your* ideas are rewarded. And can you speak up about that? No, you cannot. You'll be labeled a sniveling, jealous warthog, and relegated to getting a job in some backwater laboratory, creating new flavor combinations for corn chips. If you're lucky."

"All right," I said. "That's a well-articulated reason number one."

He took a deep breath. "Honestly, Agent Crown, reason number two is because there is absolutely nothing in it for me." Looking around, he spread his hands as far as the restraints allowed. "You can't really punish me much more than this."

I felt more than saw Fife's eyes on me. This had been a last-minute trip. We'd been given nothing to negotiate with. I wasn't even sure *who* had the power to offer anything in exchange for Steffan's help. If ever in my career I'd spoken entirely out of my ass, it was right now.

"Not everyone spends their entire sentence here," I said. "After a few years it's possible to get shipped to a more, uh, comfortable facility."

Parks leaned forward. "I'm listening."

"Well, cooperate fully, and we'll look into shortening your stay here until you're transferred."

This caused him to bark a short laugh. "Vague answers for two hundred, Alex."

I spread my hands. "Hey, I'm not the attorney general. I'm not even a lawyer. But I do have connections with very powerful people. They get what they want most of the time."

"Uh-huh. And what does *cooperate fully* look like to you?"

"For starters, everything you *do* know about the Arcetri. No bullshit, no cherry-picking. Then I want you to tell me everything you know about Jaclyn Stone. And, if it comes to it, I'd want you to testify against her."

He shook his head. "Seems an awful lot to pay for what you're offering."

"No, it's not. I'm the one who has to convince a bunch of hard-asses to move you. Seeing as how you tried to murder the family of a congresswoman—and, by the way, about ten thousand other people—I'd say I have my work cut out for me. All you have to do is sit back and tell me what you know. Now who has the harder job?"

Nothing was said for a long time.

In a softer, gentler voice I prodded him one more time. "Look, Steffan, it's not as if you're ratting out someone in the mob. Then you'd have to watch your back for the rest of your life, even in here. You said yourself the Arcetri's not even an official organization, so there can't be some code of honor you're protecting. What's the worst they could do? Cancel your subscription to *Scientific American*?"

A smile turned up on the corners of his mouth. "It's comments like that, you know, that inspired the formation of the club in the first place."

I chuckled and held up my hands in a sign of surrender. "You're right." Then I leaned forward again. "So what's it gonna be? Are we sending you back to your cell?"

He threw another glance at Fife, then nervously rubbed his hands together. "What kind of assurance do I have that you'll keep your word?"

"Assurance? Just my word that I'll do everything I can. You don't know me, but I'm asking you to trust me, Steffan."

He sat still for the longest time. Then: "I want out of this place within the year."

I took a long breath, and nodded. "All right. Now tell me about Jaclyn Stone. Is she part of the Arcetri?"

Parks sighed. "All Jaclyn ever lacked was the right bio-formula to make the kind of impact she wanted. If she now has that formula . . ." He paused. "Then you're in big trouble."

20

———————

The ride back to Denver flew by, but that could've been my adrenaline. After initially wasting our time with bullshit posturing, Steffan had filled the rest of the hour with heady talk. Some of it I'd expected. Much of it I had not.

"All right," Fife said, deftly maneuvering the sports car through traffic. "Let's assume he's telling the truth about everything. And, for the record, that's a bold assumption, because these cats *live* to screw with federal agents. It's often the *only* thing they can live for. But let's assume it's all gospel."

"Then it fills in a few gaps," I said.

"Enumerate, please."

I humored him and held up my hand, ticking the fingers up with each point.

"One, it explains how a tech-nerd like Jason Deele comes up with a ground-breaking new agricultural formula and product seemingly overnight. Because it wasn't overnight. He didn't walk away from phone apps and gadget-gear and suddenly develop a new strain of soybeans. Jaclyn Stone had a head start, probably by several years.

"Two, it explains their unlikely partnership."

Fife raised a hand, putting me on pause. "You mean the partnership of Deele and Stone."

"Yeah. Talk about two people who could never have met organically, pun intended. They couldn't possibly have run in the same circles. For my money, Stone sought him out, made him a proposition, and closed the deal."

"And three," Fife said, getting in on the act. "They were actually perfect for each other. A scientist with a product that only works if used in conjunction with a deadly fungus—that's not something you can just shop around—and a loose-cannon tech boy wonder who's always on the lookout for another big score."

"Huge score, underlined," I said. "Who knows how many hundreds of billions of dollars it could eventually be worth?"

"Is there a fourth point?" Fife asked.

"Yeah. The fourth point is that Jason Deele is a crazy son of a bitch who won't let a little thing like corruption and death on a large scale stop him from this gold mine. He couldn't be a more perfect partner for Jaclyn Stone: He's a psychopath with billions to invest." I shook my head. "She probably couldn't believe her luck."

We drove in silence for several miles. I replayed some of Steffan's comments. I couldn't tell him what we suspected of Stone, but just our presence at the prison told him she was up to no good. The feds don't come sniffing around for misde-meanors.

When he begrudgingly revealed information about the Arcetri, he did so only in regard to Stone specifically. I wanted more on the group, but for now would have to be satisfied with what he was willing to share.

"For most of us," he'd said, "there was egregious damage done to our careers. I don't expect you to understand why I did what I did, but you at least can acknowledge I got a raw deal from a lot of people. So I lashed out. To me there was justification."

"And Stone?" I asked.

He opened his mouth to answer, stopped, and then gave a shrug. "How do I say this? What she went through . . . wasn't that bad. I mean, sure, she got screwed by some people, and I think her former partner went way too far in her lawsuit."

I finished his thought. "But not enough to explain criminal activity."

He leaned forward in order to scratch an itch on his cheek, a challenging move with your hands shackled to a table. "I've met Jaclyn a couple of times. And each time she struck me as a scientist with a different agenda, if you know what I mean."

"I don't."

"Well, look, I may have strayed from my original work—"

I raised my eyebrows as if to say *No shit*.

"Yeah," he said. "But if she's finally developed something dangerous, I'm not sure it was entirely an act of revenge."

"Meaning?"

"Meaning I'm no psychiatrist, but Jaclyn is the type who'd do it for no reason other than to see how it worked. On people."

Now, racing down the highway in the passenger seat of the Mustang, I considered the fact that we might have gotten a deal on psychopaths this time: Buy one, get one free. And the idea reminded me of a conversation I'd had with our Q2 shrink, Miller. When I'd asked him once why there weren't more partnerships between dangerously sick people, his answer intrigued me.

"Contrary to what you might think, two psychotic personalities don't double the potency of the psychotic acts; they're more likely to cancel each other out. Two unstable elements will often destroy one another."

If Miller was right, then this evil marriage between Jason Deele and Jaclyn Stone was rife with danger for one or both of them. It would be a dream come true if their partnership blew up; at the very least it would save me a lot of time and potential danger. The problem was I couldn't count on them to implode before they'd fully implemented their plan.

"I've got to get back to Washington," Fife said as we neared the rental car return at the Denver airport. "What's your next move?"

"I've been thinking about that. With Deele flying back to South America, it might be a good time for me to snoop around that lab of his. The one he didn't want me to see without him."

"You know it'll be guarded, right?"

"Thank God I'm a stealthy bastard."

I MANAGED a ninety minute nap on the return flight to Houston. Thank you, window seats.

Back in my hotel room by ten, the first order of business was an upload. No way I wanted to lose my conversation with Steffan Parks.

At midnight I set my alarm for 2 a.m., grabbed another quick nap, and was back in my car, dressed in all black, before 2:30.

Poole had come through again. I plugged in the address

she'd uncovered for the lab and set off. Deele's claim that it was "not far" turned out to be the truth. My software predicted I'd be there in 45 minutes. Houston's traffic would at least settle down overnight, right?

Normally this first trip would be all about pure reconnaissance. Rushing in could be a recipe for disaster. As Fife had so astutely observed, it's not like the place would be dark and quiet. There were bound to be security people crawling around.

But truth be told, I was a spy in desperate need of some spying. Sometimes in my profession I get lots of it, but then I'll have long stretches where nothing gets my heart racing. Christina doesn't ask much about my experiences, but one time she got a big laugh out of me. We were on the couch, watching a James Bond movie—the one with Pierece Brosnan where he's shot at about a thousand times by guys with machine guns and never gets hit with even a single round—and she asked how real-life spies handle all the non-stop action. I think beer came out my nose.

If only she knew how often we had our thumbs securely planted up our asses. It ain't glamorous, and our hair never looks as spectacular as Brosnan's after our fight scenes.

At the moment I was itching for something dangerous. I'd endured a lot of travel lately and plenty of talking. For Christ's sake, I even sat through a Powerpoint display. I needed action, no matter how risky.

A small backpack filled with a nice collection of special tools occupied the seat beside me. My trusty Glock 18, delivered to my room by a Q2 courier along with the backpack, lay on the seat as well. I hoped it wouldn't sing tonight.

At ten past three I pulled to the side of the road two blocks from the lab. It was an industrial area where most of the buildings had bright security lights circling their perimeters. I studied a satellite photo, then pulled back onto the street. A slow drive-by was in order.

Deele's property occupied its own block, which meant it shared no space—not even a parking lot—with any other business. The building itself was set back from the road and fortified against an assault. The fence surrounding it was not only tall, but capped with razor wire. Signs every thirty feet spelled out the dire consequences of trespassing, but it would take quite an effort to get to that point. A guard shack defended an entrance from the road, with a solitary figure perched inside. Powerful floodlights bathed the parking area and the building. There would probably be one or two armed security types patrolling outside, and more waiting within.

It wouldn't be impossible to get in unnoticed; after all, the government trained me to do things like that. And I did have my bag of toys.

I turned a corner and drove another block, then pulled over and stepped out. With the backpack over a shoulder and the gun in my waistband, I crossed the street and headed toward the target.

Near the fence on the backside of the building I knelt and scoped out the property. As expected, besides the lonely guy in the guard shack there was one more trooper patrolling the grounds. He looked to be going through the motions, probably as unhappy with his work as you'd expect of a guy walking back and forth in a desolate field in the middle of the night. His presence helped, too; it meant motion detectors likely weren't in use outside. All I needed to do was slip past him with a distraction. That was easy enough.

Pulling wire cutters from my pack, I snipped a small section at the bottom of the fence near a pole, just enough to squeeze through. Once inside I lay prone, estimating the distance to the building's shadow at about 150 feet. When the sentry passed me and reached the limit of his route, I found the fob to my Jag and thumbed the red panic button.

It did not disappoint. The obnoxious horn cut through the stillness of the night, reverberating off nearby structures. I didn't wait for the guard's reaction; I knew what it would be. I bolted, only looking around as I neared the sanctuary of the shadow. Sure enough, the man's feet were planted, and he stared through the gloom in the opposite direction toward the disturbance. I shut off the car alarm.

So simple, and yet so effective.

Everything I needed was conveniently nearby. A utility door was placed not twenty feet from the secure junction panel I needed. Picking the lock on the panel was a breeze, revealing an array of connections. Retrieving a small device from my pack, I hooked its alligator clips in the appropriate spots, dialed up the code I wanted on the tiny LED screen, and hit the engage button. Just like that, the building's alarm system was mine. It was now in stand-by mode, which meant no squawking with a problem because, to the system, there *wasn't* a problem. It was just resting.

Any and all cameras inside and out would be essentially paused; looking back later—assuming they had a reason to look back, which I did not intend to give them—it would be a seamless splice. The only way they'd be able to tell would be the jump in the chronometer readings. But they'd have to be looking for it.

The guys on the 2nd floor at Q2 headquarters didn't get *everything* right. But they nailed it with this stuff.

I glanced back at the security guard. He was stopped, and it looked like he was texting. Jason Deele would've been beside himself. I chuckled and slipped over to the door, which was embarrassingly easy to pick.

Inside, I found myself at the end of a short hall. The dim, almost sensual mood lighting, meant I wouldn't need the night-vision glasses tucked into my pack. I crept to a branch in the hallway and peered around a corner. There was no one in sight, and, other than an electrical hum, the place was crypt-quiet.

The next step normally would be to make my way to whatever I was looking for. The problem here was that I had no clue what that was.

Which had never stopped me before.

Priority number one: To nose around and get away without being detected. This was pure reconnaissance, and it would help my case immensely if Deele never knew his playground had been compromised.

Any motion detectors that might exist were disabled, as were the building's cameras. That still left the likelihood of some gun-toting clown walking around. I mean, other than me.

Staying low, I advanced to the first darkened room I saw with an open door. It held nothing of interest. In fact, at first glance nothing at this end of the building seemed important at all. But across the way a glass door beckoned, and by nature I'm a sucker for beckoning. I hurried over.

Pay dirt. Literally. Through the glass I saw row after row of raised planter beds, flush with thick growth. This was Jaclyn Stone's playground and, if Sarah Eklund was right, Stone's lab of horror, too. The room, a large, indoor greenhouse, stretched back through the gloom. There was a lot happening on the other side of the glass.

I looked down at the modern keypad lock, and figured one

of my Q2 gadgets could handle it. But I froze when I heard a voice nearby.

It was a man, and he was singing. Not belting out anything, but the kind of singing you do almost under your breath, especially when you're not completely sure of the words. The song was faintly familiar, but his rendition was horrid. He wasn't in sight yet, but was definitely approaching from another hallway. I glanced around for cover, found little, and decided the best move was to get inside the greenhouse.

As the bad singer neared, I scrambled through my pack and pulled out an oddly-shaped tube that reminded me of an old-time car cigarette lighter. Placing it against the side of the keypad, I twisted the top. It began the laborious process of reading the guts of the lock and finding one of the codes that worked.

All the while, Adam Levine's biggest fan got closer and closer. He'd be around the corner in seconds.

Finally the tube vibrated and displayed a five-digit code on its small LED screen. I punched in the numbers, whisked open the door, slipped inside, and closed it behind me. At the same time a dark figure came around the corner and I dove to the floor, turning my face away. I held my breath.

The room was dark, and I had to hope the security guard wouldn't examine the floor through the glass. I heard his singing much more clearly now, and I'd been right: Maroon 5. At least it was one of the good songs from their early days.

I heard the door knob rattle as he checked it. Apparently content, he ambled away, still softly singing. I waited until his voice faded before getting to my knees.

A flashlight would come in handy, but with the mall cop on patrol I couldn't risk it. I pulled out the night-vision glasses after all. With them securely in place, I discovered the room was even deeper than I'd thought. Overhead, running the length of the planter boxes, an array of irrigation tubes were braided amongst a complex scaffolding of lights, which for now were dark. After checking the glass door again, I hunched down and made my way along the center row of planters.

The smell was pungent. This was basically an entire farm packed into a relatively small space. The blended scent of organic growth and fertilizer was overpowering until my senses acclimated.

I didn't recognize the first few species, but assumed they were derivatives of basic wheat. I fiddled with a section of tomato plants, tempted to sample one—until I remembered this wasn't a farm, it was a laboratory. There was always a chance some of these innocent-looking vegetables could be toxic.

I still didn't know exactly what I was searching for. Villains aren't exactly helpful, and they never place a sign over their dirty work that reads, *Hey, federal agent, it's right here.*

But on the next row over something caught my eye.

Two six-foot planter boxes were bunched alone, with empty space on each side. They both held what looked just like the soybean plants I'd seen in Iowa. You could tell from the gear around them they'd received extra love. I had a feeling these might be either the samples of the new miracle plant, or perhaps a spin-off.

I pulled off my glasses and stared at it, wondering what I could get away with. After lengthy consideration, I decided a cleanly-snipped stem would have to do. I found one on the backside of a growth. It held several leaves and pod clusters. With a knife I removed it and placed it in a baggie, which then went back into my pack.

Glancing around, I found what looked like an upright

medical cooler. It, too, was locked. But peering through its glass doors, I knew I'd need another souvenir.

Picking this lock the old-fashioned way, I pulled one door open and took a chance with my phone's flashlight. Rows of viles sat alongside other scientific gear. A box of microscope slides would be interesting, but I couldn't chance taking something that was likely catalogued and would be missed.

Then, in a glass box, I spied a flask. The liquid inside was clear, but it didn't take a genius to know it wasn't water. Someone had gone to a lot of trouble to keep it isolated: A locked building with heavy security, a locked room, a locked cabinet, and a separate box inside that. I glanced toward the door, then extracted more items from my pack.

Putting on latex gloves, I removed the flask and inserted a syringe, capturing 3 cc's of the liquid. I repeated that with a second syringe. Then I replaced the flask, carefully stoppered the syringes, and placed them into a secure kit. All of it went back into my pack, along with the used gloves.

There was probably much more I could do here, but I couldn't push my luck, either. I'd gotten further than I had any right to expect. Time to slink away.

The singing guard was silent when I pulled open the lab door. That meant he was either in another part of the building, or quietly absorbed in something nearby. The hallway to my exit door was across open space. I'd have to be patient. So I peeked through a crack in the door another minute.

The patience paid off. To my left a light came on in an office and a guard—probably the same guy—walked in and disappeared. This was my chance.

Closing the greenhouse door behind me, I hustled over to the hallway. Just as I got there I heard the office light snap off. A voice called out. "Hello?"

I pushed myself flat against the wall, out of his line of sight. A moment later he said it again: "Hello?"

He was unsure. He'd spotted what he thought was motion in the darkness. If he'd actually identified me as a moving person he'd spring into action.

While he contemplated what he'd seen, I tiptoed down the hallway to the door. There was a guard outside as well, but I couldn't risk staying inside any longer. I silently pushed the door open and stepped out.

The door closed behind me with a soft click.

Moving to my right and dropping to my stomach, I searched the grounds. I couldn't see the patrolling guard, which concerned me. I felt the familiar surge of adrenaline, and ate it up.

There. He came around the corner and walked past me, not fifty feet away. I stayed motionless in the shadow. When he got beyond me I saw him once again pull out his phone. Now he walked while looking at the screen.

The guy was a burglar's dream. I got to my feet and moved to the junction box. Within 10 seconds the clips were off and everything put back to its original state. One more glance toward the sentry confirmed he was still texting, so I picked my way across the open space to the fence. Once through the opening, I used a roll of 12-gauge wire to reconnect the chain-link fence to the post. Again, someone would have to look for the damage to ever know it had temporarily been a convenient doorway.

After packing up everything, I walked back to the Jag, smiling. Behind the wheel I broke into the Maroon 5 song.

What can I say? The damned thing was stuck in my head.

21

———

I awoke at ten with bright Texas sunshine sneaking through a tiny gap in the hotel room's curtains. That sliver of light must always find your face. It's a law.

There were two messages waiting. One from Fife, the other from Quanta.

I called the boss.

"I saw your message from early this morning," she said. "You had a busy night."

"And a busier day in store. But before we talk about that, when can you have the courier here?"

"She's en route."

"Great," I said. "I'll be interested to see what the lab nerds discover in the samples I took away. Although I think we have a pretty good idea what they are."

"I see you've also requested she bring your new identity, including passport."

"Yeah. Deele's trying very hard to crack the U.S. market, but he's already established in Paraguay. I'd like to know if he's killed anybody down there, and what else he's up to." I paused. "What I don't have is a contact in that country. My last one was killed by a drug lord about a year ago."

She considered this. "All right. I can set you up with someone. But I need you to hear what I'm saying right now."

Quanta rarely lectured. She didn't need to. She was a quiet leader, the only kind I respected. I'd served once under a ranting fool, early in my military career, and my reaction nearly landed me in the stockade. Only the benevolence of another superior officer saved my ass, probably because I'd saved his on a mission against some really bad men.

Not that I had a warm, loving relationship with the living enigma known as Quanta. But as much as she might piss me off occasionally, I still respected her leadership. So I quietly listened.

"There's a reason we tend to keep you within our borders," she said. "Q2 is a shadow organization within our own government; explaining it to a foreign power is not something we ever want to attempt."

"So I shouldn't blow up anything," I said.

"I know that's asking a lot. But it's more than that. The person I'm putting you in touch with isn't sanctioned by the government of Paraguay either."

I raised an eyebrow. "Oh. Are you saying he's a member of Paraguay's version of Q2?"

"*She*. And, in simplified terms, yes. I can't say more than that. If she wants to reveal anything else, well, I'll leave it up to her. But check your ego at the border, Swan. Gamez is an accomplished agent, and she'll be under no obligation to do anything for you that she's unwilling to take on. *If* she agrees to help, it'll only be as a favor to me. Are we clear?"

This gave me pause. Backstory on Quanta was like a precious gem: very rare and extremely difficult to dig up. If this agent owed her a favor, there was a personal connection from their past. It was a past I'd always been curious about.

But a question also came to mind. "How much does Agent Gamez know about Q2? Will she know . . . um, what I am?"

"No. She, nor anyone else down there, even knows the name of our organization. As far as she'll be concerned you're a special agent working for me, as part of a covert arm of the government. That's all. And, knowing Gamez, she won't ask for anything more."

"Understood," I said. "I'll play nice."

THE CALL to Fife could wait until after my exchange with the courier. This time it was a man in his late twenties with a scraggly beard and filthy clothes. A great cover, if you ask me. Assuming it *was* a cover. We swapped code phrases in the doorway under the guise of delivering food. And the guy actually handed me coffee and a bag of donuts. If there was a Yelp page for Q2 couriers, I'd give the slob 5 stars.

He left with the stuff I'd pulled out of Deele's lab. After closing the door and taking a bite of a chocolate donut, I skimmed through the packet at the bottom of the bag. Some *guaraní*, the local currency in Paraguay, plus two credit cards and a passport issued to one James Frank. I grimaced. Another phony cover with two first names. I tossed it all on the bed and called my favorite FBI agent.

"You think the juice is maybe the same toxin used in Iowa?" he asked after I caught him up on my late-night theatrics.

"We'll know by tonight. By that time I'll be catching a plane for South America."

"No shit," he said. "Sorry I can't go with you this time. I love it down there."

"I'll bring you a refrigerator magnet," I said. "What about updates for me? Any more squawking from the deputy secretary?"

"As a matter of fact, yes."

I sighed. "Now what?"

"She says you obstructed her step-daughter from making any progress in Houston."

"She actually used the word *obstructed*?"

"More than once. The word is big with politicians, you know. Also said you've still provided no data or analysis of any substance. And who can argue with her? We all know you really *do* suck at analysis. Oh, and she added that you're vile and uncouth."

"She did not."

"Okay," Fife said, "I made the last part up. But it sounds like something she'd say."

"That just cost you the fridge magnet. Anything new on Culbertson, or on Deele's muscle, that guy Wood?"

"Swan, we got nothing. It's frustrating as hell. We know Wood did it, we know Deele ordered it, and we can't prove a damned thing. You're gonna have to come up with something pretty soon to tie it all together."

"Think the toxin from his lab will be enough?"

Fife let out a long breath. "Honestly? I doubt it. I think you're going to have to catch him in the act."

"Great."

He laughed. "The nation is counting on you, Eric Swan. Don't let us—"

I hung up on him.

. . .

James Frank checked in at Terminal E 90 minutes before the flight departed Houston. Bless Poole's heart, she'd snuck me into first class. That was worth way more than a fridge magnet. It would be at least a shot glass or an airport hoodie for her.

I found a quiet little alcove at the far end of the concourse with a row of empty, uncomfortable seats. From there I made a call to Christina.

"Sounds like you're at an airport," she said. "Should I guess where you're going?"

"You wouldn't get it with 100 guesses. But I'm curious where you'd start."

"Mmm. How about Mobile, Alabama?"

I laughed. "The last time I was in Mobile was in the service. My buddy Drew and I got our asses thoroughly kicked by some guys at a biker bar."

"I'm sure you had it coming."

"I'm sure you're right. I think I bad-mouthed Lynyrd Skynyrd."

"So where *are* you going?"

"Babe, in one hour I leave for Paraguay."

"No shit."

"Funny, that's been everyone's response. How's your belly? And what's that you're eating?"

"You heard that? It's crackers with some brie. And the belly is fine. My back's starting to hurt, though. Which is weird. I'm not even that big yet. How's the assignment coming?"

"Oh, you know, same ol'. Chase bad guys, save the world." I paused. "I miss you a lot on this trip. Keep wondering what you're up to."

"You're sweet. I miss you, too. And we have some shows to catch up on. If you don't get back soon I can't promise I won't watch without you. Speaking of which, when *will* you be able to get home?"

"Depends. If I bite it in South America you'll see me this weekend. If all goes well, maybe another ten days? We'll see how active this particular bad guy is."

Ours wasn't your traditional marriage. I mean, how many people casually discussed their itinerary with a spouse based on whether or not they got murdered? For us it was just a semi-normal component of everyday life. And death, for that matter. In a way, our *laissez-faire* attitude toward it all is what kept us sane through the whole insane arrangement.

"I'd offer to bring you something," I said, "but I don't think I can bring back food. Want me to ship anything to you? Any special culinary delights I should look for?"

She thought about it for a moment. I heard the crunch of another cracker. "I'm interested in some of their soups, but I don't think they'd pack well."

"All right. How 'bout I just give you an epic back rub and foot rub when I get home?"

"Hey, don't make me cheer for you to get killed right away."

Like I said, not your traditional marriage.

First class air travel is one of the most awkward delights you'll ever encounter. You're spoiled beyond belief, with steaming hot towels to cleanse your hands before a luxurious meal is placed before you, complete with a linen napkin. Not to mention the endless flow of booze, should that be your choice. The seats are wide and comfortable, nobody reclines a chair into your nose, and the flight attendants refer to you by name. Mr. Frank, in this case.

I'm surprised they don't have an attendant in the bathroom to assist with personal hygiene needs.

But I said an *awkward* delight. Because even though it's plush and extravagant, you never quite feel you've earned any of it. Every time I experience first class I want to apologize to the flight attendants and tell them not to fawn over me; I ain't worth it.

Then there are the steely looks given to you by the other passengers passing through first class on their way back to steerage, where they'll be packed in tighter than a mosh pit at Lollapalooza. Unable to officially abuse you with their words, their eyes say it all: *I hope you choke on your steak, asshole.*

I try not to make eye contact. I feel guilty sitting there in my leather chair, eating warm mixed nuts from a crystal bowl and sipping my free cocktail as they struggle to the back with a rowdy child and his ragged little Sponge Bob carry-on bag.

I put on my headphones and gazed out the window, pretending to be mesmerized by the activities of airport workers darting around the tarmac on their muscular vehicles.

Settling back, I thought about the various characters who'd require attention before this case wrapped up. The most obvious, of course, was Jason Deele. It was easy to get too comfortable around him, because outwardly he lulled you to sleep with his effortless smile. Nothing about his demeanor scared me—which is what scared me. A gut feeling told me I'd see the real Deele before too long. And it likely wouldn't be as pleasant as his smile.

There was Conor Wood, the former military man who now played the part of Deele's killer-on-a-string. We'd yet to exchange two words with each other but, as with his boss, I felt a day of reckoning was drawing near. It would be painful for one or both of us.

Also on the opposing team lurked the inscrutable Jaclyn Stone. At times approachable and expressive, she could also come across as reticent, cold. From the very beginning my instincts warned me to be on alert with this brilliant scientist, and my conversation with inmate Steffan Parks reinforced that apprehension. He'd tagged her as one of the more threatening members of the Arcetri. I didn't take that lightly. My brief exposure to the limits of their vengeance was enough for me to take them—and their members—seriously.

Dr. Stone and her patron, Jason Deele, appeared to have their own separate agendas, and had apparently formed an alliance to achieve their individual goals. She wanted to prove something, and he intended to profit from it. It added up to a frightening combination of two volatile and determined personalities.

By the time we were airborne and the flight attendant had dropped off another adult beverage, I was thinking about the people on our side of this battle. There was the dynamic Sarah Eklund and her blustering step-mother, Deputy Secretary Halloran. I could empathize with FDR and Churchill; managing your allies was as much of a task as confronting your enemy. Sometimes even more aggravating.

I had to hope they'd both stop fighting me and provide valuable assistance when the time came.

For the time being the only accomplice I could trust was Agent Fife, and he'd be nowhere in sight if shit hit the fan in Paraguay.

As for this latest unknown element, Agent Gamez? I had no idea. But I was about to find out.

.   .   .

SHE WAS WAITING for me at the airport in Asunción, the capital city. And she was nothing like I expected.

In her late 50s or early 60s, she was of medium height, short, graying hair, and a hard physique that spoke to either hours in a gym or a rough-and-tumble life on the street.

"Mr. Frank? I'm Ramona Gamez," she said with a reserved smile. "Welcome to the land of peace and justice."

"I'll do my best to honor both."

Now that the dumb passwords had been exchanged, she led the way to a car. This was certainly not a Jaguar. I tossed my small bag into the back seat of her battered Chevy and climbed into the passenger seat. She jerked the car into gear before I even had my seat belt fastened. She did not use hers.

Once on the road she rolled down her window and lit a cigarette. She offered me the pack. I declined.

"How's my friend Quanta?" she asked, accelerating and changing lanes without a glance over her shoulder. Her English, spoken in a rough, deep voice, was impeccable. That took me off the hook; the population in Paraguay is more likely to speak a mix of Spanish and Guaraní. The Spanish part I was comfortable with.

"Her usual warm, gregarious self," I said, rolling down my own window.

Gamez laughed. "She's a *cabrona*. I don't care about her job title or how much money she makes. It doesn't change a thing."

"How long have you known her?"

"Oh, a long time."

Just the vague answer I expected. It would be pointless to ask more about the relationship, and we both knew it. So I changed the subject.

"How much did she tell you about Jason Deele?"

She flicked some ash out the window and turned onto a street toward San Lorenzo, one of the larger suburbs.

"She didn't have to tell me about Deele."

The surprise must've played all over my face. She grunted a smile.

"Jason Deele has been on our radar, as you Americans say, for almost a year."

"Has he been misbehaving?"

She shrugged. "Not to be cynical, but in many parts of South America *misbehaving* is relative. It's almost how business is done." She glanced at me. "That's pretty much why I have a job."

"Are we talking corruption?"

"Oh, corruption wasn't invented here. We may have employed it more than you're used to, but you'll find corruption in every government in the world. Including yours. For years people have wondered why the citizens of Paraguay don't do something about it."

"And? What's the answer?"

"The answer is that it's not so easy to change a system that's entrenched after more than a century. A lot of very rich and very powerful people have built the kind of political and criminal structure you don't just tear down with a bulldozer. And it's not all internal. There are powerful outside forces who make it very difficult."

She looked over at me, the hand holding her cigarette resting near the window.

"This country is not just the geographic center of South America, Mr. Frank. It's a hub for all of the shitty business going on around us. This city you're in right now is a strategic base for some nasty people."

I glanced at the buildings we sped past. "You make it

sound hopeless." Then I looked back at her. "Yet here you are. Somebody must want to fix the system."

"I think of them as silent partners. A few people high enough in office to pull some strings here and there, funnel some money so it's not officially accounted for. Enough to fund one more organization to fight back. All very . . . what's the phrase? Very hush-hush."

I grinned. "We have a lot in common. What specifically is *your* job?"

She took a quick drag before flicking the butt out the window. "I'm more involved in the area where corruption intersects with coercion. You understand what I'm saying?"

"I surely do. Paraguay didn't invent that, either."

"No. But some have made an art of it. And their coercion sometimes involves body counts."

"Like Mr. Deele?"

"Like Mr. Deele."

22

———————

Gamez drove me to a hotel where I checked in, dropped off my bag, then met her in the cafe across the street. A glass filled with dark coffee sat in front of her while another cigarette glowed in an ashtray to her left.

"Would I like that?" I asked, indicating her coffee.

"Probably not," she said, lifting the cigarette to her mouth.

I ordered one from the server and got down to business.

"Jason Deele was likely behind the death of a government agent in the States. Now you tell me he's contributed at least one body bag in Paraguay. What's the story?"

She leaned back in her chair.

"He showed up nine months ago. Followed the standard protocol for registering to do business. Introduced himself and one of his associates to several people in our Ministry of Agriculture and Livestock. Said all the right things, shook some hands—"

"Lined some pockets?"

"No doubt. But nothing outrageous. I'm told he made it

clear his focus was clearly on the soybean industry and introducing a new breed that would flourish."

"Is that welcomed here?" I asked. "I mean, cocky American showing up, offering to show everyone a new way of doing something?"

Gamez made a face that said *who cares*? "If you're asking if it insulted people, the answer is no. This country already has a thriving soybean trade, but one thing it lacks is a solid base for research and development. Importing the technology doesn't wound anyone's pride if it makes a profit." She took a long drag on her cigarette, then, while exhaling the smoke added, "Again, I'm sure that's true everywhere. Billions of dollars in an offshore account will buy a lot of salve for hurt feelings."

The server placed my glass of coffee in front of me. I held it up and took a sniff, which made me wonder who'd boiled the sweaty gym socks and mixed them with coffee beans and turpentine. I soldiered on and took a sip.

"Jesus," I said, setting it down. "What the hell is that?"

"Private blend from the cafe's owner," Gamez said, smiling. "I told you you wouldn't like it."

"Would it help if I added cream?"

She shook her head. "That would make it undrinkable."

"What's the difference?" I said under my breath. I pushed the glass away. "Tell me about this other person Deele brought with him. Woman?"

"Name is Stone. Scientist of some kind." She said the word *scientist* with a hint of disdain.

"Yeah, Jaclyn Stone."

Gamez nodded and took another drink of her coffee. Either one acquired a taste for it, or her taste buds had withered long ago.

"From my investigation," she said, "I discovered Stone was able to convince several people that her formula, or whatever it is, could increase their production and ward off the kind of diseases that have wiped out plenty of crops in the past. We're a landlocked country, which means our transportation costs are higher than nations who have a port. Tell the right people you can increase their output and prevent disease? You'll get a lot of people on your side right away."

I studied her face. "A lot of people. But not everyone."

She nodded once.

"And that's where death makes an entrance," I said. "Who'd he knock off?"

"The head of a family controlling one of the larger soybean concerns was strongly opposed to changing anything. Mr. Ruiz fell and hit his head on the side of the pool at his house. He was found floating face down."

"So it looked like an unfortunate accident."

"Then his number two vowed to uphold the position of Mr. Ruiz. That gentleman had a tragic car accident."

"The unluckiest company of the year."

"And no way to prove anything. Of course, within a week the company signed an agreement with Jason Deele and their plants were in the ground within a month."

"And thriving."

Gamez waved a dismissive hand. "I'm not a farmer. I'm not a botanist. I couldn't tell you if Deele's product is any better than what's been growing here for decades." She picked up her coffee. "But once he had his deal, no one else died."

Outside an argument broke out between the driver of a car and a bicyclist. We watched their shouting match for a minute. Then I pulled the coffee toward me and made another attempt. It was just as horrible.

This brought a laugh to Gamez. She waved over the server and ordered a regular coffee for me.

"I'll tell you what has me confused," she said when we were again alone. "Both Quanta and you have only mentioned soybeans."

I squinted at her. "Yeah. So?"

"Well, I have an inside connection with one of the conglomerates working with Deele. And my source tells me the soybean crops are just the beginning."

My heart sank. "What else?"

Gamez gave a half shrug. "Anything else that can be grown." She paused. When she spoke again, she sounded almost amused. "You didn't think he'd stop with dominating just one piece of the action, did you?"

An hour later I got back to my room, exhausted from the long travel. Gamez had other business to handle and said she'd let me grab a few hours of sleep before we met again to discuss the best move.

At the moment that move eluded me completely.

It was something we'd feared, even something Sarah Eklund had warned could happen. Jason Deele and Jaclyn Stone wouldn't be satisfied with the billions they'd make with one crop. If you became the top supplier for almost all of the world's biggest cash crops—to forge what would ultimately amount to a food monopoly—you'd become not only the wealthiest person on the planet, but the most powerful. People dance to your tune when you control their sustenance.

On one hand it sounded not only implausible, but impossible. Who would let that happen?

And then, lying on my hotel bed, staring at the ceiling, I

wondered: Once it snowballed, how could anyone *stop* it? The only strains of corn, wheat, and soybean able to resist a deadly disease? What was the alternative? Worldwide famine on a level never before seen in history?

Other crucial factors played into it. Jason Deele was young enough to have 20 or 30 years to gather his momentum. He had the funds to get traction in a variety of locations, and, once his system was up and running, it could easily pay for expansion. Worldwide expansion.

There was also the X factor of Stone. She provided not only the know-how to create both the problem and the solution, but was motivated to smash everyone who, in her eyes, had held her down in the past. I didn't yet know everything about the troubled minds within the secretive Arcetri, but I knew enough to fear the potential power of their bitterly-inspired anger.

First Steffan Parks. This time Jaclyn Stone.

Was there another member, silent at the moment, capable of lashing out in an equally-diabolical way?

This wasn't going to help me sleep. I had to relax.

The last torturous thought before I managed to drift away was a sharp rebuke for my own naïveté. I'd stood inside one of Stone's greenhouse labs, had seen row after row of viable crop strains, and yet didn't immediately recognize that these other varieties would follow the same pattern she'd developed with soy. What a fool I'd been. Did I assume the other species were just hobbies?

After mentally berating myself, I dragged out the tools needed to upload. As exhausted as I was, sleep would have to wait. All of this was much too important to risk losing.

. . .

IT WAS late afternoon when I awoke. Any rejuvenation the nap might have produced was lost within a throbbing headache. Sitting on the edge of my bed, I popped three pain pills. It couldn't be the travel; I'd circled the globe numerous times and always enjoyed it. For a split second I wondered if it was the tar-like coffee I'd sampled with Gamez, but surely I hadn't ingested enough to cause this reaction.

It was probably something minor, exacerbated by the flight. Technology might allow me to invest into new bodies, but it didn't coat me with teflon. I got sick as easily as the next person. It irked me nonetheless; I'd always been horribly impatient when it came to illness, but doubly so in the midst of a dangerous assignment.

After a moment's hesitation, I swallowed a fourth pill.

A text from Poole flashed across my phone's screen: *Got info. Call when convenient.*

I opened a diet soda from the room's mini-bar and, using the encrypted satellite connection with my tablet, placed a video call.

"Got a lab report on the sample I took from Houston?" I asked.

"A preliminary report. They'd like to run it again."

I frowned. "Okay. Is it not the disease that killed the crops in Iowa?"

"Well, it is and it isn't. I've sent you the initial analysis, but I've also sent the report to Sarah Eklund under an FBI cover. The people in our lab suggest you talk with her since this is more her specialty. We have as many questions on this end right now as answers."

There hadn't been time for the pills to take effect, and now the middle of my forehead felt like a dagger had pierced it. Poole noticed.

"You okay? You look like you're in pain."

"Just a mother of a headache. It'll pass. Anything else to share?"

"Quanta wanted to make sure you were getting along okay with Agent Gamez."

I rubbed my forehead. "Poole, between you and me, Ramona Gamez is borderline frightening. I don't know if it's a lifetime of doing espionage work under a South American regime, or if she's just a born hellcat. Everything about her is living on the edge."

Poole was quiet a moment, then said, "But you're getting along okay?"

Even through the pain I had to laugh. "Yeah. She's solid. We'll get along fine. Tell mother not to worry."

I signed off and opened the file on Q2's lab results. It was like a foreign language to me, so I placed the next call to Dr. Eklund, this time without video.

"Hello, Agent Swan," she said. Her voice was neutral.

"Doctor," I said. "I understand you got a copy of some lab results this afternoon."

"I did. I just finished looking at them."

"Well, as funny as this sounds, I need you to translate them for me, if you wouldn't mind."

It appeared any goodwill we'd established during our dinner in Houston had been nullified by the way I shut her down at Deele's presentation. But I couldn't worry about the perceived slight right now. I'd done what I believed was right; I hoped Eklund would move past it.

"First, may I ask where the sample came from?"

I hesitated. She didn't need to know this information, but, at the same time, I *was* asking for her help. I couldn't have it both ways.

"I lifted a few cc's from a secure greenhouse lab overseen by Deele and Stone."

"*Lifted.* So you stole it."

"Well . . . I suppose technically I could take it back. If I just *borrowed* it would that make a difference in your analysis?"

The silence on her end was long enough to make the point that she was over my act. I had to be careful, because Sarah and her beastly step-mother were supposed to be on my side. For the time being I blamed my irritability on the headache.

Her voice had a cold, crisp edge. "What I see in the report is remarkably similar in genetic makeup to the fungus that killed the crops here in Iowa."

"*Remarkably similar,*" I said. "How close are we talking? Could it be an entirely different disease that just happens to share traits with what you encountered?"

"It will take some more study," she said. "But I'll tell you what I think. This is a toxin that's based on a particular platform. At the core it's the same platform found in the disease that wiped out the fields here. This is either a mutant, or its been intentionally modified to the point where it probably wouldn't take down a crop of soybeans. I mean, it wouldn't do them any good, but it wouldn't cause the same destruction."

I leaned against the headboard of my bed, one hand massaging my left temple. "But it could potentially wreak havoc with a different species, I assume."

"We don't know that. I'd need the actual sample rather than results on a piece of paper."

I sighed. "Okay. I'll get some of it shipped to you immediately. If you have it by tomorrow morning, how long would it take for you to get your own results?"

"Maybe a day."

"All right. Text me exactly where you want it to arrive and I'll make it happen."

"Great." Then she added, in a somewhat-warmer voice, "I appreciate it."

We ended the call. A moment later she sent me the lab address, which I forwarded to Poole with a note asking for a rush. Knowing the way she operated, Poole would get it on a private plane to Iowa within hours.

I walked to the window and tried unsuccessfully to open it. A breeze sounded good, even therapeutic, but apparently security in the hotel trumped my need for fresh air. I gazed out at the city as dusk settled in and a succession of twinkling lights competed with the heavy shadows.

Somewhere in that sea of humanity two very sick and dangerous people were plotting monstrous evil. And somehow I knew time was running out.

23

———

Of course she was smoking. Gamez stood against the side of her car, took a long puff when she saw me approach, then dropped the butt into the gutter and stamped on it.

"How was your beauty sleep?" she asked.

"You can't tell by looking?"

She gave one choppy laugh. "Get in. Let's go play spy games."

Buckling my seat belt, I saw her give a curious glance before flooring it out of the parking lot.

"You never wear a seat belt?" I asked.

She shook her head.

I chuckled. "You drive like a maniac without a seat belt, you smoke like a tire fire, and you drink coffee brewed straight out of the bowels of hell. I can see how nothing in the spy world could possibly worry you."

She lit another cigarette. "Oh, plenty worries me about the job. But only when I have to rely on someone else."

"I'll try not to let you down."

"You won't let *me* down. If it comes to it, I don't sacrifice my life to save visiting agents. I prefer to live to fight another day."

You had to appreciate her honesty. It was blunt as hell, but at least she let you know up front that she wouldn't clean up your mistakes if the cost was her life.

It was another aspect of the investment program I often thought about. Ramona Gamez had one life to give; for me it was reshuffle the cards and play another hand. Of course that influenced how I played the cards dealt to me. How could it not? I could afford to go all-in when the situation called for it. There would always be another hand, another opportunity to gamble.

Miller and I once discussed whether or not this made me unnecessarily reckless. We never arrived at a conclusion, but I suspected it had more than once. What was more important, however, was whether or not my indifferent attitude toward life had resulted in some other poor sap forfeiting the only life *they* had.

The answer was: Not directly. But yeah, I'd stormed in before when it may not have been the smartest play, and others had paid the price.

What can I say? Sometimes you just have to act on your instincts, and react when there's little or no time to ponder consequences. Besides, the job automatically came with inherent risks, not only for me but for those around me. I did my best to act wisely, but sometimes shit just blows up in your face. It's called collateral damage, which may sound like an ice-cold observation, but it's a totally candid and realistic one.

The thing that haunted me about it was the fact I knew going in *I* got to hit the reset button and play again; the person with me had no idea.

Gamez told me to settle in, the ride would take about half an hour. That gave me a chance to probe a little more.

"Did you meet Quanta here in Paraguay, or somewhere else?"

At first it seemed she was going to ignore the question, but after a long silence she said, "Here. Not too far from where you're staying, actually."

I waited out another silence, using the time to rub my temple again.

"We were both young agents. Neither one of us had ever worked with a foreign partner on an international case. And in all the years since, I've never met another agent who came close to her." She threw me a glance. "No offense."

"Well, you haven't seen me at my best."

"And I hope I don't. That'll mean we've run into a shit show. I'm at an age where I'd prefer to use my wits more than my weapon."

"Sorry to get personal," I said, "but why are you still doing this?"

"You mean why haven't they moved me into a facility or something?"

"I hear they can be pretty swanky. And who knows, you might meet a kind soul who digs retired spies. Lots of action in those places, I'm told."

"You're a funny man, Agent Frank. Although that's a pretty obvious bullshit name. What do your friends call you?"

"Eric. And we detoured away from the Quanta story."

She smiled. "Oh, I can't talk too much about Quanta. But I'll give you this: If you work for her, you're only seeing the administrator. So let me tell you something. She'd probably give anything to swap roles with you. It's just that a lot of spy organizations are run by damned fools, too many without much—if any—real experience in field work. You need to know she only took jobs at the top because otherwise they'd be mismanaged to hell."

I turned and looked out the passenger window. Nothing else needed to be said.

"WHAT IS THIS PLACE?"

I was curious. Were we getting something to eat, picking up her dry cleaning, or were we about to *go play spy games,* as Gamez called it?

She'd parked in a pretty ratty-looking neighborhood, killed the engine, and sat still, peering into the gloom. I kept my voice low.

At first she didn't respond. Then, with a calloused finger, she pointed toward a door in the long, dingy building off to the right. Of the half-dozen doorways I could see, it was the only one with a functioning light of any kind. An odd, orange light bulb emitted barely enough juice to cover more than a few feet.

Gamez checked her phone for the time.

"Another minute or two. If the light goes out, we move."

It did, and we did. She led me down the rutted sidewalk, past storefronts mostly abandoned, some boarded. A man stumbled toward us, clearly drunk. We separated and he passed between us, continuing his wandering ways, carrying on both sides of a conversation.

Gamez passed the illuminated doorway and kept walking. Two doors beyond, she gave a cautious glance around, then reached for a different door, pulled it open, and we were inside. She closed the door, bolted it, and used the light of her phone to guide us down a dark hallway. At the end another door awaited.

This time Gamez gave a single soft tap. The door opened, revealing a giant.

He had to be six-eight, and probably tipped 300 on the scales. With one quick scan I got the impression 280 of it was muscle. He would scare the living hell out of anyone. He scared me.

I was grateful he was on our side.

Gamez spoke to the man in Guaraní. Really all I caught was *Frank*. Then she turned to me.

"This is . . . Well, you couldn't pronounce it. Just call him Peach."

I gazed up at the monster. "Call him *Peach*?"

She smiled. "He probably won't answer anyway. He's not crazy about Americans."

So maybe he *wasn't* on my side.

"Great. Tell him I'm Canadian."

"Doesn't care for them, either."

I grunted. "We don't need to be besties. Just tell him not to step on me." Looking around, I uttered the same question I'd asked outside: "What is this place?"

She moved past the Hulk toward a table set up with a small lamp and scattered electronic equipment.

"It's a surveillance post. I told you we were gonna play spy tonight."

I joined her at the table. A quick glance told me it wasn't the most sophisticated of equipment. I kept my mouth shut. Gamez, however, read my thoughts.

"We don't get the kind of money allocated to us that you might. But we make do." She indicated a small video screen.

"There's a shot inside Deele's local lab, two blocks east of here."

My mouth dropped open. "Wait. You have a camera inside his lab? How the hell did you pull *that* off?" Then I turned to Gamez. "For that matter, how do you *continue* to pull it off? Deele must have some of the most sophisticated security gear in the world. How can he not know this is here?"

She crossed her arms. "Which question do you want me to answer first?"

"Take your pick." I looked back at the screen just as it went dark.

"There's part of your answer," she said. "It's a very small camera and transmitter. French made. Based on some technology you might be familiar with: the STC?"

I sat down on one of the chairs and gave a slow nod. It made sense now. Sometimes during an assignment I'd undergo a quick procedure to insert an STC. Formally, it's a subcutaneous tracking device, a small wafer hidden beneath the skin. It allowed the eggheads on the 2nd floor at Q2 to follow me anywhere.

It also operated on a rotating frequency system, changing every time it came on the air. The STC generally would send out a short, encrypted blast for just a few seconds, once every 15 minutes. The rest of the time it was dead, at least by any ordinary measurement. No signal, no sign of life at all, which made it practically impossible to locate.

If this small camera operated in basically the same way for Gamez, it would come alive for only a few seconds every so often and fire images to a receiving station. Otherwise it, too, was dead. I liked to call it Zombie mode. Of course, it wasn't ideal; we'd love to have non-stop video images 'round the clock. But that was much more likely to be discovered. The trade-off was getting limited images, but remaining invisible.

"Okay," I said. "I'm still surprised he hasn't found it yet. But how did you get it in there in the first place?"

"The landlord for this particular building found himself in a predicament involving his oldest daughter and a certain drug lord. He was encouraged to allow us access through the roof."

"*Encouraged*," I said.

"Well, you know. We've come a long way toward cleaning up corruption, but some techniques still come in handy." She gave a wink.

I gazed at the other gear strewn across the table. "Audio, too?"

"In two locations. We couldn't risk any more."

"And what have you found?"

She sat next to me, then leaned back to open a small fridge, pulling out two Korok Red Ales and handing one to me. Either Peach didn't drink or Gamez didn't want him drinking on duty. With his size the beast could've downed a 12-pack before getting a buzz.

Gamez took a long swig of her beer. "At first we didn't find much to concern us. It took Deele a while to get an OK to even import his plants, but still quicker than normal. Probably made somebody rich in the process."

"Oh, that's a sure thing," I said.

"Nothing unusual happened at first. Typical appointments with the Ministry for approvals, a random meeting with some of the larger players in the soybean industry. I didn't get involved until the Ministry got a call from some politician in the U.S."

I had the beer halfway to my mouth and stopped. Slowly

lowering it, I said, "Let me guess. Deputy Secretary Janet Halloran."

"Oh. You know her?"

Now I took a drink and nodded. "Haven't had the pleasure of meeting face-to-face, but she's chewed my ass out on the phone. I hope she's courteous to our friends in Paraguay."

Gamez shrugged. "I haven't personally spoken to her. But the laws of physics are the same in both countries. Shit will always roll downhill. She spoke to the Ministry and, from what I understand, did not have nice things to say about the man."

I chuckled and took another drink. "She doesn't have nice things to say about me, either, if that matters. All right, so you got a heads-up that Deele was trouble. Then what?"

"I didn't jump too high or too fast right away. I mean, he's a billionaire with a soybean hobby. Why should I care? But then, just like with Ruiz, there was another tragic accident that, to me, didn't really seem like an accident."

"This is starting to sound familiar," I said. "Who died this time? Someone in the farming industry, I imagine."

"An attorney. Very involved in the battle between small, private farmers and the big soybean organizations expanding across the country. He was very successful in pushing back against some of the large developments that have taken place over the years."

I frowned. "So what are you saying? That this time Deele didn't kill someone who stood in his way, really; he knocked off someone who stood in the way of the people he wanted to do business with?"

Gamez finished her beer. "Uh-huh. He came in, got to know some important people, and then did them a favor, you could say."

"And they responded by purchasing his product."

"Correct. Of course, we have no evidence he was involved in the man's death, but—"

"But you know he did it."

She nodded again. We sat silently for a few moments while I caught up with her in the beer-drinking department.

"Okay," I said. "What's happened lately?"

"Mostly quiet. No more deaths, or at least none we can attach to Mr. Deele. I think he made his case pretty quickly and hasn't needed to strong-arm anyone else. Of course, when your Deputy Secretary heard about the untimely accident of Mr. Escobar, she turned up the heat. Demanded we create a file with Interpol. Demanded a lot of things, actually. But there's not much I can do besides watch him. At the moment he's obeying all of our laws and restrictions. Frustrating, but that's the way it is."

I could relate. There was nothing more frustrating in our work than knowing someone was guilty as hell—guilty even of murder—but not having the evidence to officially act. Now, granted, there are times I've stepped over the line of propriety in order to pursue justice. My only defense is that I'm paid to save lives from really, really bad people who *never* play by the rules, and sometimes the only way to prevent innocent deaths is to use my experience and training to make a critical call. Believe me, you don't want to know about it. People rarely want to know how their team's good guys fudge the rules; they just want us to keep their lives healthy and happy.

It comes down to this: If you don't know how I'm doing that, you're spared having to make a moral judgment. You just go merrily on your way.

In a foreign country, however, it would have to be Ramona Gamez who did the ethical line-hopping, not me. Something told me it wouldn't take much of a push for her to do just that.

I set my empty beer bottle on the floor next to my chair. The alcohol wasn't helping my headache, but it wasn't making it worse, either. "The only way we're going to get any action is if we initiate it. Are you game?"

"Sure."

"Both Deele and Jaclyn Stone know me, so I have to stay behind the scenes," I said. "We should set up a meeting for you."

Gamez gave a half smile, glanced at Peach, then back at me. "We're not beginners, Eric. When I heard you were coming down I started that process."

"Oh. And?"

"Have another beer. My appointment with Jason Deele is tomorrow afternoon at two."

24

I slept poorly, but chalked it up to travel, the beers, and a monkey mind that refused to shut off. On one hand I was exhilarated that Gamez would make contact with Deele, but I also felt antsy just waiting on the sideline. I wasn't trained to be an observer.

But obviously I couldn't show my face.

The plan looked like this: Gamez made an appointment as an agent with the government's Ministry of Agriculture and Livestock. She'd be Ms. Medina, and she had 'additional questions' that needed to be cleared up with Mr. Deele. He'd been told that several farmers had raised a stink, and the gentleman from the USA would hopefully be able to assuage those concerns. The insinuation, of course, was that the best way to soothe something of this nature involved the ol' cash handshake. This was totally speaking Deele's language. If the only problem was money, he'd happily make certain farmers feel more comfortable with the situation.

Gamez would show up ten minutes late because, she told me, that was how it was done. She'd wear a wire and I'd listen from my hotel room. Her ultimate goal was to convince Deele she was interested in making everyone happy, but she'd need to know more about this crop disease he'd warned farmers about. That would be her entrée to Dr. Stone. In my opinion, Stone was the weak link, and the most likely to spill something she shouldn't.

Not that she was any less villainous than her partner, but Deele had played the ruthless game a little longer. This was essentially Stone's first time at bat.

The wire had me worried.

"Don't you have anything like this?" I'd said to her before we left the surveillance post, holding up one of my series-8 business cards.

She took it, looked at my fake name printed on one side, turned it over, then looked back at me.

"A bug?" She shook her head and handed it back. "No, we don't have that. But I like it."

"If we put off your appointment another day we could have some flown down for you with your phony identification."

"No. We're going in. I'm not going to take a chance that he cancels if I put him off."

Now I lay on a ridiculously hard bed, listening to traffic outside the window, wondering where everyone in San Lorenzo could possibly be going after midnight. In about 12 hours Gamez would walk into the lion's den, and it would help if I was well rested.

At three a.m. I rolled over and checked my messages. Nothing from Poole nor Quanta. Nothing from Christina. I set the phone back on the nightstand and stared at the ceiling.

. . .

GAMEZ MET me at the hotel at 11. If she was nervous it didn't show. Of course, she'd worked with Quanta in the early days, so her blood could probably cool nuclear rods. Besides, this was an easy assignment; Deele wasn't on guard. Yet.

We walked to an outdoor cafe where she immediately lit up a cigarette.

"We're on for two o'clock," she said. "Confirmation from Ms. Capaldi."

"Yeah, Deele's right hand," I said. "Where's Peach?"

"He's setting up the listening equipment in your room."

"Oh. He's in my hotel room right now?"

"Don't worry. He'll stay out of your underwear drawer. I think."

I looked at the menu while I said, "Where did you find him, anyway?"

"Peach? Oh, I've known him all his life. That's why I trust him."

She hadn't answered the question, but that was pretty much her style. I changed the subject.

"We're sure now that Deele's objective is to use the soybean success as a way to get his foot in the door. But ultimately he'll go after all the major cash crops. And not just in the Americas, but around the world. Global extortion, you could say. Anyone who doesn't want to play ball will find themselves with a bunch of withered and dead crops."

"And starving people," she added.

"Yeah. Lots of those."

She focused for a minute on her cigarette and the people walking past the cafe. Then she said, "You know, Eric, what I find most interesting about this case? Just how easy it's been for Jason Deele."

The server had set down a basket of small, cheese-flavored rolls. I took a bite. Then another.

"What do you mean?" I said through a mouthful of bread.

She stubbed out her cigarette. "I mean, what he's doing is diabolical, but the *idea* is not far-fetched. He's introduced a sort of cancer to the world of food crops, and he's already prepared with the antidote. So what I can't figure out is—"

"Why hasn't someone already done this?" I said, finishing her sentence.

"Exactly."

I took another bite. "It's a damned good question."

"And do you have an answer?"

I wiped my hands on a napkin. "The only answer I have is not a very pleasant one. Because you're right, what he's doing isn't comic-book crazy, or something from a mindless action movie. Anybody could've done it. Jason Deele and Jaclyn Stone may not have been the first to think of it, but they're at least the first to put it into action."

She stared at me, then gave a slow nod. "And they might not be the last."

"That," I said, "is *my* biggest concern. And why we have to stop them. Cold."

At 1:30 I was back in my room after the quick lunch with Gamez, followed by a walk to release some tension. There's something tantalizing about walking around an unfamiliar city, surrounded by people you not only don't know, but will never know. I tried to do it on every assignment if given a chance. The charge from that experience, alone in a sea of strange faces, unsure of what's to the left or the right—and not caring —gave me a rush.

For the longest time I didn't understand why, but it finally occurred to me. Getting lost in a new city, and passing by so many nameless characters in my personal play, I understood that I was seeing everything in a new, fresh way that none of the people around me could. It was all so boring and predictable for them, pure wallpaper in their steady, scripted life, that they no longer saw all the things I could. This play was just for me, and they were extras. They came on and off the stage without even seeing the set.

But I was unencumbered by their dull routines. I was free to see everything, hear everything. Even the smells were new experiences for me, while the natives around me felt no stirring of excitement.

That's what walking alone in a strange city meant to me. Like I was given a gift nobody else around me had anymore. They wouldn't receive that gift until they, too, escaped their ordinary surroundings and ventured out. Granted, getting away didn't create this euphoric experience for everyone; some might be terrified to strike out into the unknown. But for inquisitive creatures like me, it's a dopamine blast. It's why sometimes my walks stretched for hours.

Not this time.

In the room I found the gear Peach had set up. I spent a few minutes getting a feel for it, but it wasn't too complicated. The first thing I did was install a patch to Washington so Poole could record the whole thing.

Then I sat back and waited.

The meeting would take place at the private villa Deele had obtained for his occasional visits. The operative word there was *private*. About 20 minutes outside of town, the gated home itself wasn't large enough to qualify as vulgar, but the land around it was expansive, providing a nice buffer for visiting billionaires. Gamez intended to dictate everything she saw until she was ushered inside.

A little after two o'clock she checked in with me. I slipped on my headphones and sat forward.

"Pulling up to the property," she said. "Not much visible in the way of security. Two men in a guard house at the gate. Hold on."

I listened as she announced herself to the security men. They went through the routine of checking for her name on a list, and even making a call to the house. Seemed like overkill for an appointment, but it may have been done for show, purely for the image it presented to visitors. No one, including Ministry flunkies, just waltzed in to see the Great and Powerful Oz.

"Okay, I'm through," she said. "They were very specific about where I should park." She scoffed. "Lots of control issues with these guys."

I heard the engine die, the door open, and then the crunch of her steps on gravel as she approached the door. After the call from the front gate they were awaiting her.

"Hello, I'm here to see Mr. Deele," she said, and I noticed she added a believable accent to her English. Damn, she really was very good.

She was ushered inside and urged to make herself comfortable in what I assumed would be a formal living room or study. Then things were quiet for a few minutes. Gamez had to assume the room was under audio and video surveillance, so there was no commentary from her. We all had to be patient.

I leaned over to the minibar, pulled out another diet soda, and cracked it open. Maybe the ingredients were the same from country to country, but it certainly tasted different. A little better, in fact.

Looking back at the equipment, I took a long gulp. At least the burp was the same in every country.

"Ms. Medina," I heard a familiar voice call out.

"Yes," Gamez said. "You are Ms. Capaldi, I presume?"

"It's wonderful to meet you. Thank you for driving out this afternoon. Could we get you something to drink? Water? Tea?"

"No, thank you. Will Mr. Deele be along soon?"

"Well, unfortunately he's been called away at the last minute."

I set the soda down.

Gamez's voice was tense. "He was called away? And yet this meeting is very important."

Diana Capaldi put on her soothing, let-me-fix-it voice. "It absolutely is important, Ms. Medina. Which is why Mr. Deele has authorized me to speak for him, and has given me the power to approve any arrangement I feel would be—"

"This is an outrage," Gamez said, her voice almost frightening. "I expressed the importance of our conversation when the meeting was arranged. Now to discover that Mr. Deele has pawned me off on a *secretary*?"

"Well, Ms. Medina, that's not exactly—"

"How *dare* he come to this country to do business, then show such total disrespect for the ministry controlling his ability to do that business."

Capaldi was uttering the expected apologies, trying to defuse the situation. But I'd pretty much tuned out.

This wasn't a case of Deele being called away at the last minute. He'd had no intention of making this appointment. And he hadn't cancelled because he *wanted* the Ministry official to drive all the way out to his rented villa. While he . . . what?

That was the question. Why would Jason Deele set up an

appointment if he never intended to show up? What else on his agenda would take priority?

I took another drink of the soda as I worked through it.

The only answer that made sense was that Deele, after the success he'd already achieved in Paraguay, felt it was below him to grovel any more to the government. This was his power play, a way for him to say *I've already got your most powerful farmers on my side.* If the Ministry and other farming conglomerates wanted more in the way of kickbacks, he'd leverage his growing influence to show them who was in control. It sounded just like him.

Gamez was still huffing and puffing, but I could tell she now was just playing a part. She was ready to leave.

I pulled off the headphones and tossed them onto the table. Deele and Stone wouldn't be at another meeting. They'd be at their local lab, investing more time in their most important assets: the bionic beans and their associated toxin. I could discuss that with Peach, who was monitoring the lab from his post in the vacant building, but I'd stupidly neglected to get his personal contact info. He hadn't seemed anxious to share his digits with me anyway.

It meant I'd just have to get out there and look into it myself.

25

───────

Quanta was once again out of pocket. According to Poole she was in a meeting that had already lasted more than two hours.

"Come on now, don't make me beg," I said over the satellite phone. "Give me a hint what it's about."

"You know I couldn't do that, even if I knew."

"You're killin' me, Poole." I looked out the window of the ride share, wondering if the neighborhood would look familiar as we got closer. My lone visit with Gamez to the surveillance post had been late at night.

"All right," I said, "just let her know I'm on my way to check on our naughty American friends."

A text came in from Gamez, asking where I was. I told Poole to hold on, then replied to Gamez that I'd get back to her in a moment.

"Have you uploaded lately?" Poole asked when I finished.

"This morning. Why?" I laughed. "You got a bad feeling I'll get blown up or something?"

The driver glanced at me in his rearview mirror. I'm sure

he understood every word I said, but without Poole's side of the conversation it was just a string of weird sentences.

"No," Poole said. "I just know it's important to have the most current data, just in case."

"Yep, just in case. Well, we have recordings of everything else that's important today, so no problem."

"And you've got a series-8 on you, I take it?"

"Yes ma'am."

I promised to check in again when I was finished, then ended the call. The driver threw another look my way, so I just smiled and complimented his collection of beads hanging from the mirror.

Gamez answered on the first ring.

"So, a wasted trip for you," I said.

"Maybe. At least it told us that Deele has no intention of sucking up to the government once he gets a foothold in a country."

"Right. So I'm making an unannounced visit myself."

That sank in with her for a moment. "Okay," she said. "Is that wise?"

"We'll find out."

"I'll meet you there," she said.

"No. It's better if you're not involved this time. On a bunch of levels. Let the American handle this one while you and your people remain clean."

Yet another glance from the driver, but what exactly could he glean from my side of the conversation?

Gamez fell silent. The vibe coming through the phone radiated her displeasure. And I couldn't blame her; some hotshot cowboy comes riding into her country and then makes a dangerous—and potentially stupid—move without her? She had every right to be pissed.

But it wasn't going to stop me from doing it. Sometimes an operation needed an assault team to ensure success; other times it required speed and stealth, and called for one person. Gamez would know that, even if she didn't like it in this particular case.

The driver pulled over and seemed perplexed by the address. It was an intersection in an industrial neighborhood with a handful of people walking around, not one of whom looked as out of place as I did. I tipped him with cash and, when he thanked me, I gave the standard A-okay sign with my fingers. I hoped the gesture translated well in Paraguay. For all I knew I'd just suggested he make love to his dog.

I waited until he drove off and turned the corner, then did an about-face and walked the other direction. If Poole was correct—and when wasn't she?—then I was three blocks from my target. I passed some blue-collar workers going the other way, each of whom gave me a curious look. But no one spoke a word.

Four minutes later the address was right in front of me. I stopped and pretended to check something on my phone. With furtive glances, I mentally catalogued a squatty building made of brick, smaller than most of the others around it. There was a main entrance I had zero interest in. At the far end a crude loading dock looked enticing.

There was no way Deele's hastily-arranged space in this Asunción warehouse district would have nearly the security upgrades found in his Texas lab. But it wouldn't be alarm-free, either. I'd brought along my small pack of goodies to handle the easier stuff.

As I straightened up to put my phone away, a large shadow fell over me. I looked up.

Into the face of Peach.

"Oh, for Christ's sake," I muttered to myself. Then, without raising my voice or making a scene that might draw attention, I said emphatically, enunciating each word like I was speaking to an idiot. "Go back. Understand? Go back to the listening post."

When he didn't move or say anything, I tried it in Spanish. This time with an almost-comical pantomime of him walking away.

He crossed his massive arms as if in defiance. Then, after staring at me for a moment, he said in crystal-clear English: "Your Spanish needs work. Better stick with your mother tongue."

I probably gawked for a second, then gave a small laugh. "Well, use it or lose it, amigo, and I haven't had to use Spanish for a while. You know, you could've indicated that you're able to string sentences together."

"More fun to watch you make a fool of yourself."

"Right." I threw a glance at the building to see if we'd drawn any attention, but everything was quiet. "I suppose Gamez sent you. She just couldn't let me do this alone, eh?"

"Guess not. So what's the plan?"

"I thought you didn't like Americans."

He shrugged, which, given his size, was an intimidating act on its own. "You have good hamburgers and video games. But that's about it. So *no* plan, right?"

I could grow to like this giant slab of smartassiness. He was like a 300-pound version of me.

Nodding toward the loading dock, I said, "Entry point there. That's as far as I've got."

"Okay," he said. "I suggest we walk back the way you came, cross over, then head back toward the entrance. Keep talking to me the whole time."

"There's an alley we can use along the right side, near the dock," I said. "Let's go."

By the time we made the loop and approached the alley, I'd learned about Peach's favorite drink, his guilty-pleasure TV show, and made an attempt at his real name, which he asked me to never try again.

Looking as casual as possible, we turned down the alley, then, once clear of the front side's line of sight, stopped to survey the scene. The building wasn't in the best condition, which led me to wonder what could really be going on inside.

But my instincts about security were correct. I nodded toward the low roof of the building and Peach followed my gaze. An obvious camera was aimed at the loading dock and the secure door beside it. That left plenty of space unwatched.

"Look for a power panel," I said. "Just stay out of the camera's zone."

Peach edged across the alley to the corner of the building and peered around the back. With his head he indicated pay dirt. Joining him, I saw the box mounted against the wall. It took about a minute to hook up the clamps and run a quick test.

"If we run into trouble, remember where these are," I said, tapping on the clamps. "All right, let's go." We moved toward the security door. I fumbled in my pack and removed the lock pick set. Sounds fancy, but you can find them online for the cost of a good bottle of bourbon.

Before starting, I gave two mild raps on the door. After 30 seconds I went to work and had it open. I slipped inside, followed by my hefty sidekick.

The condition inside matched the worn-down exterior. Through the dim light I took in ragged walls with multiple holes in the drywall. The light fixture in the ceiling was a solitary bulb with no cover. At the moment it was turned off, assuming it worked at all. The thin strip of windows near the top were crusted over with filth, which explained the crappy lighting. We'd evidently entered a seldom-used storeroom.

"Where are your cameras set up?" I whispered to Peach.

"There's a hall through there," he said, pointing toward an interior door. "It'll be about halfway down on the right, facing the back side of the building."

"What else is in this place?"

"Two offices and a kitchen area, both on the other side of the hall and closer to the main entrance. The rest is unused. Deele rented the entire space but barely uses half of it."

"So we should be able to get to the lab without being spotted."

"Assuming no one's in there," he said.

We moved to the storeroom door, which was locked. With a groan of irritation I noticed that, for security reasons, there was only a handle on our side. There was no way to pick the lock. This would slow us down for a bit if I took the hardware apart.

"Hold on," Peach said, pushing me out of the way.

He wrapped one giant paw around the handle and, without even exerting himself, lifted up and snapped it right off. The pieces came away in his hand, exposing the latch inside.

"You're handy to have around," I said in a low voice. "I've never worked with a circus strong man before."

I pulled the door open a crack and peered through. Light spilled into the hallway from several rooms up ahead. The door to the lab, however, was open, the room dark.

I motioned with my head and tiptoed down the hall. The sound of voices came from farther ahead, but out of sight. In the background I heard low music playing, which so far had masked our entry.

Another camera perched about halfway along the hallway, but, if my gadgets outside were doing their thing, they'd continue to broadcast an empty hall. In just a few quick steps we were inside the lab.

I looked around. "Peach, this place is a goddamned mess. I couldn't tell from your video feed, but Deele can't be using it for any real science. There's no way he'd risk billions of dollars on any work done in here." I chewed on my lip for a moment. "It's just a cover, in case anyone does a cursory inspection. But I'll bet he *is* using it as a storage facility for some of his product. Otherwise why bother having it in the first place?"

Voices got louder and we stood still. They faded, apparently going the other way, toward the building's main entrance. We went back to sniffing around.

"What about this?" Peach whispered, pointing to a cabinet before him.

I walked over and looked through the glass doors. A lot of routine materials, including gloves, syringes, and a bevy of empty test tubes held in racks. But on the lowest shelf, tucked toward the back of the cabinet, another rack had a familiar look.

The same types of vials I'd found in Houston. There were five of them, stoppered and sealed.

"This could be some of the jazzy juice," I said. "The malignant mix. The pestiferous potion. The—"

"All right, I get it," Peach said. He tried the handle to the cabinet, but it, too, was locked.

"This, I got," I said. The lock-picking set came back out, and within seconds I had the door open. Reaching in, I pulled the rack out and held it up to the dim light. To my untrained eye it looked similar to the junk I'd stolen in Houston, but who could tell?

I handed it to Peach and relocked the cabinet.

"Let's not press our luck any more," I said. I headed for the door, then took one last look back. A black binder caught my eye.

"Here, take this," I said, handing him the vials. After hesitating, I stuck my phone in my pack and handed that to him as well. "Start back for the car. I'll be right behind you. If by any chance we get split up, make sure Gamez gets this to Quanta. That's important."

He gave one nod, then moved down the hallway toward the storeroom. Just as he reached the door, I heard more voices. And one of them I knew for sure.

At that very moment, Jason Deele popped out of an office. He couldn't have ID'd me, but he certainly saw movement as I ducked back into the lab. I heard him shout for help.

Shit. Now the black binder would have to be forgotten. I had to make sure Peach got away.

I grabbed hold of a tray containing several large glass tumblers and beakers, and shoved it to the floor. The sound of breaking glass was probably enough to alert Peach, but, to make sure, I tipped over an entire table. That should've captured the attention of everyone in the building, and provided Peach enough distraction to get away.

It brought the bad guys, that's for sure. The first through the door was a man I didn't recognize, but I put him down with a hard kick to the gut and a heel to his jaw. Then, turning around, I rushed over to the cabinet where we'd found the samples. With one large heave, I tipped it over and it crashed to the floor. It might take a while before they could sift through the mess and discover their samples were gone.

After that three more men rushed in, including Conor Wood. He wasted no time trying to fight; he held his gun out straight, aimed right at my nose. I retreated a step and held up my hands with a slight smile.

"All right," Wood called out, and that brought Jason Deele from around the corner. He cast a quick glance down at the unconscious man on the floor, surveyed the damage in the room, then settled his gaze on me. It took him a few moments, then his eyebrows went up.

"Well, it's Mr. Ryan Thomas. Very far out of his territory." He took very deliberate steps to come face-to-face with me. "I guess this means you don't really work for D.M. Cash. Right?"

"The bastards fired me yesterday," I said. "I came down here to beg you for a job."

He smiled. "And then decided to destroy as many things as you could."

"I get clumsy when I get nervous."

Over his shoulder, Deele said to Wood: "Look around. Quickly. See who else might be with him." Then he reached back and stopped his henchman before he could move. "And find out why this didn't show up on video."

Wood bolted from the room. I had to believe that by this time Peach was gone, and hopefully he'd remembered the clamps on the junction box.

From the hallway Jaclyn Stone entered the room. Her eyes immediately darted to the shattered cabinet strewn across the floor. She uttered a curse and knelt down next to it, careful to stay out of touch with the liquid mess. A moment later she looked up at me. There was absolute fury in her eyes.

Deele scanned the debris. "Was this really necessary, Mr.

Thomas? Of course, that's not your real name." Then his eyes narrowed as he faced me again. "A better question is: Who do you really work for?"

"I'm actually a writer for a magazine called Pea Pod Monthly. I was hoping I could interview you for a cover story titled *The Wonder Boy of Soy*."

He merely stared, shifting his focus on me from eye to eye. Then Wood came back into the room and said, "He's alone. Broke in through the storage room. And the video system seems to be working perfectly."

Deele finally broke eye contact with me and said to Wood, "I'm sure people know he's here. Get him out, and take him to the alternate site. Search him first. I want to know if he's wired or has any tracking device on him."

Wood put an iron grip onto my bicep and yanked me toward the door.

The next few minutes were not fun at all.

26

The table reminded me of the kind you see in movie morgues. It was a cold slab of metal, and the restraints dug into my neck, arms, legs, and torso. Struck me as overkill, but then I didn't know exactly what they had in mind.

Oh, and I was nude.

My clothes had been violently torn off during a hectic search. When my shirt fell in tatters, I'd watched the series-8 card flutter from the shirt pocket to the ground. When they gathered up the clothes and hauled them out of the room, the card was ignored. That meant Poole would at least be an audio witness to everything about to happen. Poor thing.

I'd been driven to this building—wherever it was—after being bound, gagged, then crammed onto the floorboards in the backseat of a car. One of Wood's pals, a guy I recognized from the airplane hangar in Houston, sat in the backseat and kept a foot pressed down on my head for the duration of the drive. Once arriving at the soon-to-be torture chamber I'd been punched a few times to loosen me up before the search. Then off came the clothes.

I was now freezing but couldn't bitch about it with the gag still in my mouth. They left me alone for a long time.

In these instances my mind often surfed around and through the various tough scrapes I'd encountered through the years. Being bound and gagged isn't so frightening when it's happened to you enough times. And I'm not counting the fun Friday nights after too much tequila.

The worst had been near the end of an assignment in New Orleans. Much like this time, I'd given myself up so a Treasury agent could escape with her life. She'd bravely tried to reverse the roles, and I couldn't exactly tell her why it was better for me to risk death than her. In the end I'd done the only thing I could do in the situation: I pushed her out of a slow-moving car. I'm sure it hurt like hell, but it allowed me to drive into the trap and allowed her to limp away.

Those guys had eventually strapped me to an old, smelly picnic table of all things and gone to work on me with knives. I'll spare you the details, which I remember in this case because I survived. Well, until right after I was rescued by one of the chunkiest sheriffs you'll ever meet. He got me to a hospital before some of Q2's specialists, the folks in Sanitation, arrived on the scene and got me to a secure location where I could upload. Then we pulled the plug and I invested into a new body. The whole thing was grisly, and them good ol' boys had made sure I suffered plenty.

For the record, I was back eight days later and took three of them out with shots to the head while they sat there eating gumbo, or crawdads, or something. Didn't even mention the picnic table; just finished the job, even if I *was* a little behind schedule because of their backwater bayou antics.

Thinking about old cases inevitably led to the ones that left me angry and frustrated. And those all had one thing in common. Well, one *person* in common.

His name was Beadle. He was the only son of a bitch I could never seem to nail. And it wasn't like I hadn't had my chances.

Beadle was the mastermind of masterminds, better suited for the planning of large crimes than the actual execution. He rarely made an appearance during his capers, preferring to wait behind the scenes after plotting every move like a chess master staring at the board. I'd faced him down more than once, though, including a recent case in New England.

And he'd wriggled off the hook every time.

Beadle was Moriarty to my Sherlock, the Joker to my Batman, Newman to my Seinfeld. And yeah, I was obsessed with catching him. During one of my sessions, Q2's Dr. Miller once laughingly referred to it as my Beadle Mania.

I hated to admit it, but *that* was funny.

One of these days, I always told myself. One of these days.

But it wouldn't be today. Lying on the cold metal table with a tight gag quickly shifting from uncomfortable to downright painful, I figured I'd better prepare myself for the new body that would soon be coming my way. In situations like this what bothered me the most was the delay it would cause in my work.

Of course, I'm one of the only people in the world to ever say that death put a crimp in their schedule.

Noise behind me snapped me out of these thoughts, and a moment later Jason Deele came into view at my side. He looked down at me like someone surveying an insect they're preparing to squash. And, given his psychopathic personality, that was probably an apt comparison.

He tugged the gag out of my mouth and took a long, deep breath before speaking.

"You're not with D.M. Cash, obviously. And you're following up in South America, which means you're probably not FBI. I'm trying to think of who might employ a man of your talents, and coming up empty. Wouldn't care to satisfy my curiosity, would you?"

"Not buying the writer bit, eh?" I said, trying to work my jaw to get some feeling to return.

He looked me over from top to bottom. "You don't have the physique of someone who sits behind a desk. Not that it's *that* impressive."

"Well, remember, it's very cold in here. Besides, you won't hurt my feelings; it's just a rental."

Deele crossed his arms and looked down at something in his hand. It was the series-8 card. "James Frank," he read. "Well, a man of a thousand identities. All of them phony, I'm sure."

He set the card on the table next to my shoulder. Then he took in another long breath.

"Dr. Stone has picked through the mess you left behind, and she says some of her work is missing. Granted, most of it is a royal mess on the floor, but some of it has mysteriously vanished."

"Well, I was parched, so I drank a few beakers you had locked up. Please tell me it wasn't dangerous."

He raised an eyebrow. "Probably wouldn't sit too well with a human digestive system."

"I'll bet it's hell on soybean roots, too."

After a moment he chuckled. "I have no intention of satisfying *your* curiosity. I just needed time to see the full status of the property you destroyed. You had a partner or two, they got away, you didn't. I'm not sure what your real occupation is, but I don't believe you or they have any official business with either the government of Paraguay or the U.S. And, while you've been a nuisance, there's nothing in their possession that changes anything with *my* business. So there's no reason you can't simply disappear."

"I can think of one very important reason," I said. "I have one season left on *Game of Thrones*. You can't leave me hanging, dude."

"Are you through with your act?"

I grinned at him. "Jason, if you pull my string I can go for days. But since I get the feeling you're planning something truly unpleasant for me, at least tell me a couple of things. I mean, I'm obviously not going to share it with anyone."

"Why should I?"

"A going away present?"

When that brought no reaction, I added: "Because even though you're going to kill me, you have to admit I've been great company. Much more fun to talk with than Dr. Frankensoy."

He laughed despite himself. "Dr. Stone is a brilliant scientist, and for the time being she's very useful. But yes, I'll grant you she's not the most entertaining conversationalist." He put his hands behind his back and gave me a slight bow. "All right, what would you like to know?"

Inwardly, I celebrated. Like most psychotic killers, Jason Deele couldn't resist the attention. And every syllable I coaxed out of him could provide a helpful clue that was being transmitted by the series-8 card lying near his feet.

"Why in the hell did you give up high-tech for goddamned plants?"

He looked surprised by the question, and for a moment it

appeared he wouldn't answer. Then he leaned down close to me and said in a low, ominous voice: "People didn't *have* to buy my gadgets or my apps. But they gotta eat."

"Fair enough. And yet you hold starvation over people's heads. Why? You have more money than you know what to do with, and you've accomplished so much. Why this turn?"

He actually seemed to consider the question. Once again I noticed his body grow rigid and his eyes expand. It was creepy. I was curious, wondering what physiological changes were actually taking place to produce this odd reaction.

A moment later he blinked, then said, "Everything that came before was my childhood. Playing games. Creating games. I was 25 years old and still a child, building electronic playgrounds for other adult children. I grew tired of investing my time and energy into creating *distractions*. Creating diversions for people who were bored for the 17 hours a day they stared at screens.

"So I sold my business and spent two years thinking about how I could transition from providing junk food for the mind into providing real sustenance. I'd conquered the world of mind candy and set my sights on conquering the world of real nourishment. The kind that would still be necessary if all the world's computers and phones went away."

He crossed his arms. "So I invested my time and money into finding someone who could develop the products I wanted. And instead of waiting for the world to gradually notice what I'd done, I decided to, um, hasten the outcome."

I scoffed. "You realize, of course, that Jaclyn Stone has her own agenda. You've hitched your wagon to the wrong horse."

"Look back through history," he said. "No partnership is permanent. I'm not banking on this one being permanent, either."

"You'll part ways? Or will she get the Culbertson treatment?"

His eyebrows arched. "Ah, the bumbling fool from the USDA. I heard he turned up dead. Now how did *that* happen?"

"He tried to put the squeeze on you," I said. "And nobody squeezes the great Jason Deele, right?"

He gave that an impatient wave. "In my younger days I would've tried buying my way out of that nuisance. But somebody like that doesn't stay bought off anymore. They'll always come back, looking for a refill, like it's an all-you-can-eat buffet. Agent Culbertson was a greedy hog, and like someone once said: pigs get fat, hogs get slaughtered."

I laughed. "And what do you expect is going to happen to you, Jason?"

Leaning over me, he said, "I'm going to control the world's food supply, Mr. Thomas. So no one becomes a pig or a hog unless they deal with me."

He straightened up. "Now, that's enough talk. I've got things to do, and, thanks to your own little act of terrorism today, I've got a vacation cabin that needs my attention."

With that he moved out of my field of vision, and all I heard were hushed voices from somewhere in the back of the room. I began to prepare myself for the end. Well, the temporary end.

I'd uploaded in the morning, so when I opened my eyes in the basement of Q2 in a new body, these last several hours of my life would be spliced out. I called it the lights-out period. My memory went from lying on a hotel bed, the blink of an eye, and then I was staring at the ceiling on a table, not too dissimilar from the one I was currently strapped to.

And yes, it was freaky as hell. I'd like to say I was mostly used to it by now, but, as you can imagine, it was still a jolt. It always helped if there was either a witness who could fill me in on the final hours, or a recording. It looked like I'd be relying on the series-8 audio to fill in my missing gaps this time.

About five minutes dragged by. I was still cold, but also beginning to sweat. Nerves will do that to you. I may be slightly conditioned to absorb a killing, but I wasn't superhuman; I still got nervous.

Then I heard the sound of a cart rolling into the room. It reminded me of the cart our middle school janitor would wheel around the hallways, laden with his cleansers and tools. When this one came into my peripheral vision, I expected to see some sort of hammer or saw, or something dreadful. Deeply sick killers like Deele often felt they had to make some sort of statement.

When I saw what he had, my breath caught in my throat.

It was a terrarium, the kind you see in pet stores for keeping hamsters. But this one did not have a hamster.

It housed four large, brown spiders. They each had a leg span of about five or six inches, with soft, fine hairs along those legs. They didn't appear happy. That made five of us.

I couldn't see Deele, but he'd walked up behind me and now spoke in a soft voice.

"You might remember I told you I started collecting poisonous spiders when I was a child. And in the last two days I've added these beauties for my collection. So, yes, you can add illegal smuggling to my list of crimes.

"Your new playmates are members of the genus *Phoneutria*. That's a Greek word, Mr. Thomas. It means *murderess*. I mean, isn't that just perfect?"

My voice came out in a croak. "Yeah, it's wonderful."

He laughed, his voice still soft. "Their more common name

is the Brazilian Wandering Spider. Some call it a Banana Spider. And you have every right to be afraid. These lovely creatures are considered to be among the most deadly spiders on the planet. Now, of course, you'd probably be okay if one bit you and there was time to get you to a hospital for some antivenom. But, sadly for you, you're all tied up at the moment. And I doubt you'll be limited to just one bite."

I did everything I could to hold back an audible groan; I hated giving Deele any satisfaction. Which, when you got down to it, was stupid, because he was about to get loads of satisfaction whether I made noise or not.

Spiders didn't terrify me like they did some people. But I didn't enjoy finding one in my bed, either. And I certainly never wanted to come across something that looked like this, let alone a four-pack. All I could do was eye them and try to control my breathing.

"You know what I love about these beautiful specimens?" Deele said. "They don't bother with traditional spider activities like building webs. No waiting around for them, just hoping something will fly into their trap. No, take a good, long look at these magnificent animals. They're hunters. They move about on the jungle floor, looking for something good to eat. That's where the *wandering* part of their name comes from."

Now Deele moved to my side and knelt, looking into the terrarium. He seemed to be mesmerized by his four new pets.

"I've seen some other poisonous spider bites, how the infection grows and the pain they can inflict." He turned to face me. "But I've never sicced a spider on anyone before. You're like a test subject so I can see just how bad it is. You know, without having to watch some dumb video."

I tried to keep my voice calm. "And how many do I have to fend off?"

"How many do you see?"

I turned my head back so I faced the ceiling. "I'm guessing I won't get off as easily as Peter Parker."

Deele laughed. "No, you will certainly not turn into a superhero. Sorry."

He stood up. "Let's see what happens."

THERE WAS A TIME, not long after I broke the news to Christina about what my job entailed, when she asked me a question I could never truly answer. She wanted to know how I prepared emotionally for death.

Perhaps I always prepared the same way. Perhaps it was different every time, depending on the method and the surrounding circumstances.

But, I explained to her, the actual act of death and its associated preparations were always lost in the lights-out period. Since it happened after I'd uploaded, my memories were reset, and I'd never recall how it came down at the time.

It's something I've thought about. And it's not like I'm some kind of expert; the fact that I don't remember my death scenes removes that possibility. But how I prepare doesn't matter, and it couldn't possibly be helpful as a primer for anyone else. I get to do it over and over again; it may be damned terrifying, and it may be more painful than most endings, but somewhere in my mind I know it's temporary, and I know I won't remember the pain. That tiny edge gives me the strength I'm not sure anyone else would have.

Like almost everything else with the investment program, it makes me a cheater.

This time, lying on the table as Deele and his cronies began preparing to serve me up to a handful of deadly spiders, my thoughts happened to turn to the same source of serenity I often fell back on.

Christina.

I closed my eyes for a moment and conjured an image of her face. If there was anything good from this failure, it was the knowledge I'd see her again in just a few days.

Before I left Washington again on a mission to stop Jason Deele. If necessary, to kill him.

He spoke again. "I guess I'm so curious about this, and I'm hoping you are, too. Come on, open your eyes, Mr. Thomas."

I did. The first spider, the largest, was now in a foot-tall glass tube. Deele brought it over and rested it on my right bicep. There was now just a thin piece of glass between the spider and me.

"I'll need to get him sufficiently worked up," Deele said. "Here goes."

He slid the bottom panel of the tube away, and suddenly I felt the feathery touch of the eight legs on my arm. The spider froze, probably as scared as I was. If that was possible.

Now my breathing picked up again, and I wondered if I might hyperventilate. I heard short, barely-audible gasps, like a child beginning to wind up into full whiny mode, and realized it was me. I tried to relax.

Until Deele shook the glass tube, then tapped on my arm in front of the spider's gaze. It didn't have any effect; the jungle killer seemed confused, backing up against the tube, and then finally raising its front legs.

I couldn't watch anymore.

"They're basically timid creatures," Deele said in his soft voice. "They really only attack if they feel threatened. So let's threaten the little guy."

That's when I felt the bite. It was a sharp pain, and I sucked in a mouthful of air. In a matter of moments I felt a burning sensation in my arm. It quickly began working its way toward my shoulder.

"That's one," Deele said. He slid the glass bottom back under the spider and lifted it away. Then he leaned over to examine the puncture marks.

"Fascinating," he murmured.

A minute later he was back with another spider. This time the canister was placed on my chest. And this spider was apparently ready to fight; the bite happened in less than ten seconds.

There was a third. And a fourth.

And there were shock waves of pain.

I heard Deele's voice again. "I think we'll let you sit with that for a bit. It might take a second round."

Then his face appeared above me as I labored to breathe through the shock.

"Too bad we won't get to fly again." He smiled. "But at least you won't need that helmet."

27

I woke up in a familiar place, along with a headache that had also become routine.

The basement lab at Q2 headquarters didn't have much personality to it, although I'd made the request multiple times. The people with the checkbook didn't seem to think it needed warmth. To them it served its purpose and that was good enough.

But here I was, so something had gone wrong. My last memory was of lying on my bed in a hotel room in Paraguay, uploading. For the time being I assumed I'd been killed in the line of duty, but hey, sometimes it was just a routine car accident. I'd never know until I went to debriefing. Hopefully there'd be enough of a recording to catch up.

I recognized a friendly voice.

"Hello again, Mr. Swan. Welcome back."

It always took a moment to get the vocal cords up to speed, but I eventually croaked an answer. "Hello, Sherilyn. Long time no see."

She was my favorite lab tech, the one who'd most often nursed me back into shape over the years.

"I'll let you have a couple minutes," she said. "Then we'll go through the checkup. Here, take a sip of water first."

A straw was placed on my lips. It was cool and delicious.

Over the next fifteen minutes I got the feel for what it was like to exist in this new body. On first examination it felt strong, but they almost always did. I felt a chipped tooth on the left side, and the nose had most definitely been broken at some point. Maybe more than once.

When it was time to sit up, Sherilyn helped me. I was a little more stout than usual this time. Sherilyn told me I was now 5-foot-9, and a quick glance down the length of the body reminded me of those guys who do the rings during Olympic gymnastic competition. It was *that* kind of stout.

I could live with that.

Actually, I *had* to live with that. I didn't get to choose my own bodies.

Next came the short, easy walk. The muscles felt okay, but the guy had experienced at least one round of knee surgery. The scar was impressive, but didn't seem to impact my mobility.

"Try doing a few stretches, and some range-of-movement exercises," Sherilyn said.

"Seems okay," I said, testing the limits. "I'll need those special headache pills, please. That didn't used to be a thing, but it's happened a few times in a row now."

"How bad?"

"Just annoying."

She pursed her lips. "Probably nothing important. I'll be right back."

What I didn't verbalize was the new feeling I had. Other

than the headache, my cognitive abilities seemed to be ahead of the usual pace. Devya Nayar had insisted that she'd made improvements. I didn't know if this was a product of those changes, or if I'd managed to somehow secure a body that just naturally acclimated better and faster.

And the cynical side of me wondered if those improvements were too little, too late.

By the time Sherilyn returned with the pills and more water, I'd repeated all of the exercises and had started on some of the more difficult cognitive tests. Those took more time than the physical checkups, and with good reason; an agent had to not only be able to get out of danger with their brawn, they had to be able to think their way out, too.

I spent hours with Sherilyn and two other techs, going through everything on the checklist. Eventually they gave me a thumbs-up, and I went directly to one of the sleeping pods for a good three hour nap.

QUANTA WOULD MEET with me after I'd caught up on the case. It began with written reports from Gamez in Paraguay, including her actual observations and her speculation. Those helped to fill in the blanks from the lights-out period. It ended with the disgusting audio captured by a series-8 card during my subsequent execution at the hands of Jason Deele.

He'd killed me with spiders? I'd been through a lot over the years, but this was a new one.

Sick bastard.

Gamez made it clear she was pissed that Quanta's agent had acted impulsively, forcing her to place her own assistant in danger. Apparently Peach had joined me for a raid on Deele's lab in Asunción, which, although ultimately deadly for me, had resulted in Peach getting away with important lab samples. I'd be briefed on those later by Quanta.

I listened back to my final conversation with Deele at least five times, but only suffered through the actual spider bite segment once. Nobody needs to hear their own death more than that.

I tried parsing as much as I could from the madman's words. I was drawn to his little speech about evolving from the *distractions*, as he called them, into food production—a more grownup calling, he reasoned.

To understand that his plan to poison food crops was motivated by a desire to hurry up the goddamned process was revolting. But what might be within his words that could help to track down his primary stash?

He'd basically spelled it out for me with one sentence as I lay strapped to the table: *I've got a vacation cabin that needs my attention.*

Was that an allusion to something important? Was he just being cryptic for the sake of drama?

When I got the call to join Quanta in her office, I gathered my notes and took the stairs to the fourth floor. I noted the impressive leg strength in my new model.

The boss sat at a round table in her office. Poole was beside her.

"Ladies, good afternoon," I said, taking the chair across from them.

"No problems with this investment, I take it?" Quanta asked.

"Your people did good this time," I said. "I feel like my eyes are too close together, but I'll get used to it."

Quanta ignored the sarcasm, but I saw Poole absorb my observation. She was intrigued by the whole process, but rarely asked personal questions, especially in front of the boss.

"So where are we with Jason Deele and Jaclyn Stone in the last three days?" I asked. "They're back in the States, I presume."

"Arrived last night," Poole said. "But neither have been seen since they climbed into a car at Houston's airport."

"We have plenty, obviously, to pick up Jason Deele," Quanta said. "And we certainly will. But I don't want to simply arrest him for the murder of an agent in Paraguay or even the death of Agent Culbertson. Not yet."

"What specifically are you looking for?" I asked.

"For one thing, a direct tie between the poisoned crops and his supply. We're hoping he'll lead us to his official stash so we can prepare a full case on him."

I frowned. "I thought I found the connection in the lab in Houston. And what about the samples Peach took out of the Asunción location?"

Quanta shook her head. "This is where Deele and Dr. Stone have been clever. Those strains are similar to what was used in Iowa, but they're not an exact match. Thanks to the samples you've acquired on two continents, we've been able to combine research between Sarah Eklund and our people on the 2nd floor. We can give you some notes to read on the plane, but I believe Dr. Eklund will do a better job explaining it to you."

"All right," I said. "Any more news about Deele's actions in Paraguay?"

"No. After the scrape with you he disappeared for a couple of days. We're concerned he may have been plotting his next move in South America. Perhaps Brazil or Argentina. Agent Gamez has a contact within the Argentinian Ministry of Agriculture. She's there right now, working on it."

"She's an interesting character," I said. "Someday I'd like to hear the story of how you met."

When she didn't answer, I added, "Please have her pass along my appreciation to Peach. I don't know his real name, but he did a great job. She must be proud of him."

Quanta said, "Oh, I know she is. That's her son."

BEFORE I COULD LEAVE I was ordered to spend a half-hour with Miller. It was standard procedure, and even I agreed it was a good idea. When your mind is continually transferred from one body to another, it's probably smart to make sure that mind isn't veering off the road.

Which, truth be told, had been my biggest fear from the beginning. The brief time I spent with Devya Nayar didn't exactly fill me with confidence. But so far in this body I *had* begun to feel normal at a faster clip, so maybe she'd swapped a couple of variables in the equation and was indeed working to prevent me from becoming a monster.

Miller started with my gruesome execution, and the question was interesting.

"Does the manner of death play a part in your recovery in the next body?"

I squinted at him. "Do you mean if I get shot, is it easier to get back up to speed than if they cut my throat?"

"Or slowly poison you with spiders," he added. "Yes. Have you thought about that?"

"Well, yes and no. You know I'm pushing hard for God Maker to get the entire experience uploaded, so we can eliminate the lights-out period. But then I wonder if the actual murder would be too horrific to ever get past."

"So although you *think* you want the whole experience, you're saying you really don't."

"I'm saying it would be nice to be able to cut and paste the parts of the experience that would be helpful, and to delete the parts that would make me a drooling idiot. Although drooling idiot probably isn't in the psychology handbook."

"No, that wouldn't be very compassionate."

"But going back to your question," I said. "I'd say no. Maybe at first it played a part in acclimating to my new body. Now it's like swapping your car lease every so often."

He looked down at his notes as he responded. "You don't really believe that. I've known you for a long time, Swan. We wouldn't have had all these talks over the years if it was that simple to you. So why are you avoiding the question? It's not really like you."

I remained silent for a moment before answering. He was right. It wasn't simple for me at all. In fact, it was mind-blowing in its complexity. Wrapped up in all of it was my burning desire to understand the transition across that threshold. To know what my parents had experienced, to know what my sister experienced at that very moment. Would I be able to *feel* they're in a good place? Or *any* place, for that matter.

Would I get the satisfaction I hungered for? Would this particular search, like my obsessive hunt for Beadle, ever bring the results I so desperately wanted?

All of that raced through my mind before I answered Miller.

"Your question is valid; I just think my answer would be different from anyone else's. While this may be just a job for someone else—like Parnell, for example—for me it's a job and a journey, all rolled into one. A personal journey. And that means the manner of death will never slow me down like it might another agent. Rip my goddamned heart out while it's still beating, and I'll get right back up the first chance I get."

He scribbled something on his pad, and for a moment I thought his expression was one of concern. I never saw that with Miller. Then he defused the tense moment with a line:

"Well, it's not really *your* heart anyway, right?"

I laughed.

But I also left the meeting feeling that something between us had changed.

I TEXTED Christina on my way home and let her know she'd find a new me walking in the door. That was a courtesy we'd decided was mandatory after an awkward incident the first time it happened.

When I left the stairwell on the 7th floor and opened the door to number 700, she was waiting on my side of our twin condos.

"Let me see," she said, crossing her arms and adopting an expression of hard appraisal.

I did a slow spin. "You like?"

"What are you now, like five-seven?"

I adopted my own hard look, but one of outrage. "Hey! Five-nine, lady. And did you not notice the muscles?"

She laughed and came over to embrace me. "I did, babe. You look terrific. Really bad hair, but terrific."

A glass of wine was already poured for me, and Christina had a mug of tea. We plopped onto the couch and sat right up against each other. I rested a hand on her leg.

After a minute of silent appreciation, she said, "If you're here with a new body then I'm assuming you have to get right back to it. Tonight?"

"Tomorrow morning," I said. "Very early. Thank you for taking off tonight to be with me."

"Of course. So tell me how it's been for you going back to work. I know you weren't sure you'd ever do it again. Has it been okay? I mean, up until the part where you got killed."

I sipped my wine. "It's been pretty good. I haven't had much time to sit and stew on all the stuff that built up over the years."

She thought for a moment. "Well, maybe it means you're not so worried about it anymore, right?"

"Maybe. But I had six weeks of worrying about it, and this new case has been a tonic. Although I could get morose again before you know it."

She nestled her head down on my shoulder. "I've seen you upset, sad, and really pissed, but I've never seen you morose." She squeezed my arm. "I'm glad you're working again."

"Even though I got murdered?"

"Uh-huh."

We both laughed for a moment and enjoyed the scene out the large window.

"Enough about my dumb job," I said. "Tell me about the little one percolating inside you. All good?"

"Couldn't be better. At least according to the doctor. I'm happy with everything, and I know Antonio and Marissa are very excited. They haven't even bugged me about my diet in the last week."

"Babe, that's so good." I wanted to ask her something, but wasn't sure if I should at the moment. We only had a short time together before I left again.

Finally I decided to go ahead.

"I know how you felt when you decided to be a surrogate. But, now that you're several months along . . . well . . ."

"Am I regretting that I have to give it up? No. I mean, don't get me wrong, Swan, I'm thrilled to be doing this, and I really do feel a close bond with the child. But I know my role in this, and I'm at peace with it."

We fell back into silence. And I spent a long time thinking about the last thing she'd said.

28

———————

Fife met me at the Des Moines airport. I was totally prepared to screw with him since he wouldn't know my new body—except Poole had texted him a photo along with the flight information.

She was so efficient that she inadvertently wrecked great practical jokes before they got started.

"So nice of you to finish up your little vacation and come back to work," Fife said.

"Had to. I missed your face."

"Hard for me to miss yours since it changes all the time."

He grabbed my bag and started walking for the parking garage. "I heard about how you bit it in Paraguay. Damn, Swan, sometimes you find the most bizarre ways to die."

"Just taking one for the team, my friend. What do you have to report here in the Hawkeye State?"

"Just got here this morning," he said. "Haven't had a chance to meet with Sarah Eklund yet, but she wants to connect as soon as possible. She's convinced something bad is about to happen."

"So am I."

We reached the car and Fife threw my bag in the back seat. A minute later we were driving away from the airport.

"Did Sarah tell you what she based her feeling on?" I asked.

"I guess before he even got back from South America, Deele was pressing again for some cooperation from Iowa farmers. I don't know if your snooping around got him antsy or what, but he's almost demanding an answer to his latest proposal."

"She thinks he's going to take out another field or two, doesn't she?" I asked, rolling down a window and breathing in the fresh air.

"And I don't blame her," Fife said. "Besides his success in South America, this is the only state where he's tried to get a foothold so far. I don't think he wants to throw in the towel after investing so much time and effort. So yeah, I wouldn't be surprised if he dropped a pretty big toxic bomb somewhere around here."

"All right, we might as well go see Dr. Eklund right away. Does she know I was killed in Paraguay?"

"The word was passed along to your very good friend, Deputy Secretary Halloran, but with no details. Halloran informed her step-daughter."

I nodded. This was one of those somewhat-awkward instances where changing horses in the middle of the race got confusing. Sometimes we simply said I'd been caught up in a different case, and the new guy would be taking over. That wouldn't work this time, mostly because of the intense pressure Halloran was asserting from Washington. If we'd told her Eric Swan had been reassigned, she'd blow a gasket and say we weren't respecting the gravity of her case.

So instead she got the news I'd been killed, and had been replaced with a new agent by the name of Gumm. I doubted any condolences would be forthcoming from the Dep Sec, and I didn't expect the pressure to let up, either.

I HADN'T SEEN Sarah Eklund since she stormed out of the conference room in Houston. Now she looked tired. It was a reminder that this case with Deele, as serious and draining as it might be, was only one of several issues she had to deal with. She led us back to her office, which still came across as an organized mess. Bright sunlight pressed through the large window behind her desk, forcing her to tilt the blinds.

"Let me start by saying how sorry I am to hear the news about Agent Swan," she said. "He and I had our ups and downs, but he was a good agent, and I know he was determined to bring down Jason Deele. I hope he was able to find something in South America that will ultimately help us succeed."

It sounded so much like a prepared speech that I could only nod. And yet I couldn't blame her; for professionals like Fife and me it wasn't unheard of to lose agents in the field. For someone like Eklund this was straight out of a movie. She'd now seen two federal agents lose their lives in a span of days. It slammed home a reminder just how dangerous this game was, and she was fairly deep into it. Preparing a quick statement regarding the dead agent she'd worked with made complete sense. The woman was probably freaking out.

I needed to put her at ease.

"Dr. Eklund, I've followed the details of this case very closely. Agent Swan left extensive notes, including his personal thoughts on everything. I know he made contact with

Jason Deele more than once, and he even managed to get inside Deele's laboratories, not just in the U.S. but in Paraguay. I'm up to speed on everything that's happened, so there will be no lag whatsoever in pursuing justice."

She offered a weary smile in gratitude.

Fife said, "We share your concern that something is brewing. We've examined the work you've done on the samples, but maybe you'd like to clarify how they're similar and yet different."

Eklund took a deep breath. "The toxin used to kill the crops here in Iowa and the samples found in Paraguay basically come from the same family of fungi. You could look at it like they're distant cousins to the main virus, as if they've evolved onto a different branch of the family tree. I think Dr. Stone developed one primary strain, which we might consider the ancestor. Then she uses common supplements and some genetic tweaking to isolate these other strains into their own line."

I took all of this in. "So you're saying there's a set of grandparents somewhere who have a variety of offspring. They're all capable of killing, but we need the original formula to prove that Stone and Deele are responsible."

"That's right," Eklund said. "Think of it like the genetic tracking that companies do when tracing your ancestry. They follow merging lines back up the family tree, finding where everyone connects. That's what we're trying to do."

"We need to find the missing link," I said.

"Yes. Do that and you'll be able to connect all of the dots to prove Deele and Stone are behind it all. Right now they can claim pure coincidence."

I tapped a finger on the arm of my chair. If we really were working under a deadline, we needed some kind of break. We didn't know for sure Deele would make his next move in Iowa. It could be in another state altogether. Or in a different country.

And yet I had to agree with Fife; something told me he wasn't through with the good people of Iowa. I'd spent enough time visiting with Miller to understand certain traits in the psychotic killers I pursued, and one of those was an almost stubborn determination. To alter their plan would be acknowledging that someone had got the better of them, forcing them to pivot.

No way Deele would back down from a challenge. He would conquer Iowa's lucrative agricultural market before he moved elsewhere. Now it was a matter of finding him.

And his pantry of poison.

Fife and I grabbed an early dinner at a steakhouse. Few of the tables were occupied yet, so we requested a large booth away from anyone else.

"I know he's coming here," I said. "And when he does we'll follow him to his secret stash."

"Unless he's already here, somewhere," Fife said. "He essentially disappeared once he landed in Texas."

The server dropped off a basket of rolls and cornbread. While meticulously buttering a slice of the cornbread I let my mind dance around the odd bits and pieces of the case. If Deele was indeed coming to Iowa, he certainly wouldn't drive. But his own private plane was parked in Houston, and if he flew commercially we'd have an alert from the airlines.

Then there was the matter of how he'd disperse the toxin once he got to Iowa. If he really intended to make a big splash, then spreading it by hand was out of the question. He may have been able to get away with a small sample size the first time he poisoned crops, but this would need a larger platform.

The cornbread was delicious, and I prepared another slice. Halfway through the act of spreading the butter I stopped.

Fife, busy adding sweetener to his iced tea, noticed. "What is it?"

I set down the knife, but held on to the bread. I used it to punctuate my words.

"You said something in the car when you picked me up this morning."

"Yeah?"

"Yeah. You said you wouldn't be surprised if Deele dropped a big toxic bomb."

He raised his eyebrows. "I was speaking metaphorically."

"And I'm speaking literally. He's going to use good old-fashioned crop dusting to deliver his toxin."

"Well, that makes sense. But we still don't know how to track him. He could do that in the middle of the night, and this is a pretty damned big state."

I smiled. "We can track him. Get on your phone."

"Who am I calling?"

"You're calling to check on a flight plan for a man named Benjamin Hughes."

"And who the hell is Benjamin Hughes?"

"He's a pilot and airplane builder. He designed a new plane for Deele, and I got a ride in the backseat." I popped the cornbread into my mouth. "Deele is going to fly that plane to Iowa under the name of Ben Hughes, so he stays off the official records. And I'll bet the aircraft is already fitted with all the equipment needed to spray poison across soybean crops."

I pulled out my own phone and looked up my files on the

case. I shared all the details of the plane called *Amy Leigh*, including its registration number. Fife went to work.

Minutes later he hung up and gave me a big smile. "You're good, Swan. The *Amy Leigh* flew to Iowa earlier today, piloted —allegedly—by one Benjamin Hughes."

"Today." That wasn't what I wanted to hear.

"Yeah," Fife said. "He's parked at a small, private airfield about thirty miles from here. I've got one of our local guys heading out right now to confirm the plane is there."

"Let's get something to go," I said. "This night could get very busy."

29

In the car, Fife reached out to his operative heading toward the airfield. His instructions were to prevent the plane from leaving, under any circumstances. It was important to get a good look at it to see if it had been equipped for crop dusting.

"But I doubt he's sitting with the plane now," I said, noting the gathering dusk. "He has to get his supplies first, and those wouldn't be stashed at the airfield. At least I don't think he'd be that transparent."

"Unless lots of farmers stow their pesticides out there. Then it would fit right in."

"Yeah," I said. "Maybe."

But I didn't think so. Jason Deele was all about having his own storage facilities, and wasn't one to share space. If he did have the missing link somewhere in this state, it would be kept far from prying eyes.

His so-called vacation cabin. I mentioned it to Fife.

"And you don't think he was being literal?"

"No," I said. "He had no reason to mutter anything about a

vacation home. We were talking about his business. It's gotta be the place he keeps his primary stash."

We drove in silence for a mile. Then Fife said, "You know what else? We keep forgetting about the USDA agent, Culbertson. That guy was a slime bag, sure; but every report said he was a good agent, too. That's why he was able to stick around so long."

"Okay," I said. "And?"

"And Deele had him killed. Now, we're convinced Culbertson was blackmailing him. But wouldn't Deele be more likely to kill an agent who knew more than just the basic plan? Like, say, an agent who'd stumbled onto this vacation cabin?"

I stared at the broken white stripes flashing by on the two-lane road. "You son of a bitch," I finally said. "Of course that's it. Culbertson sees a way of bankrolling his retirement, and needs to strengthen his play against Deele. So he probably followed him, found the cabin, and used it as part of his black-mail scheme."

"But," Fife said, "he slipped up. He never thought the Silicon Valley computer nerd would have his brains blown out."

"Because this isn't a million-dollar deal. It's billions." I grunted a laugh. "Now we have a bunch of different puzzle pieces. We just have to assemble them."

Fife's phone rang, and he answered it on speaker. "Yeah, Danny, what have you got?"

"The plane's gone," the agent said. "It definitely landed here, but it's not here anymore."

"So where did he go?" Fife asked.

"Nobody knows."

Fife and I exchanged a look.

"What did the people at the airfield say about it?" I asked. "He had to have filed a flight plan."

"No flight plan. The manager here says the plane landed, refueled, and they were sure it would just be parked for a day or two. There's no record of it taking off."

I thought about it, then laughed quietly. "Of course."

"Hold on, Danny," Fife said, and muted the call. "So, wanna keep going and talk to the airfield manager?"

"No point," I said. "Our little billionaire used those big bucks to pay off someone at this small airfield. Even if we went out and talked with them, they won't know where he went. He just paid them to look the other way while he sailed off into the sunset. They can always claim later their records just got confused."

Fife made a sound like an angry animal. Then, after a few seconds, he told Danny to go back to the office, then hung up.

"Shit," he muttered. "Now what?"

"Now we turn this car around, find a place to sit down, and collate everything we know. Probably dig a little into Culbertson's files. And figure it out."

When we were heading back toward Des Moines I gazed out the window and watched the first few stars dotting the purpling sky. Our talk of Culbertson's murder brought home the fact that Jason Deele was a cold-blooded monster. He'd hitched his wagon to an implausible plan, one created in tandem with another psychopath, and now that farfetched idea was close to fruition. He'd offed Culbertson, then me.

I turned and looked at Fife. "Maybe you'd better let me handle this the rest of the way."

He took his eyes off the road to give me a sharp look. "What are you talking about?"

"I mean this entire operation is screwy and way too unpredictable. We're dealing with a psychotic killer who's partly methodical and partly a wild cannon. You don't have the luxury of popping back up in a new body if things go to hell."

He laughed. "What kind of bullshit is this? Things could get dangerous so I should wait at the hotel while you charge in? Maybe I'll watch a movie and order room service."

I didn't answer, and instead went back to watching the white stripes.

"Hey," he said. "Seriously. What's this about?"

"Oh, I don't know. Maybe some new tweak in the investment technology. Or maybe it's been too soon since my latest death. I just don't want some nut job like Deele or Conor Wood to pop one of the only friends I've got in this stupid business."

He threw me another glance. "Damn, Swan. If you're not careful I'm gonna pull this car over and give you a big hug."

I laughed. "Shut up, Fife, before I shoot you myself."

As more miles passed, though, I couldn't get it out of my mind.

"Let me ask you this," I said. "We barely touched on this before, but . . . why are you opposed to investing? I mean, even doing an upload for them to store. You know, just in case."

He was steering with one hand and rubbing his forehead with the other. And he seemed to really be considering the question.

"Look," he finally said. "I've been with Q2 since the very beginning. I've put in some time on the 2nd floor, got moved up to operations on the 4th, and I've kept track of you, in particular, since your audition."

"Nebraska?"

"Yeah. Part of my training is in behavioral science. I think

Quanta appreciates the fact I'm not only a cop-turned-government-agent, but a student of the human psyche. I'm not privy to any of your psychological evaluations, but I still think I understand some of the stresses you live under.

"And believe me, I've thought about requesting an upload many times. But I know I never will."

"Why?" I asked.

He let out a long breath. "I'll tell you why, but remember, I'm just speaking for myself. I'm not projecting any of this on you."

"Okay."

"I know God Maker and Quanta—and probably you—believe there's a physical body and a separate state of consciousness. And God Maker proved you can lift that consciousness out of one human shell and drop it into another. You're obviously walking proof the science works. And I won't deny that, other than your looks, you are the same pain-in-the-ass Eric Swan in this shell as you were when you left for South America in a different body.

"And yet, I can't let go of the feeling that the connection between body and mind is more intricate than that. More *intimate*, too. That we weren't built emotionally to let go of one home and trade it in for another."

He looked at me and shrugged. "I don't know. It's hard to explain. I'm probably not making any sense."

I kept staring ahead. "No," I said. "You're making way more sense than you think. And I—"

I was on the cusp of telling him all of the fears I'd carried around since the very first time I invested. The dread I toted around from body to body, afraid that I left behind little pieces of my mind each time I died and hit the reset button. I wanted to tell him how Devya had basically confirmed this was happening, before assuring me it was better now.

Yeah, it was all better now.

Right.

The only people in my life who'd heard these fears were Miller and Christina. And what could either of them say? I mean, who really knew if I was becoming a monster, even if it was incrementally? Since he already had thoughts on this subject, was it fair to bring Fife this far into my circle? He was a member of Q2. He was a great agent. And he was my friend.

I shook my head. Maybe someday. Not now.

I had to finish my sentence. "And I totally understand your reluctance."

We didn't speak about it again. But I know it was on both of our minds.

FIFE'S HOTEL room was nothing special, but it did have a table. We spread our tablets and file folders across it. Our beers sat on the floor beside us.

"Here's what we know," I said. "Deele has a place somewhere in the state, and he refers to it as his vacation cabin. I don't see why it wouldn't be an actual cabin."

"That way it could be anywhere, and be far removed from prying eyes," Fife said.

"He landed at the private airstrip here," I said, stabbing my finger to a map. "He refueled and left, heading for who knows where. But I've been in this plane, and I know it wouldn't need an actual runway to take off and land. It could be done on a long stretch of road, even a dirt road."

"Which leaves about a million choices."

"Maybe we can narrow it down a bit more. Where are the notes from Culbertson's work?"

Fife tapped on the keyboard of his tablet until he pulled up a spreadsheet. These were the official notes the FDA agent had turned into his department, and the last ones had been about two hours before he disappeared. The notes listed his activities, including addresses of the places he went. There hadn't been time to have the data transferred to a map, so I used a yellow highlighter to mark the areas as Fife read them aloud.

When we were almost finished, Fife said, "Of course, if he was planning on extortion with Deele, he'd probably leave the really important locations off this sheet until he knew if Deele was playing ball or not."

"True," I said, taking a swig from my beer and setting it back on the floor. "But he may have already recorded a nearby route before he knew the significance of the location." I put the marker's cap back on. "All right. Now, where on this map would we find the crops that were originally poisoned?"

It was Fife's turn to mark up the map. He used a blue pen and circled a spot east of Des Moines, just north of I-80. I sat back and studied everything, then spun Fife's tablet around to look at Culbertson's itinerary again. He'd spent the bulk of his time in and around the capital, but ventured out to the rural areas a few times. Glancing back and forth from the spreadsheet to the map, I looked for anything that might seem unusual. Then it occurred to me.

"Wait a minute," I said. "We're overthinking this. If Culbertson found something he could use to pressure Deele, then he'd probably stop looking after that, right?"

It took a moment before it dawned on Fife. "Well, yeah. So we don't have to worry about *everywhere* he went."

"We just need to focus on the *last* place he went," I said, nodding. "Because once he found what he was looking for, he was done. He could start putting the screws to Jason Deele."

I looked back at the tablet, then took Fife's blue pen and circled an area that had already been marked with the highlighter. "Somewhere around here."

The FBI agent nodded, his eyes darting around the areas we'd marked on the map. Then he sat back and said, "You know what really sucks about this? Culbertson really was a good agent. He could've saved all of us a lot of time and trouble—"

"And death," I said.

"And death. All he needed to do was bring his information to his bosses, or turn it over to the FBI. Instead he made an important discovery and tried to fund his retirement with it."

I called Poole and gave her the approximate coordinates of Culbertson's final expedition.

"We need an immediate infrared scan of this area. Highest priority. We're looking for an isolated cabin, and probably an airplane parked nearby."

"Right away," she said, and hung up. She didn't bother to explain how this would be accomplished. With Poole it would just get done.

"It might be a few hours before we hear anything," I said to Fife. "But I doubt Jason Deele will waste any time. He'll want to dust those crops under the cover of night. Probably between midnight and five, I would think."

I glanced at the time. "Nine o'clock now. I say we get going. We can at least get within fifty or seventy-five miles and wait for Poole's call. Got everything you need?"

"What are you talking about?" he said with a grin. "I have the country's greatest secret agent in the passenger seat, don't I? That makes me practically invulnerable."

30

———

The miles sailed past. I sipped a high-caffeine beverage and began visualizing how everything might go down in the next few hours. Somewhere in the vicinity of Iowa City or Cedar Rapids, a small team of people loaded a deadly dose of Jaclyn Stone's homegrown fungus into canisters attached to the bottom of the *Amy Leigh*.

Then, while hard-working farmers slept, their life's work would be utterly destroyed with one or two low passes overhead. They might not even hear the drone of the engines through their sleep, or, if they did, they wouldn't think much of it. Not until two or three days later, when they faced wilting crops and a devastating future.

That would lead to fresh negotiations between Deele's people and a growing number of nervous farming conglomerates, all anxious to switch their supply of soy to Deele's new miracle strain that seemed impervious to recent fungal infestations. There would be outcries from some, and accusations made by many. And those would lead nowhere; or, at best, wind up in court for years.

Deele had managed to camouflage his brazen, outrageous behavior beneath a sly coating of well-planned strategical moves. His foothold in South America lent an air of validation to his product and his program. All he needed were a few more players to fall into line and the momentum would be too great to govern any longer.

Jaclyn Stone's part intrigued me, though. Steffan Parks had warned me she was a dangerous player, and yet so far she'd been a mostly silent partner. True, she'd developed the formula, and no doubt was thrilled to see her own vindication taking place so quickly. But I couldn't help wonder if this was merely a first step for her. Just as Deele used her to build his empire, I felt confident Stone was quietly using him to bankroll what she had planned next.

She'd definitely flown under the radar. Now, as I stared through the windshield at the headlights splashing across I-80, it struck me that this lethal member of the Arcetri was just warming up. My guess was she would take her earnings from this gambit and break away to do her own thing. And if her opening salvo was this horrific, who could imagine what she had in store once she no longer answered to anybody?

We stopped at an all-night cafe just outside Iowa City for coffee and a quick bite. There wasn't much to say, so we didn't bother with small talk. Both of us understood that everything hinged on what happened in the next six to eight hours.

Poole did not disappoint. My phone vibrated just after midnight.

"Map coordinates are on their way to you. It's a cabin west of Cedar Rapids."

"Hold on," I said to her. Fife and I had already paid the tab. We hustled out to the car and kicked up gravel as we tore out of the lot. I shared the map info with Fife, who gave one quick nod.

"All right," I said to Poole. "We're en route. What's the story?"

"Property has been leased for one year under a trust that might take time to peel apart. But it's isolated, and satellite imagery shows a small plane parked about fifty yards north of the structure."

"Okay, that has to be it," I said. "Better have FBI standing by, just in case we're able to confirm everything." After a pause I added, "Probably not a bad idea to have Sanitation on stand-by, too. We probably don't want to explain anything to the local authorities."

That's what the mysterious teams in Sanitation took care of for Q2 agents who created a bit of a mess. They cleaned up. They covered up. They sanitized. Once they quietly arrived on a scene, you'd never see or hear anything in the media. I'd used them plenty of times, and to this day I had no idea how they pulled it off as smoothly as they did. I eventually decided it was simple: I was highly trained in what I did, and they were masters of what *they* did. And that was all anyone ever needed to know.

I ended the call with Poole and asked, "ETA?"

Fife looked at the map on his phone. "Forty-one minutes."

We fell back into silence. I pulled out the Glock, did a quick check, felt for the spare magazines in my jacket pocket, then stowed it all away and got my mind right.

IT DIDN'T LOOK like much. A ramshackle building, more like an oversized shed than an actual cabin. But a light shone from one window, evidence that someone was here in the middle of the night.

Fife and I knelt in a dense field atop a nearby hill. Naturally, the plants around us were soybeans. We'd parked the car well off the road a mile back and trekked to this point. So far we hadn't seen anyone walking around, but through a special pair of night-vision glasses Fife spotted the *Amy Leigh* on the far side, resting on a long straight stretch of a private road. Someone leaned against the side of the plane, fiddling with something. He was likely a lone sentry left to guard the plane, or just one of many, with the rest inside the cabin.

Things were quiet, so I kept my voice low. "Here's the way I see it. We need to find out what's inside, and we need to scuttle that plane."

"I don't know enough about airplanes," Fife said. "You handle that, and I'll start on the cabin. Meet you there in about fifteen?"

I gave a small salute and, crouching behind the plants that stood about four feet tall, made my way around to the right. It took a while to get into position on the far side of the aircraft. I peered out from a distance of 100 feet, but, in the weak moonlight, no longer saw the person who'd been waiting there.

A breeze had kicked up, which worked to my advantage; it would help to cover any sound I made scrambling from the crops to the plane. I just wished I could see where the sentry had gone.

Then he appeared. He'd been inside the rear compartment, the space where I'd endured my near-death experience during the Houston test flight. Now the man jumped out, but leaned back inside, intent on securing something. His preoccupation with the interior provided the break I needed.

Keeping low, I took off for the far side of the craft, and

covered the ground quickly. The man's torso was halfway inside the back compartment, and as I approached I saw a gun tucked into his waistband.

So this certainly wasn't some innocent farmer preparing to eliminate a few pesky grasshoppers.

With his attention still focused on the plane's interior, I veered and made straight for him. If he heard me at the last moment, it was too late. I had him down and asleep in a flash. Then, stepping over him, I stole a peek inside the aircraft's rear cabin.

The seats were empty, but several containers, about the size of suitcases, were stacked against the far side. There were also two medium-sized gym bags. One was open, the source of my sleeping friend's diligence. A quick glance revealed it held nothing more than the contents of an overnight bag. I chuckled; the sentry may simply have been snooping through one of his associate's private things. Well, then he'd had the punishment coming.

Next I knelt down and inspected the underside of the plane. There, toward the rear, I saw the mounted canisters. The *Amy Leigh* had indeed been fitted with the tools necessary for crop dusting. There could be no more doubt about Deele's mission.

The solution would be easy enough. I'd tear out some of the mechanisms attached to the canisters, leaving work that would occupy mechanics for a day or two. That should be enough time to—

A shot rang out from the direction of the cabin. I tensed, then got back to my feet.

The same faint glow leaked out of one window, but there was no movement.

Shit.

I pulled out the Glock and hurried toward the small building. It left me vulnerable, but there was nothing to be done about it. I planted myself against the side of the cabin, got my breathing under control, then edged toward the window, which was cranked open. After listening intently for a full 20 seconds, I peeked through the screen.

Agent Fife was on his knees, facing me. A ragged hole in his upper right chest had spewed enough blood to coat his upper half. His face looked drawn and ragged, as if he were on the verge of passing out. Which he probably was.

One of Deele's muscle men, the one who'd guarded the stairwell at the hangar in Houston, stood behind Fife, holding his head up with a firm grasp of the agent's hair.

That's when I heard the familiar voice.

"You should come on in," Deele called out. "Unless you want Tyler to go ahead and put a bullet through this man's head." He was out of sight, probably in the hallway to the left.

I pulled back from the window, silently cursing. I could try to make a run for it, but that would only guarantee Fife's death. And just how far could I run?

Before doing anything I pulled out my phone and hit the shortcut that would send an emergency text to Poole. With that finished, I flung the phone as far into the weeds as I could, followed by the gun.

Then I walked around the corner of the cabin toward the door. I automatically raised my hands so there'd be no confusion or deadly knee-jerk reaction. More than likely it was all pointless; Deele wouldn't possibly spare two agents who'd stumbled across his operation.

Reference Culbertson.

Yet when I stood in the doorway, hands high, Deele stepped out of the shadow of the hallway, smiling. Fife made eye contact, but he looked close to passing out. The man named Tyler shifted his gun barrel from Fife to me. A moment later I was pushed into the cabin from behind. Conor Wood followed me in.

They'd been prepared all along. One look at Deele must've conveyed my confusion, because he raised an eyebrow. "Did you think because it's an old rat trap that I wouldn't protect this place?"

He walked toward me, sizing me up along the way from top to bottom. "There are more than enough security cameras and other gadgets wired in a full perimeter. I've got way too much riding on everything." He stopped in front of me. "Who are you?"

"Bug-B-Gone Pest Control," I said. "Got a call you might have a bunch of spiders here."

The smile flickered for a moment, then disappeared altogether. I could tell he didn't know what to make of me, or the curious spider comment. But after a few seconds the corners of his mouth twisted upward again.

"You know, it doesn't even matter what your name is. But I'm sure you must've been good friends with the late Ryan Thomas. Your other partner, the bleeding one over there, isn't carrying identification, and I'm assuming you're not either. You may be with the government, or you may be working for a private business interest. Both would explain why you're so curious about what I'm doing. And you know what?"

His eyes turned cold. "You're going to get a front-row seat to everything. Would you like that?"

"Jason," I said, "somebody once told me there'd come a day when you went too far. That you'd be too bold for your own good. So maybe you should just stop right now. Our backup is on the way. You can still make things worse for yourself by doing something really stupid tonight."

"But I'm leaving," he said. "And there won't be anything here when your backup arrives. Just an empty cabin."

I looked around the room. Other than the five of us, there was nothing, other than a few pieces of old furniture. He'd emptied it of anything that might link to him.

"In the plane," I said. "The containers. You've loaded everything." Turning back to him, I said, "Why are you clearing out?"

"It's done all it needs to do for now. After our little field trip tonight we'll take it all back home and wait for the offers to roll in. And, trust me, there will be many." He called over his shoulder. "Doctor Stone, are you ready?"

A door opened down the hallway and a moment later Jaclyn Stone appeared. She carried a tablet in one hand and had a large handbag slung over the other shoulder. She barely wasted an effort in looking at me and completely ignored the bleeding man on the floor. She walked past us and out the door.

I glanced down at Fife, whose eyes were closed. I didn't know how he managed to remain upright on his knees with his hands behind his head. He looked ready to topple at any moment.

Deele looked over my shoulder at Conor Wood. "Take both of them to the plane."

Then he got right in my face. "Mystery man, you're going for a ride."

The rear compartment of the *Amy Leigh* could accommodate four people under normal circumstances, but the large containers took up a fair amount of space. Conor and Tyler handcuffed Fife and secured the cuffs to a metal ring on the bulkhead beside the left rear seat. The same was done with me on the right side. Then Conor buckled himself into the seat facing me.

In the front, Jason Deele took the pilot's seat, adjusting the headset with a sort of glee one usually saw on the face of rollercoaster fanatics just before the cars took off. Jaclyn Stone, always the stoic, sat in the co-pilot's seat, clearly dialed in to the forthcoming activity in the air, while completely disinterested in the two prisoners in the back.

The man I'd belted during my surveillance of the plane was dragged back to the cabin where he and Tyler would clean up the place before leaving it deserted. The only sign anyone had been there recently would be the fresh spatters of Fife's blood on the floor.

There were times in my career when things couldn't be

more grim. This was one. Grim and frustrating. Just as I had that thought, Fife slumped over to one side. He'd passed out.

Deele, satisfied once he had the engine revving, looked back over his shoulder at me and indicated his headset before pointing above my seat. I found another set there. My hands, although secured to the bulkhead, had just enough give for me to slip the headset on.

The tinny voice of Deele came through over the roar of the engine. "Hey, Bug man. We have two destinations on the itinerary tonight. Since you and your late partner, Mr. Thomas, have been so curious about my work, you'll get to see firsthand how it works."

"Great," I said. "And you're probably not going to be checking in with any of the commercial or military airfields during this little adventure, right?"

"Not tonight. Just a little joyride out of restricted airspace and away from commercial routes. We won't be a bother to anyone, except maybe a few folks we might awaken as we buzz overhead."

"And what poor farmer in Iowa is going to suffer for your profits this time?"

There was pure delight in his voice when he answered. "No poor farmer in Iowa is going to suffer anything tonight." With that he killed the communication in order to concentrate on the control panel.

His words tumbled around in my head. What exactly did he mean by *No poor farmer in Iowa is going to suffer*? Had we struggled to reach a conclusion that was off target? What was the point of this flight if Stone's killer fungus stayed bottled up?

And why was she on the flight anyway? Her end of the partnership started and ended in a laboratory. I could understand Deele's childlike enthusiasm for not only watching the distribution of her product, but also for physically throwing the switch to send the poison cascading down onto someone's land. It was totally in line with his villainous personality.

But Stone? She was the deadly Ice Queen who preferred to hang back and quietly concoct the deadly poison behind the protective walls of her lab.

If I'd guessed wrong, and Deele *wasn't* going to dust crops with the fungus, then everyone in this play was out of place.

Goosing the throttle, Deele taxied the plane across the short grass until it reached the dirt road. Then I was pushed back into my seat as we accelerated, barreling down the road, building enough speed to lift off. It's one thing for a plane to race down a runway, but it's disconcerting to be in a small, homemade aircraft tearing down a dirt road. It's even more unsettling when your hands are handcuffed to the bulkhead.

I threw a quick glance at Fife to my left, but he was out. I hoped he was still alive, but how much longer could he hold on? Across from me, his eyes locked onto my face, Conor Wood sat impassively, unbothered by anything.

Building up speed on a dirt road involved a lot of bouncing and jolting, and I found myself holding my breath. Then, after one serious bang that shook the aircraft, the wheels came up and everything smoothed out. The engine sang a song of sweet release as we roared upward into the starlight.

I took some calming breaths and tried to analyze the situation. Fife was at best unconscious, but probably had no chance if he wasn't taken to a hospital in the next hour or two. My hands were cuffed to the side of the airplane. A complete madman was at the controls of a plane that was experimental to begin with, while his armed henchman appeared to be counting down the minutes in his head until he could put a bullet into my brain. And nobody who could help even knew where we were.

Other than that, things were peachy.

We banked left. Gazing ahead through the plane's windshield I saw the constellation Ursa Major, the Big Dipper. Polaris burned brightly to the side.

We were flying practically due north, and Deele kept that heading for quite some time.

Now his words came back to me. *No poor farmer in Iowa is going to suffer.*

"All right," I said into my mouthpiece. "So Iowa is not your target tonight."

Deele didn't look back; instead he held up his right thumb.

Dammit. It's not like he had a case of conscience. He was just spreading the destruction around.

"Wisconsin, I assume?"

Now he answered. "Look at it this way: It's their turn."

I let a minute pass before responding. "Tell me why."

He shrugged. "Very simple. I've already given the hardworking farmers of Iowa something to think about. Once the same fungus shows up in another state, it's no longer an isolated incident. Now the whole country—hell, the whole world—gets a news flash that this particular disruption can take place anywhere. It's a disruption they're not prepared for." Then he looked back at me. "Yet."

The bastard was right. He was brilliant, psychotic, and right. By seeding the deadly fungus in multiple locations, he would put a scare into the growing community, forcing them to act. And act quickly.

I sat back and stewed on it for a bit. What stung the most at this very moment was the fact that I was acquiring all this information during a lights-out period. If and when Conor

Wood put me down, I'd wake up in a new body with no memory of this conversation. Of course, by then the desolation would've begun.

There was no choice: I had to survive this night and prevent Jason Deele from wriggling off the hook.

Through the headset I heard Deele and Stone talking. Actually it was an argument. It became clear she was—as I'd suspected—very unhappy about being along for the ride. At one point she told Deele, "I don't need another demonstration, Jason." He laughed.

They were a horribly mismatched team of killers.

Soon I felt the plane begin to drop in altitude. I looked into the cockpit to see if anything was amiss, but Deele had the stick forward. He was bringing the plane down, then banked it slightly to the right. I saw him point out something to his disgruntled partner. Probably the target fields.

He glanced back at me for just a second, then said, "Bug man, watch how this is done. It's actually a lot of fun."

After he circled some crops from a height of just a few hundred feet, he dropped even lower before straightening the plane out. He flicked a couple of switches, then held a finger over one, hesitant. As soon as he flipped it down, I heard and felt a whoosh from under my feet. It was the canisters beneath the plane, disgorging their killer contents. In just a few days all of the soybean plants below us would turn brown and start to decay.

And I'd done nothing to stop it.

Counting the two passes we made over the same crop, the spraying lasted less than a minute, combined. That would be enough.

Deele took us back up and flew for another few minutes, before dropping down and repeating the procedure over another set of crops. He was killing more than one this time, gunning for maximum terror within the farming community.

"That," he said with a chuckle, "is how it's done. I may have to write a book." He used his right hand to highlight imaginary words in the air: "How to make a billion dollars in one night." Then he laughed again.

I rested my head back against the seat. Now that the show was over, I began to wonder what was in store for Fife and me. It most likely would be a bullet. And yet Deele wouldn't want a shot fired inside his plane; bullets often passed right through a body.

The plane banked again, this time to the east, and rose to an altitude of about two thousand feet. I sat quietly, gazing through the darkness ahead, trying to watch for landmarks.

Then I saw one. A really big one. The moonlight was faint, but enough to glisten off a large body of water.

We were flying out over Lake Michigan. I began to wonder if Deele would put the aircraft down somewhere in Michigan, or perhaps Illinois. There was no way he'd venture back into Iowa. Not until the time came to accept very large checks.

"Doctor Stone," he said. "Would you please switch seats with the agent who is not bleeding all over my airplane? I want to show him something. Oh, and be careful. I'm fighting some extra turbulence right now over the lake."

If she'd been irritated before, Stone was infuriated now. She had to unbuckle, remove her headset, and squeeze back into the rear compartment. She waited long enough for the delay to register her anger, then went through the process of climbing back into the crowded space in the back.

"Careful you don't kick the console," Deele said, adding salt to her wound. A moment later she was hunched over, just in front of me.

And yet Conor Wood made no move to release my handcuffs. He sat immobile, watching as the scientist looked back and forth between me and Wood.

"Well?" she finally said, thoroughly pissed off.

Wood pushed himself out of his seat, and, with a movement so fast I barely saw it, clubbed Jaclyn Stone across the head with his fist. She dropped with a cry. As I watched, unable to do anything, he struck her again, twice, until she lay moaning on the floor of the compartment.

Then he leaned to his left and did the unthinkable. He unlocked the large door, and pulled it inward. The howl of the wind was deafening, drowning out the sound of the engines and the sobbing of the woman whose blood now mingled with Fife's.

In one fluid movement, Conor Wood grasped her by the neck and, as if he were discarding a bag of trash, hurled her body out the open door.

It takes a lot to stun me, but this qualified. I stared up at the sedate, dispassionate face of the killer. He returned the stare, unblinking.

Shit, I thought. I knew what was coming. On this assignment I'd already experienced death by multiple poisonous spiders; the thought of plummeting thousands of feet into the middle of a Great Lake sounded even worse.

I chose to speak with Deele over the roar of the wind. "Why in the hell would you do that, Jason?"

He shrugged again. "I got everything I needed from Dr. Stone. It's no more complicated than that. Keeping her around would only create an extra security threat I just don't need." He looked back at me, wearing a grisly smile. "You and your buddy pose that same threat."

Conor Wood had turned to watch his boss, awaiting a sign. He got it with a curt nod.

My mind raced, but Wood gave me no time to work out a solution. He leaned over and delivered another punch, this one across my jaw. At the last moment I'd seen it coming and went with it, enough to alleviate some of the power, but not enough to make him think he'd come up short. He followed it up with a solid blow to my gut, and another to my chest. My headset flew off, clattering to the floor.

Air rushed out of me and the cuffs dug into my wrists, drawing blood. I coughed and let my head fall forward onto my chest. With about five inches in height advantage on me, Wood must've felt he'd dominate. But this new body of mine didn't just look like a gymnast's body; it had the strength of one. While my lungs clamored for air and my head rang like a bell, I understood that I wasn't completely disabled. I kept my eyes closed and let out a low moan. It sounded believable to me.

I felt the handcuffs being released from the bulkhead. They were still firmly clasped to me, but at least my arms were free from the plane's side. I waited for Wood to lean and grab me by the neck.

He did. And I slammed my head forward into the bridge of his nose as hard as I could. I heard it crack, and his hands fell away from me. I pulled my head back, gauged his distance, and fired a hard kick into his gut. Then, pushing off with all the strength I could summon, I lunged at him, driving him back into the seat across from me.

But Wood was damned good. Blood streaming from his nose, he recovered and began trying to land blows. I blocked one, but another landed solidly on the side of my head, knocking me backwards and to the side, so that I fell against the unconscious figure of Fife.

Deele was yelling, but without the headset and against the howling of the air racing past the open door, it was a jumble of sound. He may have been trying to look back to see what was happening, but the open door created turbulence, the small plane jumping this way and that, and the controls demanded all of his attention.

Wood got to his feet and came at me. Another shot aimed at my head became a glancing blow when I ducked to my right. I brought my foot up into his groin, which hurt him, but didn't stop him.

That's when I realized the handcuffs weren't entirely a handicap.

I kicked him backward against the heavy containers and followed after him. Just as he looked up, ready to pummel me, I threw everything into a backhand, aiming with the metal cuffs. They landed hard on his cheek, gashing him open. For the first time I heard him make a noise, the sound of an injured animal. He had time to look up at me, surprise and fury blazing from his eyes. I didn't give him time to recover more. I repeated the blow, this time connecting near his temple.

His eyes rolled back, and I knew this could be the only chance I'd get. With his hands down, I landed a hard kick to his jaw, snapping his head back. Then, grabbing him by the head, I slung him as hard as I could toward the open door. His lower body slipped out, and his instincts kicked in, grasping desperately at the side of the opening. Just as I began to walk over and finish the job, he lost his grip and disappeared into the night air.

For a few seconds I caught my breath, then turned to face Deele.

He had his left hand on the control stick of the plane.

The other held a gun. Pointed at me.

Well, I'd taken enough gunshots over the years. What was one more? The only thing that pissed me off was that I wouldn't be able to finish the job. At least for now.

"That was a good try," he yelled over the rush of the wind. "And I'm not completely upset about Mr. Wood. He would eventually have become a security threat, too. Better to start fresh every so often when it comes to the hired help, wouldn't you agree?"

"You don't really want to put a hole in your fancy airplane, do you?"

"Meh," he said. "If it doesn't patch perfectly, I'll just have Benjamin build me another one. Or ten."

He laughed and began to center the gun barrel on my head.

At that moment the plane hit another patch of turbulence and his arm jerked upward. Before he could bring it back down, I lunged. I heard the gun fire, but felt nothing.

I dove into him, knocking the gun out of his hand, and he rocked forward into the control stick, sending the nose of the plane down. Bracing myself against the sudden plunge, I used the same backhand move, connecting with the side of Deele's head. He let out a yell, then landed his own blow with an elbow. I felt a tooth snap off and the taste of blood filled my mouth. Deele swung again, but I managed to dip out of the way and the punch grazed the top of my head.

He had to save his hide, however, which forced him to cut short his attack so he could try to bring the plane level again. I used the time to my advantage.

I spun to my side, still lying across the center console, and fired the best punches I could, given the handcuffs. Deele wasn't a lightweight by any stretch, and he took the blows pretty well. But a moment later I saw him look down to his left, and before I could react he'd reached down and come up with a screwdriver.

Well, shit. It's never easy, is it?

I rolled to my right, into the passenger seat as he stabbed. The end of the screwdriver embedded in my left calf, and I let out a scream. Mostly out of pure anger, I think.

All right, I decided; I was tired of shithead villains pushing me to my limit, handcuffed or not. As he reared back to stab at me again, I pulled my legs back like a spring, then shot both feet hard into his face, slamming his head into the window beside him. The screwdriver dropped to his feet.

But that wasn't enough for me. I wound up and did it again, this time so that his skull actually made a slight crack in the window glass. He turned toward me with dazed eyes, blood beginning to flow from multiple gashes in his head. It was a beautiful sight.

And yet there was another sight I longed to see.

After leaning forward and punching him hard across the jaw, I used my shackled hands to unhitch his seat harness. Then, moving back, I used every ounce of my gymnast strength to drag his squirming body out of the seat and into the rear compartment. The plane, now without anyone at the controls, was beginning to sway and dip. In another minute it would begin a spiral to the water's surface 2,000 feet below.

I punched Deele again, and blood spewed from his mouth. He looked at me, unable to comprehend, it seemed, that this could happen to him.

Grabbing hold of the front of his shirt, I brought his face up to within inches of mine.

"I still didn't bring a helmet, Jason, so no Red Baron look for me. But you'll need one more than I will."

His eyes went wide with fear and perhaps recognition. I hoped he made the connection with our previous ride aboard the plane, and our final chat in Paraguay. But, if not, who cared?

With one arm I threw his sorry ass out of the plane.

32

None of the magazines appealed to me, or, if they did, I was too grossed out by the evidence accumulated from dozens of human hands, many of which must've held food at the same time. The television volume was up too loud, blaring a program that appealed to the least-educated and most-bored segment of the population. A few seats down, someone's child was unhappy about something, and wailed.

I felt like matching him decibel for decibel.

Hospital waiting areas produce a vibe all their own. It's a strange melding of hope and sadness, coated with a thick covering of restlessness. Name the places where you'd least like to spend an afternoon, and a hospital waiting room would give hell and furniture stores a run for their money.

I picked at the bandage covering my calf, grateful at least for pain pills that worked wonders.

A pair of white, thick-soled shoes appeared in my vision as I sat slumped with my chin resting on a fist. I looked up to find the same nurse who'd asked me to kindly wait over there.

"You can go in now, sir. But only ten minutes, okay?"

I thanked her and made a dash out of the pit of despair.

Fife was gazing in a listless way at the muted TV screen in his room, which featured a sports-talk show that couldn't have appealed to much more of an IQ than the garbage I'd just escaped. The screen was crowded along the bottom and one side with scrolling updates and statistics about people who made large sums of money playing games.

"Need me to place a bet for you?" I asked when he hadn't registered my entrance.

His head fell to my side of the room, and he grunted a laugh that seemed to pain him.

"Hey, asshole, get in here. What's it been? Two days?"

I grinned and strolled to his bedside, where I didn't hesitate to grasp his hand. "What the hell, champ? How do you like this role reversal?"

"I hate it. It was much better when I came to visit and *you* were the one with tubes sticking out."

"I still owe you one. You've had to visit me twice."

He smiled, and even that seemed to cause discomfort. I'd had a good talk with the surgeon who'd operated on him, and he warned me about how difficult the recovery would be. As he'd told me, *That man is gonna hate the world for a few days.*

I pulled up a chair. "They won't let me stay long. What can I do for you?"

"Tell me what the hell I missed after I passed out on the plane. Tell me all of it."

"Oh, we flew around dom buzzed sheep for a while, then took a beautiful moonlight cruise over Lake Michigan."

"All right, jerk. What happened?"

So I told him. From Jaclyn Stone's early departure, to the

slugfest with Conor Wood, and finally the cockpit battle. Nothing caused so much as a raised eyebrow until I mentioned the abrupt exit of Jason Deele.

"No shit," Fife said in a mumble. Then he narrowed his eyes. "Is that how you reported it?"

I didn't answer at first. Just glanced past him out the window. Finally I said, "There are two reports. One is strictly internal. In that one I said we scuffled near the door and Deele fell out."

"Uh huh. What about the external report?"

"Well, you can't have one of the richest men in the country die without a news story. So after I managed to land that crazy airplane at Mitchell Airport in Milwaukee and got you whisked off to surgery, the phantoms from Sanitation showed up and worked their magic."

"How?"

"The official log at Mitchell shows that Jason Deele and two passengers touched down briefly in Milwaukee before departing again, this time for Detroit. Unfortunately their plane went into the lake not long after takeoff. It was an experimental craft, you know. Very risky."

"They crashed the plane?"

I nodded. "After removing certain containers from the back."

Fife grimaced as he tried to shift in bed. Then he said, "So now what happens?"

"Now we're treated to news reports about how the loss of a maverick like Jason Deele can't be accurately measured, blah blah blah. Some sidebars about how he lived a daredevil life that finally caught up to him."

"And we're waiting to see which two crops turn up

diseased. Sarah Eklund's people will convince the farmers it's an isolated incident, and they'll be quietly reimbursed for planting new crops after some special soil treatment."

"You've spoken with Eklund?"

"Briefly. She wasn't sure how to take the news of Deele's accidental death. I think she thinks it's bad form to cheer somebody's plane crash. But I'm sure inwardly she did."

Fife stared up at the ceiling for a few seconds. I could tell another wave of pain had rolled in. When he finally relaxed, he turned back to me.

"Thanks for saving my life, Swan."

"Hey, I saved both our lives. And the world's food supply. Don't forget that."

"Don't get cocky."

I laughed. Then I gave his hand a squeeze. "Listen, champ —I hope this little incident has at least made you rethink your decision."

"Yeah, what decision is that?"

"You know exactly what I'm talking about."

He shook his head. "You got it backwards, pal. This only reinforced everything."

I was startled, and it must've showed.

"Look," he said, his voice mellow. "Facing death doesn't make me want to upload myself into a computer hard drive. If anything it makes me more at peace with the prospect that it's going to happen."

"But—"

"No, wait," he said. "This is no judgment on *your* decision. It works for you. And I'm pretty sure you have underlying reasons that have nothing to do with the job. Personal reasons. Am I right?"

I just blinked a few times, then turned my attention back to the window.

"Yeah," he said. "That's what I thought. But see, for me, I have all the answers I need when I go home. Having no reset button makes my life more special for me. I know, it doesn't make sense to you. But it does to me. And that's all that matters."

Seconds ticked by, then a full minute. We sat there together, hands clasped like brothers, the flash of the TV screen illuminating us.

When the silence became uncomfortable, I said, "Need me to sneak in some whiskey?"

ONE WEEK later I sat at the round table in Quanta's kitchen. She placed a glass of water in front of me and took the chair directly across.

"You stayed in Milwaukee a long time," she said.

"I wasn't going to leave Agent Fife until I knew he was fine."

"But his wife was there, correct?"

"I don't care."

Quanta had no comment.

"So tell me," I said. "What happens with the contents of Deele's Houston lab? It's not all deadly. There's a lot of potentially powerful science in there."

"That depends on several factors," she said. "There's a lot to be done first with the settlement of his estate, and I'm sure that's weeks away, at best."

I studied her face. "Who are you kidding? You expect me to believe our government's just going to sit back and wait to see who gets control of those samples? I'll be shocked if you haven't had them removed already."

By not answering she confirmed exactly what I suspected. All I could do was shake my head and give a low chuckle. "Well, there's really no one around to complain, I guess. No direct heirs for either Jason Deele or Jaclyn Stone. And you know, Miller was absolutely right. He told me two psychopaths could never work together for long. Deele was pretty quick to jettison his partner, figuratively and literally."

Quanta said, "I have no doubt many more will step up to fill their vacancies."

"Speaking of which, I need you to get Deputy Secretary Halloran to direct her bark at someone else."

"And who would that be?"

"The DOJ."

Quanta raised one eyebrow. "What can Justice do for you?"

"I need her to get Justice to relocate Steffan Parks from the supermax in Colorado."

"That's an unusual request. Especially since he was responsible for your death. Are you feeling benevolent?"

"I won't be exchanging birthday cards with him, if that's what you mean. But I gave him my word I'd try to get it done if he helped out."

She tapped a finger on the table. "I've gone over the case, Swan. His information didn't help that much. A member of the Arcetri may have played a major role in what happened, but the organization as a whole was very much in the background. I'm not sure anything changed because of what he shared with you."

"I agree. I think ultimately Jaclyn Stone was dangerous as hell, but her original vision wasn't wrong. Her dream was to build stronger, more pest-resistant crops to expand worldwide food productivity. It was the implementation of her vision that was criminal, encouraged by some underlying resentment and a whole shitload of anger. All of her anger, though, was tightly focused on this project, most of which was *Deele's* baby, not hers. He couldn't have done it without her, but I don't think she would've done it on her own. He provided the structure she lacked."

"So why the sympathy now for Parks?"

I shook my head. "It's not sympathy. It's leverage. I'm going to make it clear to Steffan that this isn't a gift. It's an exchange. And from now on, when friends of the late Eric Swan want information he better pony up all of it. Any time, any subject. Or back he goes to Colorado."

Quanta studied my face. "You're creating a source in case we encounter the Arcetri again."

"That's right."

"You think his information will be that valuable?"

"Over time? Yes. In the spirit of this particular assignment, let's say I'm planting a seed I hope will reap dividends down the road. Because while I don't know everything, I know this much: We will hear from the Arcetri again."

Quanta paused a moment before answering. "All right. I'll see it gets done. I'll let the Deputy Secretary know this is the bill for helping her step-daughter."

"Thanks," I said. "Now please don't tell me you have another case right now. I need a few days."

"A few *more* days, you mean."

"Are you insinuating that one week in a Milwaukee hospital is a vacation?"

She actually smiled.

"I need you back to work. I'll give you three days, Swan."

"Which means two. What's going on?"

Quanta stood up and shook her head. "No. Take your break. Spend some time with Christina. Then we'll talk."

"Not even a hint?"

She hesitated before saying, "Cybersecurity. And this could be very bad."

I'D SHOWERED, and now I lay on my stomach across the bed on Christina's side of our dual-condo complex. Over on my side people were dropping off a new set of clothes for my some-what-shorter physique. Just one of those side effects of constantly switching bodies.

I suspected Quanta had waited to see if I brought this version back home before she bothered with the wardrobe update.

Christina was hunched beside me, working on a second coat on her toenails.

"Should you be breathing those fumes in your condition?" I asked.

"Hmm?"

"Nail polish? Is that okay?"

"Yes, it's safe. Unless you're huffing it all the time. Besides, I haven't painted my nails in ages. I'm treating myself tonight."

With the polish brush she indicated the bandage on my leg. "Do I want to know how you got that?"

"Screwdriver."

She went back to work, slowly shaking her head in disbelief. Sometimes I wondered what went through her mind when she considered her husband's job. Her questions were few and far between, mostly because not knowing much was better than knowing and worrying. At least that's what I told myself.

How anyone could live with a Q2 agent was beyond me. Christina made it work.

"Do you feel like talking?" she asked.

I squinted the one eye that wasn't buried in her comforter. "Uh oh."

A broad smile flashed across her beautiful face. "Oh, stop it. Nothing about us. Well, sort of about us, but not really."

I pushed up onto my elbows. "All right. I'm game."

She finished the final coat and screwed the cap back onto the polish bottle. Leaning over, she set it on the nightstand, then collapsed next to me.

"Just wondering if this first assignment back . . . well, if it made you glad you didn't quit. Or did it make you *want* to quit?"

I sighed. "Whatever I tell you now might be different than what I would've said yesterday. Or tomorrow."

"Kind of a chickenshit answer, wouldn't you say, Swan?"

It was my turn to smile. "Here's what I can tell you. I've been so unsure lately. And yet, babe, when I'm in the middle of it, when things are heating up—even when the game is going badly—there's not a single thought in my mind about giving it up. It's only when I get away from it that I begin to doubt everything." I shrugged. "Too much time to think about it makes me second-guess."

"That's still not an answer," she said, her eyes revealing a sincere curiosity.

"Yeah, I know. What I'm trying to say is I haven't figured it out myself. But I suppose when those doubts begin to seep into my mind when I'm in the middle of a case, that'll be a sign it's time to walk away."

I leaned over and kissed her, then did it again.

"I just can't right now. There's still too much I have to learn." I paused. "And too many loose ends to clean up."

I knew she knew what that meant. We both let it go.

Then, with a devious smile, I pushed her onto her back and placed a hand on her belly. "How would this little guy feel about some ice cream right now?"

JOIN THE SWANIVERSE - GET FREE STUFF

Eric Swan is
The Spy Who Can Never Die

With each new tale you'll learn a little more about Q2's super spy, Eric Swan.

If you'd like to be among the first to learn of each new adventure *before* they're published, just let me know where to find you.

As a thank you for joining the Swaniverse, you'll be treated to a **free** Eric Swan short story, along with other bonus treats.

It's simple: Just go to EricSwan.com.

Thanks, and happy reading.
Dom Testa

MORE ERIC SWAN BOOKS FROM DOM TESTA

Power Trip: Eric Swan Thriller #1

Swan takes on diabolical twins determined to bring down the power grid. If he fails, millions could die as the country tumbles into a dark age of chaos and anarchy.

Poison Control: Eric Swan Thriller #2

A treacherous madman is intent on poisoning the water supply. Swan must outsmart this rogue scholar before he can release his apocalyptic toxin.

God Maker: Eric Swan Thriller #3

Agent One has resurfaced, and he's kidnapped the mother of Q2's investment technology. Swan must not only battle this psychotic killer, but come to grips with his own fears.

REVIEWS MATTER. THEY REALLY DO.

Reviews are critical for independent authors like me.

We don't have mega-publishers in New York or London pumping millions of dollars into promoting our work.

What we have . . . is you. And you're very important to us.

One honest review from you can do so much to help an indie author. People *do* read them, and they *do* make decisions based on them.

So please, log on to your favorite online retailer and, no matter how brief it is, let other thriller fans know what you thought of Eric Swan.

It's VERY appreciated.

Dom Testa